the **JOURNEY PRIZE**
Stories

WINNERS OF THE $10,000 JOURNEY PRIZE

1989
Holley Rubinsky for
"Rapid Transits"

1990
Cynthia Flood for "My Father
Took a Cake to France"

1991
Yann Martel for "The Facts Behind
the Helsinki Roccamatios"

1992
Rozena Maart for "No Rosa,
No District Six"

1993
Gayla Reid for
"Sister Doyle's Men"

1994
Melissa Hardy for
"Long Man the River"

1995
Kathryn Woodward for "Of
Marranos and Gilded Angels"

1996
Elyse Gasco for "Can You Wave
Bye Bye, Baby?"

1997 (shared)
Gabriella Goliger for
"Maladies of the Inner Ear"

Anne Simpson for
"Dreaming Snow"

1998
John Brooke for
"The Finer Points of Apples"

1999
Alissa York for "The Back of the
Bear's Mouth"

2000
Timothy Taylor for
"Doves of Townsend"

2001
Kevin Armstrong for
"The Cane Field"

2002
Jocelyn Brown for "Miss Canada"

2003
Jessica Grant for
"My Husband's Jump"

2004
Devin Krukoff for
"The Last Spark"

2005
Matt Shaw for "Matchbook for a
Mother's Hair"

★ ★ ★ ★

the **JOURNEY PRIZE**
Stories

THE BEST OF CANADA'S
NEW WRITERS

SELECTED BY
Steven Galloway, Zsuzsi Gartner,
Annabel Lyon

McCLELLAND & STEWART

Library and Archives Canada has catalogued this publication as follows:

A CIP catalogue record for this book is available from Library and Archives Canada.

ISBN 13: 978-0-7710-9560-3
ISBN 10: 0-7710-9560-0

We acknowledge the financial support of the Government of Canada through the Book Publishing Industry Development Program and that of the Government of Ontario through the Ontario Media Development Corporation's Ontario Book Initiative. We further acknowledge the support of the Canada Council for the Arts and the Ontario Arts Council for our publishing program.

"BriannaSusannaAlana" © Heather Birrell; "The Baby" © Craig Boyko; "The Beloved Departed" © Craig Boyko; "Heavy Metal Housekeeping" © Nadia Bozak; "Conjugation" © Lee Henderson; "Wrestling" © Melanie Little; "The Lonesome Death of Joseph Fey" © Matthew Rader; "Law School" © Scott Randall; "Throwing Cotton" © Sarah Selecky; "Sleepy" © Damian Tarnopolsky; "Cretacea" © Martin West; "The Eclipse" © David Whitton; "Split" © Clea Young.
These stories are reprinted with permission of the authors.

The epigraph to "The Beloved Departed" is from the poem "Fragments from an Apocryphal Gospel" by Jorge Luis Borges, translated by Stephen Kessler, from *Selected Poems* by Jorge Luis Borges, published by Viking Penguin, a member of Penguin Putnam Inc.

The epigraph to "Wrestling" is from the song "The Best Is Yet to Come." Music by Cy Coleman. Lyrics by Carolyn Leigh. © 1959, 1961 (Renewed 1987, 1989) Notable Music Co., Inc. And EMI Carwin Music Co., Inc. All Rights on Behalf of Notable Music Co., Inc. Administered by WB Music Corp. Lyrics Reprinted by Permission of Alfred Publishing Co., Inc. All Rights Reserved.

Typeset in Janson by M&S, Toronto
Printed and bound in Canada

This book is printed on acid-free paper that is 100% recycled, ancient-forest friendly (100% post-consumer recycled).

McClelland & Stewart Ltd.
75 Sherbourne Street
Toronto, Ontario
M5A 2P9
www.mcclelland.com

1 2 3 4 5   10 09 08 07 06

ABOUT *THE JOURNEY PRIZE STORIES*

The $10,000 Journey Prize is awarded annually to a new and developing writer of distinction. This award, now in its eighteenth year, and given for the sixth time in association with the Writers' Trust of Canada as the Writers' Trust of Canada/McClelland & Stewart Journey Prize, is made possible by James A. Michener's generous donation of his Canadian royalty earnings from his novel *Journey*, published by McClelland & Stewart in 1988. The winner of this year's Journey Prize will be selected from among the thirteen stories in this book.

The Journey Prize Stories comprises a selection from submissions made by literary journals across Canada, and, in recognition of the vital role journals play in discovering new writers, McClelland & Stewart makes its own award of $2,000 to the journal that has submitted the winning entry.

This year the selection jury comprises three acclaimed writers: Steven Galloway is the author of two novels, *Finnie Walsh*, a finalist for the *Books in Canada*/Amazon.com First Novel Award, and *Ascension*, a finalist for the Ethel Wilson Prize for Fiction. He lives in Vancouver, where he teaches creative writing at the University of British Columbia and Simon Fraser University. Zsuzsi Gartner is the author of the fiction collection *All the Anxious Girls on Earth*, a finalist for a B.C. Book Prize and the Danuta Gleed Award, and a *Globe & Mail* and *Quill & Quire* Book of the Year. Her fiction has been widely anthologized, most recently in *The Penguin Anthology of Canadian Humour* and *The Literary Atlas of Canada*, and broadcast on CBC Radio. She has won awards for both her fiction and non-fiction, including a 2006 National Magazine Award for Fiction. She lives in Vancouver. Annabel Lyon is the author of the fiction collections *Oxygen* and *The Best Thing for You*. In addition to creative writing, she has studied music, philosophy, and law. She lives in Vancouver.

The Journey Prize Stories has established itself as one of the most prestigious anthologies in the country. It has become a who's who of up-and-coming writers, and many of the authors whose early work has appeared in the anthology's pages have gone on to single themselves out with collections of short stories, novels, and literary awards. The Journey Prize itself is the most significant monetary award given in Canada to a writer at the beginning of his or her career for a short story or excerpt from a fiction work in progress.

McClelland & Stewart would like to acknowledge the continuing enthusiastic support of writers, literary journal editors, and the public in the common celebration of the emergence of new voices in Canadian fiction.

For more information about *The Journey Prize Stories*, please consult our website: www.mcclelland.com/jps.

CONTENTS

Introduction   ix

LEE HENDERSON
Conjugation   1
(from *Border Crossings*)

SARAH SELECKY
Throwing Cotton   25
(from *Prairie Fire*)

MARTIN WEST
Cretacea   45
(from *PRISM international*)

CRAIG BOYKO
The Baby   73
(from *Descant*)

DAVID WHITTON
The Eclipse   82
(from *Taddle Creek*)

NADIA BOZAK
Heavy Metal Housekeeping   100
(from *subTerrain Magazine*)

DAMIAN TARNOPOLSKY
Sleepy   108
(from *Exile*)

SCOTT RANDALL

Law School   126

(from *The Dalhousie Review*)

MELANIE LITTLE

Wrestling   147

(from *PRISM international*)

MATTHEW RADER

The Lonesome Death of Joseph Fey   167

(from *Grain Magazine*)

CRAIG BOYKO

The Beloved Departed   177

(from *Grain Magazine*)

CLEA YOUNG

Split   200

(from *The Malahat Review*)

HEATHER BIRRELL

BriannaSusannaAlana   212

(from *The New Quarterly*)

About the Authors and Their Work   235
About the Contributing Journals   247
Previous Contributing Authors   253

INTRODUCTION

There's always a whiff of mystery, and perhaps even duplicity, to the work of literary juries – at least when viewed from without. All three of us have been there: the writer, nose pressed to the wrong side of the looking glass, marvelling at the machinations of those charged with judging our work against that of our peers. So we could lay down a bunch of jive here about the almost sinister alchemy that transpires when three headstrong lovers (and writers) of fiction meet to thrust and parry over which handful of stories, out of a dizzying seventy-five submitted to the Journey Prize this year (read blind, of course), ultimately deserve the limelight.

We could tell you there was blood on the floor.

We could tell you what we were looking for, checklist firmly in hand: Stories with sentences that flaunt and swagger, that seesaw and flirt, sentences you just might want to curl up inside of for a week; stories savage with wit and wisdom; stories that startle; stories that know when to hold 'em, know when to fold 'em; stories with complex emotional undertow, that have that requisite "X" factor – compelling the emotions as well as the mind. Although, to be honest, we didn't know what we were looking for until we actually stumbled across it – but *shhhh*.

We could wax academical about themes. Why so many stories about babies, or fear of babies? About death and near-death? And why are the guys in these stories so *weird*, the small fry so preternaturally intelligent, the women so bloody-minded? Is it just us? The state of CanLit? Something in the non-medicated, organic beef jerky?

We could. But why try to connect the dots? As American writer Jayne Anne Phillips once wrote, "Any piece of fiction that really works is a perfect example of itself." In other words, all the best stories are *sui generis* – they have no evil twins. Any confluence of theme here is accidental; we were seduced by particulars rather than universals.

So why not let the stories speak for themselves?

There's Lee Henderson's "Conjunctions," a *Metamorphosis* for the twenty-first century: "As I awoke one morning from uneasy dreams I found myself back in grade four." Hard to resist a story in which a grown man finds redemption while wreaking havoc in the carefully constructed schoolyard pecking order of a bunch of ten-year-olds.

Equally at ease with their own slant logic are Craig Boyko's two stories: "The Baby," a clever work that is as much a paean to the power of storytelling as to fatherhood, and "Beloved Departed," a tour-de-force recasting of the Orpheus myth.

Clea Young's "Split" is spring-loaded with tension, its sentences taut enough to hold a tightrope walker, as two old friends – one a new mother, the other hugely ambivalent about babies – talk about sex ("The organic track of Jed's tongue like snail-glue over her body was enough.") and who they used to be.

With "Cretacea," Martin West has created a fully three-dimensional world for his acerbic, politically jaded, historically savvy Luddite of a narrator to ride shotgun over. The smartest political satire ever set in the Alberta Badlands.

The world's tallest free-standing structure hovers like a sentinel in the distance over Heather Birrell's "BriannaSusanna-Alana," through which bright urgency surges like an electrical charge as three sisters try to reconstruct what they were up to the day a murder was discovered in their neighbourhood.

And just when you thought the second-person singular had outlived its rather short-lived welcome, along comes Nadia Bozak's "Heavy Metal Housekeeping," a wrenching ode to the travails of motherhood and to the surprisingly delicate T-shirts worn by concave-chested acolytes of Metallica, Anthrax, and Megadeth.

That's just some of them – thirteen stories in all (we're not superstitious). And no blood on the floor.

It's become an annual ritual to note that a different jury might've picked altogether different stories. This year's jury is guilty of favouring the offbeat, the witty, the *knowing*, at the expense of merely competent stories that felt overly mimetic, earnest, and that strove for moral profundity rather than moral complexity. We were suckers for balls-out-bravado. There are a few exceptions, quieter stories, less look-ma-no-hands, that spoke particularly strongly to one or two of us through a keen sense of emotional intelligence and understated eloquence.

Ultimately it was stories with distinctive, confident, authentic voices that appealed to us most. As for those stories (and there were many) that indulged in a kind of literary slumming – mucking about on the wrong side of the tracks, or hoping to trade in on the inherent glamour of sex and drugs and rock 'n roll, but ringing false – a word of advice: it's not what you write about, but *how* you write it. As the man said, there are, after all, a million stories in the naked city.

A small clutch of weirdly wonderful or wonderfully weird stories did fall out of the running (the sound you just heard – that little vibrating *zing!* – that's the heartstrings of regret) because there was something incomplete about them. Shaky beginnings, unrealized endings, punches pulled, or simply, a touch too elliptical. But we're confident we'll hear from these authors again (and again). They're the genuine article.

We could pretend we faced some tough decisions along the way. Our overall impression, though, was of broad competence but little excellence. We didn't find many stories that would change our day, let alone our lives; few had any lasting music. Perhaps that's as it should be. Excellence comes at a cost. No blood on the reader's floor, maybe, but certainly blood on the writer's, as when a dancer steps out of toe shoes, or a boxer from the ring. We celebrate excellence, as in this year's invigorating *Journey Prize Stories*, because it is rare and wonderful and hard earned.

A big thank you is due to McClelland & Stewart for its ongoing commitment to showcasing the work of Canada's undiscovered short fiction writers, and, of course, to those unsung heroes at literary magazines across the country who diligently wade through the slush piles and keep the hopes of burgeoning writers alive coast-to-coast.

Steven Galloway
Zsuzsi Gartner
Annabel Lyon
June 2006

LEE HENDERSON

CONJUGATION

As I awoke one morning from uneasy dreams, I found myself back in grade four. All summer I'd dreaded this day and now it was here, the new school year. My clock alarm went off and I patted the snooze button and just lay there with my eyes closed – 6:45 a.m. and I had to get up and go to grade four. It was somehow uniquely depressing, grade four, sort of inescapably elementary. I didn't even want to yawn and admit the day had begun. Still half asleep, I had a vague sense that some rude sunlight was coming through a window. I was getting nervous now. My bed seemed the only safe place. I didn't rise when the snooze was over and my alarm started making a fresh little electronic scream – well, I can admit it now, that's when I finally started to cry. And no one came to dab my cheeks and give me a glass of orange juice before I got out of bed, and no one pulled back the drapes – first warning me to avert my salty eyes from the sun – and no one started my tub running so it was hot and ready by the time I came to sit in it, and no one helped me pick out some nice clothes from my dresser, or iron them, or button them, or tuck them in for me, and no one made me breakfast, not even a bowl of Mini-Wheats, not even a banana was peeled for me, and no one drove me to school and kissed me on the cheek and wished me a good day. No. No, I did all that. And I drove myself to school, and I asked the secretary in the principal's office for permission to use a vacant spot in the staff parking lot because of course there was no *student* parking at Whispering Pines Elementary School.

I tried to appear nonchalant while the children of grade four gawked at me with no sign of shame – in what grade did a kid learn about shame? I looked at their soft faces and smiled in an open and hopefully well-adjusted way. Fact was, I was totally nervous. I was sweating in my new T-shirt. I scanned my classroom, nodding serenely at a poster of a monkey on a snowboard. Running along the tops of the walls was a series of cards with a picture of an animal on each and both their French and English names written below. Cow, Vache. Sheep, Mouton. Cat, Chat. Moose, Orignal. Hanging from the ceiling, a handmade thing explored our vast planetary system in Styrofoam and construction paper and multicoloured pipe cleaner. I suppressed the urge to sob.

I always hated children, even when I was one. I preferred the Bible to Sunday cartoons, cheese to chocolate, privacy to community. I kept to myself in school. I made basically zero friends.

Kids, the teacher said. She guided me by the crook of the elbow to the front of the class. I could tell by the civilized look on her face she'd been warned about me in advance. This smile she used on me she'd practised maybe all summer long. Her hand in my crook like that, and her voice so affected and brave like it was, I felt a bit more in control and a little more helpless, and I thought I might be able to learn something from a woman like this. Kids, she said, this is our new classmate. His name is Lee.

I stood there.

I'm Ms. Durant, she said, and shook my hand. She was young, maybe a bit older than me, it was hard to tell. I was a foot taller than her.

Hi, I said. Nice to meet you, I said to the class. And then I took my seat.

We learned arithmetic in the morning and that helped me relax. We did some exercises in our *cahiers*, and then a benign pop quiz, a kind of refresher course for those pupils who'd been in grade three last year and not working for an academic publisher.

I finished my quiz and sat facing the window, to daydream. A white cloud so white that I couldn't quite believe it rolled by not too high off the ground.

A girl behind me tapped my shoulder. Her name was Melinda, a pretty little religious girl (she prayed in a loud whisper before the pop quiz). I looked back, and she handed me a note folded into a kind of origami. It was one of those origamis I remembered being very popular one year and then just as quickly forgotten. There was a time when I could've made this miniature paper alcazar as well or better, but it was a forgotten art to me now. But it was odd to discover that even after I'd grown up, those same elements of childhood I'd experienced still existed in the here and now. Grade four was the origami grade.

I opened the note. It read: We want to know the answer to number 6.

When I put the note down on my desk, I looked up to Ms. Durant, who was busy at something. Only after reading the note did I remember what kind of infraction I'd made simply by reading the note. God, new to the school and already the little buggers were trying to get me in trouble. I looked at my class-mates. They were waiting to see what I'd do. No one was working. Immediately it became clear this was a test, my first of the year. Would I help them, my little co-pupils? Whose side was I on?

I shook my head, no. Of their cheating I would have no part. The origami I flattened as best I could and put inside my desk.

While they all worked, I went back to my daydreaming. The cloud was gone.

I checked my watch. It was almost time for recess. An elastic bounced sharply off my ear and a round of vindictive giggles went through the room.

Shh, Ms. Durant requested.

Soon we moved on to fractions and the kids started to look antsy.

My next mistake was at recess, before I was even outside. This was an old school, a brick tower built in the 1920s with what felt like a hundred portables sprouting from it. Portable classrooms: the ghetto of education. Our class was lucky to be in the school proper, where two sets of old doors exited to the playground, one set for boys and one for girls. Well, without even noticing I went out with the girls.

This is the girls' side, a little grade-oner explained. She pointed to the girls' washroom. See?

I'm sorry, I didn't know.

What are you doing here, anyway? she asked. Shouldn't you get a job?

Never you mind, I said.

Once outside I sat on a looping metal bar meant for bicycles and watched kids play. A mafioso of girls stood in a shady corner and discussed private matters. I noticed Melinda – the girl whose desk was behind me – standing by herself at her own set of bike bars and I thought how interesting and desirable she'd be someday, eventually making a zealot very happy. There was a game of tag in the field she seemed to regard with mild amusement. Some boys were crouched on the ground, looking serious and getting dirty. Recess was only fifteen minutes. I couldn't figure out why they thought so much could get done. Kids and dogs are alike in that they are so docile, but if you frighten or confuse them or keep them penned up in cages too long they turn vicious. They need to get out as much as they need to be in. Or they kill you.

I thought I no longer needed recess but when the school buzzer went off and I had to go back in to class, my whole body clenched. Meanwhile, a scurry of impromptu races made the kids all vanish back into their classes in under a minute, with me still walking to the door.

The principal gave me an emphatic pat on the shoulder. How are you enjoying your first day back in school?

It's fine, Ms. Wilson. It's fine, thanks.

We walked through the boys' door even though Ms. Wilson was a girl. It's a good class, she said, but they all know each other, so don't be alarmed if it takes a while for them to warm up to you.

I think it's cool kids in grade four still make origami.

She nodded, Oh, I know. Grade four is great for that kind of thing. Can I give you some advice?

Sure.

Teach the boys a code, make up a language, and send notes in it.

Good call.

Don't tell Emma I told you that.

Who's Emma?

Oh, pardon me: Ms. Durant. Ms. Wilson laughed, Ha ha, and walked back to her principal's office.

I sat at my desk and conjugated verbs. After a long time deliberating, I finally got the nerve to put up my hand and was astounded to feel my eyebrows raise too. Some kind of juvenile reflex saying, Please, do you see me?

Yes, Lee?

Can I go to the bathroom?

Ms. Durant checked over her shoulder to the clock. It's fifteen minutes until lunch. Can it wait?

I suppose it can. I turned my head back to my desk, a little flustered, and a bit sore in the bladder.

She went back to the lesson. I ran, I run, I will run, she said, writing it all on the chalkboard. Meanwhile I tried to cross my legs but the desk was too low and my knee wouldn't go over.

Before lunch, Ms. Durant handed out a form, counting out how many in each row and giving the forms to the person at the front to pass back.

Have your parents sign these and bring them back as soon as

possible, she said. No one seemed to read what was on the form so I chose not to either.

I didn't know where to eat, and somehow found it unbearable to follow the other kids into the lunchroom, so I went to my car and ate in the back seat. I'd made myself a ham sandwich. Even so I peeled the top slice of bread away to look at the meat inside, and said to myself, Ham sandwich. I ate it, disgusted with myself for such a boring lunch. I broke the straw from my juice box and tore it out of its wrapper and pierced it through the foil top and squeezed the juice into my mouth until the box was as flat as could be. I finished off two Oreo cookies and tried to remain calm. Only a few hours left and I could go home.

School let out at 3:30 and everyone scrambled to the cloakroom to put on their jackets and by the time I got to mine everyone was gone except the other pariah in the class, a boy named Derek who looked like a snowman made of skin. He was tying his laces so slowly a kind of hatred welled up in me. Even the academic press staff at their most irritating didn't make me feel this kind of rage.

I understand you drove here, Lee, he said to me. He was a mouth-breather. He looked so deeply stupid.

Derek, I said.

Derek is my name. That's right. He regarded me, up and down, like a boy. I loathed him.

It's true, I drove here, I said.

I have missed the bus again, he said. I always miss the bus.

Oh.

Now I have to walk home. He groaned. I have to walk through the high-school park.

Why not walk around it?

It's the shortcut, he said. He peered at me as if I were dense. No way I was giving this pudge a ride.

Derek, I have to go. I'll see you tomorrow.

At home that night I had a bit of a conniption. Making dinner, I'd thrown a chicken breast in the oven and put on the timer. When the timer went beep and I opened the oven door, I realized I'd never turned on the heat. Then I freaked out.

Aaaah, I screamed. The hair on my head was really on the verge of rising when the scream abruptly ended. I sat in a chair and rested my face. I took a deep breath.

I said to myself, Good god, I can't go back there tomorrow. I just can't.

I unzipped a compartment of my backpack and finally looked at the form Ms. Durant gave us that day. The upshot was we needed consent from our legal guardians for an overnight trip to a forest. I signed the damn thing immediately and crammed it back deep into the fuggy bottom of my bag.

The phone made its sound, and I contemplated not answering. How crazy was it to not answer the phone? The odds of it being someone phoning to ask me how my first day back in elementary school was were so unkindly high that I knew if I didn't answer it, that person, whoever it was, would almost certainly know I hadn't answered the phone for the very reason that I didn't want to talk with them about my day.

Hi, Lee.

Howdy, I said.

There was a silence, time for me to conjure up an image of my girlfriend sitting on her futon, having finished her own dinner and flipping through a fashion magazine with just enough energy to envy the women she saw there, and now deciding to be the first cruel person to care enough about me to ask how was elementary school.

How did school go today? She said it with a calculated lack of emphasis.

Fine, I said.

Fine? That's all?

I dunno, I said.

Did you just say, I dunno? I could hear the magazine fall from her lap. She was standing now. Her place was always a ghastly mess, the lair of an otter obsessed with prized clamshells. She liked to look out the window when she talked on the phone, always exempt from the private reality behind her unctuous lifestyle.

So, how was it?

Baby, did you know they still make origami in grade four?

What? She sighed rather too heavily. Don't you see why it's so hard to connect with you? You push me away with all this nonsense.

Ms. Durant: I was thinking about her, in all honesty. The way her lips slanted down while she thought, her slim gentle hand brushing chalk from the blackboard with a yellow shammy, her laugh, which started as a squeak and finished in a silent giggle.

It was an old desk. I got to know it well. The wood split at the corners and on its face someone long ago had carved the word KISS into it, and then later, maybe someone else, had filled the letters in with red ink. I respected desk vandalism. I also liked the green pole that connected the desk to the chair. When my hands felt too warm, I cooled them on the metal.

During art class, all the boys except for Derek got together and drew these incredibly detailed blueprints for buildings. The buildings could never be made, no logic to them, but wonderful all the same. I watched each boy take a portion of a large section of unrolled newsprint paper and start to work out plans for his wing of this enormous building. They steadfastly used rulers and incessantly sharpened their pencils. A boy named Chris was in charge. He requested revisions if designs didn't satisfy criteria he invented.

A fuzzle never uses stairs, Chris said. Make that an escalator.

What's a fuzzle? I asked.

Chris didn't answer. He chose to sharpen his pencil and work more closely on the main entrance.

Alex, another boy whom I admired for his huge mature forehead, turned to me and said, A fuzzle is a perfectly round animal that is one point one eight sixth of a millimetre.

An incredibly tiny animal. Does it have eyes?

Yes, it has eyes.

How does it move?

Without taking his concentration off his work, Chris finally answered me. It uses very sensitive feelers. It's covered in very sensitive feelers. It looks like hair, but it isn't.

What does it eat?

Datum, another boy replied.

Datum? What's that?

Chris put his pencil down, as if every moment I took away from their work cost him money. It was like talking to someone in the marketing department of the academic press where I worked. Datum is invisible speckles of floating meat, Chris managed to say.

I decided not to ask any more questions about fuzzles. I really wanted to be invited to work on the fuzzle project, but for now I was working on something a lot more mundane. With the only pair of left-handed scissors, I was dutifully cutting out construction paper and making a two-dimensional garden.

I thought I'd try something I remembered from school. I took a jar of pins from the cupboard and started piercing them through the thin first layer of skin on the palm of my hand.

Hey, guys, I said. Check this out. I held my hand up and they gathered around to see if the pins would fall.

All the boys quickly had pins in their hands. They got an idea to freak out the girls with their newfound nightmare, and naturally, being girls, they started to make a lot of screamy noise and Ms. Durant came over.

Take those pins out of your hands, she said. Who gave you the bright idea to do this? Chris?

No, Chris said. No, it wasn't me, it was Lee.

As I pulled pins from my hands, Ms. Durant stood beside me looking baffled. Thanks a lot, *Chris*, I said.

I'm a little surprised, she said.

I'm sorry, Ms. Durant. I remembered doing this when I was in school and thought –

Yes, well. Not every tradition needs to be passed along to the next generation.

True enough, I said. When she walked back to her desk, I hissed at Chris, You snitch.

Alex said, Yeah, Chris. He rolled his eyes at me, as if to reiterate to me that Chris was the worst kind of friend – a true rat.

Someone was taking my side, I couldn't believe it. I gave Alex a wink and a smile, and he liked that, but really I was holding back tears of joy.

At home I was able to work the oven, and when the phone made its ridiculous sound, I answered without hesitation.

We learned about Louis Riel, I told the director of the academic press.

Don't underestimate the skills you're learning. Be aware of the skills.

I'm totally aware of the skills. I'm meshing with the skills.

I'm serious, Lee. Please don't think if you come back from this and nothing has changed that you can expect to keep your job. We're a team, right? A *community*, Lee.

I wanted to tell him to piss up a rope, or to especially fuck himself, but I was predictably obsequious. We are a team, I said. I understand completely.

Anyway, he said, we're hoping to have you back, all refreshed and such.

We left it at that. I sat in front of the TV for the rest of the evening, doing my homework, drinking box wine until I was so drunk I couldn't brush my teeth.

School was fine. Melinda and I talked occasionally. I asked her what church she attended and was irked to learn it was something Mormon. I had no idea they'd migrated so far north, I said.

Yes, it's true, she said.

What do you do for fun? I asked.

I don't know, she said. We have Bible school, that's where most of my *real* friends are.

My real friends don't go to this school, either, I said.

After it sunk in, she giggled, and we shared that little laugh. The way she tilted her head, crinkled her cute little eyes, I could tell this poor little girl, this nice little Mormon girl, was beginning to have her first crush, the first of, I estimated, three, before she would utterly stamp away all her nigglings of religious doubt and sexual curiosity to marry a drab Mormon four and a half years older than her. She'd always remember me, though: the first boy to show her some charm and attention like no boy in the fourth grade could ever express, Mormon or normal. Too bad I was twenty-eight and she, only nine.

Buoyed by the strength of a young girl's infatuation, I decided I was going to displace Chris as the alpha male of the classroom. The little monkey king with his fuzzle worship. Chris was going down. I wasn't going to be his replacement, though. My plan was to make Alex the new leader of the boys. Alex and his wide, sage forehead would rule all. His brains and my adulthood: we were unstoppable.

My plan to overthrow Chris happened quickly, such is the way kids do everything. At an academic press it might've taken half a career, but in elementary school it took all of an hour. Basically after one lunch when Alex and I kept to ourselves, Chris began to fear he was losing Alex as a friend, so he started to buddy up to me in class, and went so far as to invite me to work on the fuzzle project. I think he figured it was better to have me on board than to lose Alex, who might initiate a mass friend exodus. But it didn't matter. It was like checkmate whatever move Chris made.

Your lines aren't straight enough, Chris muttered to me.

Sorry, I said, and sharpened my pencil. I gave Alex a wink and we smiled at each other. On one of the balustrades I was working on I added a rococo finish Chris approved of, not knowing it was actually a graffiti of code. Alex and I had invented this great code over the lunch hour and were already using it to undermine Chris and his fuzzles. My code translated simply as, Chris farts.

Alex replied by adding a wing of the building named, again in code, Chris is a farter.

There was a problem, though. I was failing. Over Christmas break I spent time with my girlfriend's family, chatting aimlessly or watching television shows I hated. My girlfriend ignored me even more than usual, moving me aside like a whining door. But I couldn't concentrate on anything besides my low letter grades anyway. I excused myself for long stretches of family time just to hide in my girlfriend's childhood bedroom and stare anxiously at the report card I kept hidden in my back pocket. I had one gold star, in music, because I already knew how to play the recorder. My only comfort came in knowing I wouldn't have to show anybody my marks. My own parents were already dead, a depressing and shameful relief.

We'd begun long division in October and no matter how much I studied, it always left me confused. What was with that little table, held up by one leg and a number underneath it? The footrest of a number beside the table and a vase of numbers somehow (how?) appearing on top. It was a total bafflement. And then on a crucial social studies test I'd mistakenly written that Lois Riel was born in Edmonton – what was I *thinking*?

The worst was Ms. Durant's comments. Unlike the other kids

in my class, I had a career to think about. I was sleeping poorly, I was constipated, and I related it all to my marks. I lay in my girlfriend's childhood bed, underneath the chenille blanket and sour yellow sheets, and looked at my report card without blinking. *Must learn to play fairly. Causes mischief. Does not play well with others.*

In January, during art class, I broke it to the others. Alex, I said, I don't think this wozzle compound is working out.

What do you mean? he said. Since Alex and I found ourselves in a leadership position, there'd been no more fuzzles. Chris was devastated but too fearful of alienation to quit altogether, and so, with Hamish and Steven, and even dumb Derek, Chris agreed to work on a project Alex outlined as a giant war compound for wozzles, an even smaller creature than a fuzzle, perfectly cube-shaped and deadly poisonous, hovering just above the earth on a magnetic force field.

I could feel Ms. Durant nearby, and hoped she was listening to the conversation. I said, Wozzles prepare, but for what? What do they plan on going to war against? Now, Chris, I said.

Huh? Chris lifted his head up. He had so little energy for wozzles that his pencil was nothing but a tiny soft nub and his portion of the compound was a dull, hazy mess of wavy lines.

This wozzle here is deadly poisonous. All you have to do is touch one and you die. What kind of defence does the fuzzle have?

Chris thought for a minute. I was worried he'd say it had no defences, a victim of never knowing a predator. But I knew if this kid was smart about anything, it was fuzzles. Finally, brilliantly, he said, A fuzzle has death-ray vision.

Boys, I said, it's time we had a sleepover. I think the fuzzles and the wozzles are about to go to war.

Over our ham sandwiches and detwizzled cheese tubes we sat at a large table in the lunchroom and laboriously developed this big survey map of the terrain where fuzzles would meet wozzles. Since both these creatures were so tiny, the terrain we decided on was a vegetable garden. It had the rugged earth terrain we desired as well as lots of varying flora and underground dimensions, potatoes and carrots, which could act as cover. We all became detailed agricultural draughtsmen, with Hamish showing some astonishing work rendering cabbage and broccoli. The job of critical appraisal was restored to Chris, and once again we were a tireless and coordinated group of sharpened pencils and vanishing erasers.

Then in gym class a girls against boys dodgeball game ended in tragedy. Forgetting completely about how much stronger I was, I whacked Melinda in the face so hard with the volleyball her whole body swung through the air and she landed in a sobbing heap on the ground.

Oh my god, I'm so sorry, Melinda.

That's it, said Ms. Durant. Detention after school, Lee. You should know better than to throw that hard. Are you okay, Melinda?

My face! she wailed.

Melinda was sent home sporting a gruesome bruise on the entire left side of her head. That afternoon was a misery. I felt her empty desk behind me, like a kind of apparition, breathing without breath down my neck. Her voice interrupted my every thought. My face! I heard her say. My face! My face!

I thought it'd make me feel very guilty, said Ms. Durant, to force a grown man to write lines, but frankly, I'm a little concerned. Didn't you read what I wrote on your report card, or do you not care?

I didn't answer right away. I was writing, *I will not throw so hard in gym class ever again*, over and over on five pages, double-sided, single-spaced.

I don't know, I said. For a minute there I totally forgot I was an adult.

I agree.

You gotta know how important it is for me to pass. My whole career is riding on me passing grade four.

Ms. Durant wore a little green sweater and she had her hair cut recently so I could see a pair of adorable rectangular silver earrings, and I wanted to comment on them but it didn't seem like the most opportune time. She said, Well, your attitude is very inconsistent.

My heart is in the right place, I said. I have a friendship with Melinda none of the other kids share with her. I hope she'll forgive me.

She's a Mormon, you know.

Nevertheless.

We were silent. I continued my lines. She leaned back against a desk, and I couldn't help but kind of desire her.

She smelled of cocoa butter. I wrote a few more lines.

Do you mind if I ask you a personal question? I said.

She blinked. Go ahead, she said. I might not answer it, though.

How was I going to ask this, I thought, and no sooner had I delayed than I became really nervous. Contrary to popular opinion, sometimes it is wise to speak before thinking. I'm wondering if, I'm curious if, well, ha ha, do you have a boyfriend?

She bit her lip and thought, intelligently, then finally, with melancholy, she said, A yes or no answer is unavailable at this time.

I went out and bought pyjamas, not having owned any for close to fifteen years, just for the occasion of this night's sleepover, and my finger was at the doorbell when Alex's parents answered, both of whom I'd met at parent-teacher interviews. A very dormant couple, from what I could tell. I had bags of chips in my hands, flavours I didn't even know existed, like Chicken Fried Rice, Guacamole, and BBQ'd Steak. In my back pocket was a rolled-up *Playboy* – I thought it about time the boys learned something more about life than just wozzles and fuzzles.

I'm sorry, Lee, Alex's father said in his pale and exhausted voice, like a man suffering from near-death ennui. He said, We've decided we can't allow you to attend this sleepover.

Don't be absurd, I said. The conversation already seemed infinitely familiar from my days at the university press as I learned to dodge the scholarly cudgel of my halfwit boss.

You're an adult, the man said. It sets a weird precedent. I'm sorry.

Don't be sorry. Just let me in.

His parents stepped aside, and I removed my shoes at the entrance. Sit down, I said. They sat down on their couch next to one another, and his mother clapped on a living-room light.

Look, I said. Alex is a very talented and intelligent young boy. He does well in school. You shouldn't limit him.

I don't think it's appropriate for you to give us advice, his mother said, on how to raise our son. You're a grown man and you met him as a *classmate*.

Don't let that reflect on Alex. Here, I said, and pulled a little transparent pink box from my pocket, opened it. These are ear plugs. I thought you might end up needing them. Also, I gave my girlfriend your number, so if she calls, I'll be in the rumpus room downstairs.

Things got started kind of slowly on the designs for the war because the boys paired up and pretended to fuck each other after poring through the *Playboy*. They called each other by the names of girls they adored. Oh, Jane, Hamish exclaimed from atop Steven. Oh, Mary, Steven replied. It was puzzling but I sympathized, and chose not to disrupt their fantasies. Little kids experiencing love for the first time. It was lewd and adorable simultaneously. I sat somewhat uncomfortably in a far corner and rummaged through old video games that looked about as joyful as a collection of broken phones.

At about 8:30 p.m. I decided to go upstairs and call my girl-friend.

You're calling me from a sleepover, she said.

Think of it more like a retreat, or working late. We've got a project on the go.

I've started seeing someone else, she said.

This comes as a complete shock, I said.

I called Melinda after that, concerned for her health.

You're calling me from a sleepover, she said.

It's this fuzzle versus wozzle war. We're working late. I called because I'm worried about you and wanted to apologize. Are you okay?

We gave me a Tylenol. Have you heard of that?

Tylenol? Yes, I have.

Yes, so I had one of those with ginger ale.

I am very sorry, Melinda.

It's dodgeball. It happens. God has forgiven you and so me too. Who is at the sleepover?

Oh, you know, I said, the boys.

Is Chris there?

Yes.

Could you do me a big, *big* favour?

What's that?

Could you, she paused. Could you tell him I like him?

My eyes kind of bugged out. Sure, I said. You bet, Melinda. Bye.

Oh, no! she squealed and giggled. Okay. No, call me tomorrow, okay? And then she hung up with a series of fumbles.

I went downstairs and studied the progress we'd made on the war. We were pretty much ready to start waging. I sat down with Chris and told him the news. He went so pale, I thought he'd faint.

Well, do you like her? What should I tell her?

I like her, said Chris. I do like her, he said again as if it really had never occurred to him before. Let me look at that *Playboy* again, he said.

It wasn't until Sunday I remembered we had our class field trip into the forest on Monday. That evening I went over the camping checklist, interrupted by the blurting sound of my phone.

We've filled your position, the director of the academic press said.

I'm completely shocked, I said.

We got busy. We needed someone.

I'm sure you were very busy. An academic press is a busy place.

I'll give you a good recommendation.

For what? Grade five?

We took a big yellow bus into the forest. Us boys all went and sat at the back and when we drove over a serious bump, the littlest ones, Steven and Hamish, would pop so high their hair would brush the ceiling.

Whee, they said in unison.

Careful, Ms. Durant yelped out over the megaphone.

Chris and Melinda sat in a seat together a few up from the back, and our spy Alex reported they were holding hands but not speaking very much.

It's often more complicated to talk, I mused. It's better they just enjoy each other's silence.

The forest was about thirty minutes from the city and included two large, square fields separated by a column of trees, like a long, extremely narrow forest. It was very unnatural. We set up our tents in the line of trees, and made hamburgers and hot dogs over open fires and sang songs I forgot even existed and the kids didn't know. Ms. Durant had a guitar and she sang and played at the campfire until it was time to go to bed. Her voice was beautiful and I became so relaxed. No job, no girl-friend, away in the forest and only a song to keep me from falling straight to sleep under a night filled with gold stars.

Alex, tucked into his brown bag, looked so small and new, I was reminded again of how much older and how much taller I was than any of my friends. Not that I wanted to be young again, or even small, but there was nothing in me that yearned to rejoin the world I'd left behind last September. The phony world of so-called grown-ups. I no longer considered myself back in grade four. For me this was, by virtue of all I'd gone through since I was nine years old, an entirely original grade.

Next morning Ms. Durant and her teaching partner announced we'd stage a game of capture-the-flag, and would split up into two teams. The morning air was just beginning to warm, and by the time we had the teams organized we were down to our T-shirts and the sun above us was a gleeful yellow. I was on the red flag team with Alex as my leader, and it turned out that Melinda and Chris were both on the blue team – likely to get lost in the trees until a winner was announced. Our teams split up, each taking a field on either side of the column of trees, and went off to hide our flags.

Leaning on the wood beam of a fence, I watched as the game began and kids started racing off in all directions, climbing into bushes and getting lost and coming out covered in thistles and sap, being chased by someone on the opposite team. Every now and then a kid would get tagged and put in our prison. Thanks to his wozzles, here on the field, Alex was a confident and brutal tactician. My pulse raced when I saw a child come close to our flag, but what with the incident during dodgeball I was less than eager to get in there and start frightening kids. Better we lose than I smack someone else upside the head.

Ms. Durant came over and leaned on the wood beam with me.

Hello, she said.

Your kids are great, I said. You give them such good guidance. Look how well they play compared to those kids from the other class.

It's true, they're an energetic bunch. And how are you?

I'm enjoying sitting here and watching, I said. I'm proud of our strategies. I'm giving plenty of moral support.

I didn't know what else to say so we fell silent and watched the kids. Almost foolishly, I wanted my team to win, but it was looking desperate. I counted my teammates and figured we had little more than our defence left.

Ms. Durant said, I hope Alex is somewhere close to that blue flag, because if he's in prison your team is sunk. You've got no one else.

What do you usually do with your summers? I asked her.

Me? Well, I go to the art galleries and museums and talk to curators and whatever. I read art magazines and history books.

That sounds really great, I said. I like galleries too. I like museums.

She smiled. Just then, Alex came out of a row of trees, huffing, his face bright red. He saw me standing here and looked furious.

What are you doing just standing there? he screamed. We're getting clobbered.

What am I supposed to do?

Well, run! he told me. You're the fastest person on our team. We need you. I'm only one wozzle, he said. I can't do everything myself.

I don't know if I should, I said.

I looked at Ms. Durant for a hint. She was so beautiful, but she was my teacher. My grade four teacher. I thought, If only – if only – and we stood there, on the other side of a fence from the kids in my class, and I really didn't know what to do. Could I kiss her? Should I run?

Go on, she said. Your team needs you.

You're right, I said. I gave her a light pat on the back – it was an impulse, but it felt good. I hopped over the beam and ran over and met Alex on the field. I was a secret weapon. I put an arm on Alex's shoulder, my ally, my little friend. I kneeled beside him.

Okay, boss, I said. What do you want me to do?

Get that damn flag, he said.

I took off. And fast, I tell you. Because that's how you play the game.

SARAH SELECKY

THROWING COTTON

This past New Year's Eve, sitting on the loveseat in front of our little tabletop Christmas tree, I poured us both a glass of sparkling wine and told Sanderson: I think I'm ready to do it.

He kissed the top of my head and asked, Are you sure?

This is my last drink, I told him. I am officially preparing the womb.

Now it's the May long weekend. Sanderson and I have driven four hours north to Keewadin Lake, a cottage that we've rented every long weekend in May since we were at Trent together. We share it with our friends: Shona and Flip, who have been married even longer than we have, and Janine, who found the cottage for all of us almost ten years ago. I have a stack of first year composition papers that still have to be marked, but I left them at home so this could be a real holiday. I have a strong feeling about this weekend. I think this might be the weekend we conceive. I'm trying not to get my hopes up, but my instincts are usually good.

We get to the cottage late, nine o'clock. It's already well past dark and we're all very hungry. I can smell tension between Flip and Sanderson like something electric is burning. They both retreat to the living room. We move into the kitchen. Shona is an amazing cook, and she likes to do it. It's always been my job to sort the linens out when we arrive. But I feel particularly irritated that neither of our husbands has offered to help in the kitchen. These are progressive men. They know better than that.

Right in here, Shona says to me, even though I didn't ask her anything. She digs out a yellow packet of spaghetti from the bottom of one of the boxes. Told you! she says.

She also finds a pot with a lid, a can opener, and cardboard tubes of salt and pepper left over from the last people who stayed here.

A knife, she says, distracted. Were we supposed to bring our own knives?

I remember the drawer from last year and show her.

I don't think they're very sharp, I say. We should have brought a good one.

This will work, Shona says, and selects one with a plastic handle and a pointy, upturned blade. It's not like we're carving a roast, she says. She starts slicing cloves of garlic on one of the speckled stoneware dishes. Each time the blade strikes the plate, the sharp sound makes me wince.

The sun was down by the time we got here. Now it's too dark to see anything. When I flick on the porch light, I disturb a fluster of moths. I cup my hands around my face and look out the window. There's a dock with a little motorboat tied to it and an apron-shaped beach. There is a pale glow that looks as if it's radiating from the sand.

The linen closet is where it always is, in the main hallway. I pull out musty-smelling sheets and threadbare pillowcases for both of the beds upstairs. For Janine's bed, on the main floor, I pick out the pink-and-orange-flowered ones. Janine loves colour more than anyone I know. She's a graphic designer, but at Trent she studied English Lit like the rest of us. Not counting Sanderson, of course. She was actually enrolled in Sanderson's drawing class in her second year, but she withdrew when I told her I was sleeping with him. Those first years with Sanderson were more awkward than I like to remember. Our age difference was much more shocking when I was twenty-two years old. Now I'm teaching English at Ryerson and he's moved to the art history department at York and I can't remember the last time I felt scandalous. I drop the flowered sheets off first, leave them folded on the edge of the mattress in her room.

She's not coming, Flip calls to me when he sees me there. Didn't she call you? I told her to call you.

She didn't call me. I hug my chest and follow his voice into the living room. I look back and forth between Flip and Sanderson. Janine didn't call, did she, Sand?

He shakes his head and fills his glass with more wine.

Did she say why?

She said she had a family thing.

I started dating Sanderson two semesters after I finished his class. I was the one who asked him out. We met in East City, across the river, at a small café not far from the Quaker Oats building. There was a woman wearing a red apron who served us coffee in thick white cups. I put two packets of sugar in my coffee and a long dollop of cream. He told me, You have a good eye. But you need to trust the line when you draw. He had silver strands of hair at his temples. I thought this made him look debonair and sophisticated. Now I think it's safe to say he's going grey.

I wish you wouldn't drink so much this weekend, I tell him.

We just got here, he says. It was a long drive.

Flip is stretched out on the chair, even though the chair itself doesn't recline. His body is slouched down so his seat reaches the edge of the cushion and his head is pressed into the back of the chair. His long legs are crossed at the ankle. It doesn't look comfortable. He takes up most of the living room.

I can tell you why she's not here, Sanderson says to me.

He rubs the side of his sandpaper face with one hand. He hasn't shaved for three days. He says the stubble makes him feel like he's having a more authentic cottage experience, so he cultivated it before we arrived. His beard is still dark – there's a patch of grey on his chin, but the rest of his face still grows a mix of dark reds and browns. Earlier this week, watching him sleep, I picked out the different colours sprouting. They grew like a pack of assorted wildflower seeds.

She feels threatened by your choice to have a child. She's withdrawing from you so she doesn't feel – he trails off.

Lonely and misguided, hopeless, bitter? Flip finishes for him.

Exactly, says Sanderson. She doesn't want to feel threatened.

Wait. *My* choice to have a child?

Flip ignores me. I can see now that he is stoned. But, but, he says. Janine must feel lonely and threatened already. Otherwise she'd be here, right? Whoa. I think that's a paradox.

Did she tell you that?

No, says Flip, looking at me again. I think it was her grandmother's birthday.

I glare at Sanderson. He looks pleased with himself.

The sound of the knife cutting on stoneware stops. I go

back into the kitchen to open a bottle of seltzer. My choice to have a child. Okay. What I really want is a glass of red wine. Sanderson, of course, has the whole bottle next to his chair.

Shona hands me a glass from the cupboard above the sink. You want some lemon?

I want what you're having. I look at her glass of wine on the counter. But yes. Thank you. Lemon.

Shona is getting her master's degree at the Ontario Institute for Studies in Education at the University of Toronto. She has told me stories about the kids she's working with in her practicum. For instance: there is a boy who is obsessed with chickens. He calls himself the Chicken Man. Occasionally, he clucks to himself when he is drawing at his desk. When he's excited, he calls out, Chick-*EN*!

Shona has this quality. She observes the world more carefully than I do. She is slow to make decisions or judgments. She will listen to you ramble, and when you are finished, you feel like she has just told you something important about yourself. She is going to be a remarkable teacher. I hope that my son or daughter will be able to study with her.

Shona slices a lemon in half and squeezes it over my glass. Have lots, she says, it's cleansing. She rinses her hand under the tap, blots it with a dishcloth. Cloudy tendrils of lemon juice work their way into the water. I can hear the fizz of small bubbles rising and breaking the surface.

I look up. Did you know Janine couldn't come this weekend? I ask her.

Flip told me. Birthday party? Something.

I think it's strange. That she didn't call me.

Shona doesn't answer. She reaches up and pulls her ponytail apart to tighten it, and I catch a whiff of lacy, pungent garlic. Her oval face with all the hair pulled back is like an olive.

I say, Sanderson says Janine got her dog because I decided to have a baby.

She was looking into the breeders before that.

Yes, but. She didn't actually get Winnie until after I told her. And Sanderson thinks this is important.

I look into my glass and focus on the bubbles that cling to the sides.

There's never the perfect time to have kids, I say. Right? You just have to jump right in. You never feel one hundred per cent.

You make a convincing case for it, Shona says.

Janine's latest project is a font that she's made entirely out of pubic hairs.

I'm still working on it, she said on the phone the last time I spoke to her. Parentheses were easy. But I need an ampersand. I haven't even done uppercase yet.

I could hear a reedy whine from Winnie in the background. Then she said, I was sitting on the toilet one day and I saw a question mark on the tile by my foot. The most perfect question mark.

In your pubic hair, I said.

It's important for me to keep the letters genuine. I don't want to mess around with the natural curls.

Right. That would be missing the whole point.

No! Off! Mama's on the phone right now! Janine said. Anyway. I think it looks good. Almost gothic, but still organic.

I wish that I could be more like Janine. She doesn't even

pretend to care about anything other than herself, and we all love her anyway. I shouldn't be so surprised that she didn't call me about this weekend.

Wait a minute, Shona says in the kitchen, raising her wineglass and pointing at it with her other hand. Where's the rest of this? Is Sanderson hogging the wine?

In the living room, Flip and Sanderson have started to argue.

Sanderson leans forward in his chair in a half-lunge. His white sweatshirt has a logo with two crossed paddles on the chest, and a few spots of red wine that he won't notice until tomorrow morning.

Flip's face is tight. He says, If smokers came with their own private filtration systems, they could breathe what they exhale themselves. But we haven't invented that yet. So we stop smoking in bars.

Nobody's forcing you to breathe smoke.

Yes they are. In a bar, when there are smokers, it's everywhere.

Sanderson nods his head, leans back in the chair. Listen, he says. If I don't want to see a monster truck derby, I don't go to the arena. Get it?

You don't have to be an asshole.

You used to be a smoker too. I don't see where you get off.

Shona interrupts. Honey, leave it, you're stoned. Sanderson, pour me some wine.

Marijuana is different, Flip says.

They've been smoking in bars since the beginning of time, Sanderson mutters into his glass.

I don't like to see them fight like this. Sanderson thinks Flip needs to stop smoking dope – that it's making him dumb. Shona told me that Flip cringes when he reads Sanderson's emails because of the spelling errors. It's so important to each of them that the other appears intelligent. As though Sanderson's own intelligence is threatened when Flip appears dim-witted, or the other way around.

I get the bottle myself, since he's not making any move to do it. I pour some for Shona. Then I pour the remaining trickle into Flip's glass. Shona made dinner for us, I say, and turn to Sanderson. Say thank you.

Don't talk to me like I'm a child, he says. Then he flashes a wine-stained smile at her. Thank you, Shona.

There had been a student in the fall semester. A young woman named Brianna. She's very bright, Sanderson told me. Her technique is rough, but inspired. He'd call me in the afternoon, sometimes as late as five o'clock, and tell me that he was going to miss dinner. He never lied about where he was. He'd say they were going for drinks, grabbing a bite. He was helping her with her portfolio. One night he took her to Flip's bar. That's how self-assured he was. Flip told me that he saw them share a plate of calamari. That the woman fed him a ring from her fork. He said, The way she leaned across the table, Anne. I don't know.

I have always known this about Sanderson. He's one of those men who can keep his loving in separate compartments. He can love two women at once and not feel that he's betraying either of them. But when we got married we promised that we'd tell each other about our attractions, that there wouldn't be any secret affairs. I can understand having a crush. It's lying about it that bothers me.

It's ten o'clock when we sit down at the wobbly kitchen table to eat. The pasta should have been cooked for another five minutes. It sticks to my teeth like masking tape. But the four of us are so hungry we finish most of the noodles anyway, use up the whole pot of sauce to cover the piles on our plates. Flip mops up the last of it with a slice of garlic bread. Sanderson is quiet, possibly craving a cigarette. Shona is the only one who has wine left in her glass. I wrap my ankles and feet around the cold metal chair legs and silently will Sanderson not to open another bottle. It's cold in the cottage, even though the candles on the table make it look cozy. I could go put on some socks, but Sanderson already took my bag upstairs and I'm too lazy to go up there. My belly feels full and tight from too much pasta and bubbly water.

So, have you picked any good baby names? Flip asks me.

I heard someone in Calgary named her daughter Lexus, I answer.

I think it's exciting, Shona says. I'm living vicariously.

Flip looks at her. You want one too now?

This is how it happens, Sanderson says.

Shona looks at him. What exactly do you mean, she asks.

We all want meaning in our lives. We all want to feel significant. Why else would we choose to have babies? It's our mortality thing.

Flip says, You have a mortality thing happening already?

Shut up, says Sanderson.

I try saying this out loud: I just think it's time. I feel ready. I don't want to wait until I'm old to have a baby. I want to be a cool mom.

Shona says, I hate to say this sweetie, but I don't think a mom will ever seem cool to a teenager.

What do you think is old? Flip asks.

I just feel ready right now, I say.

Sanderson pushes his chair back from the table. He says, If I'm not ready now, I'll never be ready. It's time to throw cotton to the wind. He picks up his plate and brings it to the counter, plugs the drain, and turns on the hot water tap. Did we bring dish soap?

Shona points. Underneath.

Caution, I say.

What?

Everyone is quiet for a moment. Then a round, hollow, and breathy sound comes from Flip, who is trying to hide his laugh in his wineglass. It sounds like the fossilized call of a loon. Shona rolls her eyes at him.

It's throw caution to the wind, not cotton, I say.

You know what I mean. You don't have to make fun of me, he says.

No, it makes sense. You just throw cotton to the wind. It starts blowing around, right? Because of the wind? I start laughing, knowing that I should stop if I don't want to start another fight.

Sanderson ignores me. He looks in the cupboard under the sink and finds a bottle of green dishwashing detergent. He squirts some into the sink and there is a sweet apple smell. A white foam begins to grow on the water. Flip and I make ourselves stop laughing. We all sit at the table and watch Sanderson do the work.

You're going to quit smoking when the baby comes, right? Flip asks him.

Sanderson looks pained. Yes, Flip, of course I will.

Shona gathers the rest of the plates on the table and stacks them in front of her. She places the three forks on the top plate, which is covered with splotches of red sauce like a lurid Rorschach test. I think it would be nice, she says, for our babies to grow up together. She rests her hands on her belly.

Flip stares at her. I think we should wait, he says. Until you start teaching. You'll get maternity leave when you have a job. He touches his upper lip with his thumb. We could get a dog first.

Like Janine, says Sanderson.

Janine's dog is a baby replacement, Shona says. I want the real thing.

Flip holds the edge of the table with his hand. No, no. I'm way too irresponsible.

Shona sighs when she brings the stack of plates to the sink. You're just a scaredy-cat, she says. If I got pregnant, something would click for you. You'd get another job.

I say, What's wrong with working at a bar? Bartenders are respectable people.

You know what a baby means. The money. There are those trust funds, those babies with the little graduation caps. No. Not until my own student loans are paid.

Shona laughs. Stop it, you're killing me. Paying off our student loans!

Sanderson turns off the tap and swishes the water with his hand. There's the bumping sound of plates swimming against stainless steel. Shona is beside him at the counter. She puts an arm around his waist and leans against him. He braces himself against the counter with one hand and holds her weight. Look at Sanderson, she says to Flip. He's not a scaredy-cat. I bet he still has student loans. Don't you, Sandy?

I glance down at my stomach, the way it makes a small ball of itself when I sit. It looks flat when I'm standing, but there's a little roll when I'm sitting down. I fix my posture in the chair. My belly changes when I straighten my back, but it still rests in a small lump on top of my legs. It's not a pregnant lump, it's just a weak abdomen, too much for dinner. But I try to imagine what it would feel like. When you're carrying a baby, you must feel like you're always carrying around a little Christmas present.

I'm actually all paid up, says Sanderson. But I had scholarships, so.

Flip stands up and fills my field of vision with his long legs, his green plaid torso. Sanderson is older than I am, he says. He's much more mature.

Don't you forget it, Sanderson says. Now excuse me, all of you, but I'm old, and I need a cigarette.

Don't turn on the porch light, I tell him. You'll attract the moths.

When he goes outside, I reach over the table for what's left of Shona's wine. Flip waggles his finger.

Oh drink it, Shona tells me. It's not going to hurt anything. If Janine were here, you'd be drunk by now anyway.

This winter, when she bought a new condo downtown, Janine sent an email: I'm throwing a housewarming party. Just for us. Come at eight, stay till late. It was the coldest night in February, steam swirling on top of Lake Ontario because the air was so much colder than the water. When I blinked, my eyelashes stuck together, frozen. We arrived with housewarming gifts: a bottle of Tanqueray Ten, a jar of vermouth-soaked olives, a shiny silver martini shaker.

Janine opened the door and there was a gush of warm air in the hallway. The entranceway was a bright lacquer red. All along her wall, a line of tea lights glowing in glass saucers. She wore a short sequined cape on top of a black dress. It fell just above the elbows. A capelet. I felt the air melt around my body, my face defrosting. Janine had sparkles brushed along her cheekbones.

You brought cocktails! she said. She took the tall bottle out of my arms.

You look gorgeous, I said. I'll have a virgin cosmo.

Virgin my ass, she said.

Great paint job, I told her.

Like it? It's the same shade as Love That Red by Revlon. I had it specially blended and shipped from this place in Oregon.

It's hot, Sanderson said.

Inside, Flip and Shona were already drinking, sitting on chrome barstools. Shona stirred pink juice in a glass with her finger. They were talking about the ways people learn. Shona had just come from class. She said, There are three ways that we all learn: we're either auditory, visual, or kinesthetic.

I'm visual. I know I'm visual, Janine said.

Shona said, We learn in all three ways, but we lean one way most of the time.

I went over it in my head: It's hot, Sanderson had said. He didn't say to her, You're hot. But that's what I heard. I had just come off the pill at that point. My hormones were still stabilizing.

I walked to the back window. There was a good view of the Gardiner Expressway. A string of red tail lights curved away from me, and the cars made small movements as they braked and accelerated. From this distance they looked like I imagined blood cells would look, moving through a capillary.

Flip came up behind me and said in my ear: Hello, I'm kinesthetic. What are you?

Sanderson was at the bar looking for a shot glass. Janine had filled the martini shaker with ice cubes. The bottom half of the shaker was already cold grey, frosting from the inside out. Her sequined cape, the martini shaker, the barstools, Sanderson's hair: I turned around and saw everything in silver.

Janine said, You're visual too, Sandy. She flickered her fingers on his chest to illustrate her point. He wore a white T-shirt with a.silk-screened drawing of a swing set on it.

I think I'm all three of them, I said. I can't just pick one.

Now Flip, he's auditory, Sanderson said.

And how would you know? Flip asked from across the room.

Because you talk so much.

Fuck you, said Flip.

Then in a soft voice, Flip said to me, How are you doing.

I leaned into him. Ooh, I said. Is that velour?

Touch it, he said. I petted his sleeve like it was a puppy. His arm felt warm through the plush. I stopped at his wrist and held it with both of my hands.

Don't be mad at Sanderson, I said. He's just wired that way.

With the girls, you mean.

It's not serious with Brianna.

Well good. As long as it's not serious.

I looked at him. We're human beings, I said. It's normal to flirt. We can't help being attracted.

Flip took his arm out of my hands. You don't have to explain it to me, he said.

I just love Weimeranders, I know, Janine was saying. She had brought a dog book out to the bar. She pressed the spine open with the palm of her hand. But my space is so small, she said.

What do you guys think about this one? Is he too cute? Would you laugh at me if I got a terrier?

We'll always laugh at you, darling, said Shona.

What kind of terrier? Flip asked.

It's called a Cairn terrier. And it's oh-my-god cute. But then I would be one of those women, wouldn't I? Janine made a face. She held a fresh Tanqueray martini. The glass caught the light from the halogens overhead. It glimmered in her hand. There were three olives speared on a silver pick.

Shona said, Janine, you're already one of those women. Don't fight it.

If you see me with a Burberry dog coat, okay? You have permission to smack me.

Can you make me one of those, I asked Sanderson. With onions if she's got them.

On the fridge door, middle shelf, Janine said. She smiled at me. Virgin.

You want one too, Flip? Sanderson said. I'm pouring.

Flip looked at him. I'm kinesthetic, he said. Read my body language.

That night in the cottage I dream about a blizzard. Janine and her dog Winnie are trying to dig something out of a snowdrift. When I wake up, it's still dark out, and Sanderson has stolen all the covers. I'm freezing. I lean over, grab the pile of comforters and blankets on the floor beside him and pull them over the bed evenly again. He's wearing the blue boxers I gave him for his birthday last year. He sleeps on his side, one arm under the pillow, the other stretched out in a straight line away from me, his hand almost touching the night table. His hand is curled as though it could be holding something very small, like a pinch of salt.

I flatten myself against him, wrap my body around his lower half. I lift up my T-shirt and press my breasts into his skin. Tease my hand over the front of his boxers. The skin on Sanderson's neck is damp and bristly against my lips. I promise God, the Universe, the baby itself: Please let me have you. I will love you like nothing else has been loved before. Sanderson exhales a sour cloud of undigested wine.

There's a sound downstairs. Outside, on the deck: soft thumps, like falling potatoes. I stop the prayer and hold myself perfectly still. A rustling against the glass, a bump against the kitchen doors. It sounds like someone is trying to break in.

I whisper Sanderson's name, grip one of his hips and shake it so that his whole body rocks the mattress. He makes a noise like he's slurping something through his mouth.

I wrap a fleece blanket around my shoulders and shuffle across the hallway and peek into Flip and Shona's doorway. Flip is sleeping on his stomach, face pushed into the pillow, facing Shona. Shona is splayed on her side like a pressed flower, arms and legs draped over Flip's body in the effortlessness of sleep. Now that I am fully awake, I can hear the thumping sound for what it is. Paws, jumping on the wood of the deck.

I go down the stairs slowly, starting on tiptoe and rolling to my heels so I won't scare them away. A family of raccoons. Three small ones rolling like bear cubs on top of one another. Close to the glass doors, a large raccoon – the mother, naturally I think it's the mother – sorts through the remains of the plastic

Dominion bag that we had used for garbage. The leftover spaghetti noodles seem to emit moonlight, making an elaborate pattern of loops and curls. I fold myself into the armchair and watch the little family make a huge mess. I look for letters in the patterns of noodles, try to spell out the letters in my name.

When Flip comes down, he sees me bent over in the chair with my face in my hands staring out the window.

Anne, he says. What's wrong. What's happening.

I look up at him. He has a T-shirt on, boxer shorts. His hair like a pile of twigs.

The raccoons got into our garbage.

He follows my gaze to the window. Shit, he says.

It's our own fault. We should have thought.

Flip rubs his head. You couldn't sleep either?

I just saw you. You were sound asleep.

I need a snack, he says, and goes into the kitchen.

The mother raccoon stops what she's doing for a moment and stands on her hind legs, her paws held in front of her. It looks like she's watching me. But I haven't turned any lights on. It's perfectly dark, we're concealed in here.

Flip comes out with a plastic honey bear and a spoon. Scootch over, he says, and sits next to me, half on the seat cushion, half on the arm of the chair. He squeezes the honey bear over the spoon. There is a shine in the dark when the honey flows out. He slips the spoon into his mouth and closes his eyes.

Flip.

Mm?

Do you know something.

What.

No, I mean, do you know something that I don't know.

Have some, he says.

He fills another spoonful and brings it to my lips. He doesn't let go, even as I work my tongue over the spoon, licking all the sweetness off it. Then he slides it out of my mouth.

There, he says. Is that better?

His bare leg touching mine on the chair. It could happen so easily.

You can tell me, I say. Janine and Sanderson. Am I right?

Oh Anne, Flip says.

I won't tell him you said anything. I figured it out on my own. I just want to know for sure.

There's nothing between Janine and Sanderson.

If there's nothing, then why isn't she here this weekend?

Anne. She wanted to be here. It really was a family thing.

I stop talking. Flip is resting the honey bear on his knee. He plays with the pointy cone on top of its head with his index finger. Circles it first one way, and then the other. When his finger gets too sticky, he puts it in his mouth. Looking at me as he does this. I feel my nipples tighten into hard french knots under my T-shirt. He leans over and drapes his arm around my shoulder. His face is very close to my face. I can breathe him. He smells like toasted bread and Ivory Soap.

I let my head fall back so he can kiss me. I notice differences: the softness of his lower lip, the way he cups the side of my face in his hand. That his face is smooth, even at this time of night. It is the first time in nine years that I have kissed anyone but Sanderson.

There, he says, and pulls away from me. That's what I know.

My eyes have adjusted to the dark, but they take shortcuts, turn shadows into shapes. It's too dark to see anything clearly. The shapes adjust when I think differently about what I'm looking at. When I stare at Flip's shoulder, the darkness clusters in front of my eyes and I can turn it into a perfect sphere. It crawls with darkness and I think about what Flip's shoulder should look like and then it morphs into a shoulder again. I remember an old drawing lesson, something Sanderson told me years ago. When you're drawing an object, you need to stick to one viewpoint. Set the object down and sit so you can see it without moving your head very much. You always want to have your head in the same place whenever you look at the object. A small movement can make a surprisingly big difference once you start drawing the details.

You should go to bed now, I say slowly.

Is that really what you want me to do.

Yes.

Fine, he says, and he pulls me off the chair and I go with him to the couch and we make love there. We move quietly and quickly. He says my name as he inhales. It sounds like and, and, and. When we're finished we don't say anything. We lie on the couch together breathing honey. My arm is stuck in a crevice between the couch pillows. I feel something gritty rubbing against my elbow. Flip moves first. He slides his hands down along my hips and rests his head on my chest before he stands up. Then he goes upstairs and I can hear the water running for a minute.

I find my way into the kitchen and without turning any lights on, I feel for a plastic bag in the drawer. I bring it outside onto the deck. The raccoons have pulled everything out and thrown it into piles. I crouch and scrape up the noodles with my hands. The wood looks stained even when the garbage is gone. I'm still in my bare feet. I know I should be cold, but I can't feel it.

MARTIN WEST

CRETACEA

A White Tail deer went down over a wire fence and lay sprawled in the middle of the road right on the centre line. The animal contorted on the pavement with a broken leg in the shadow of the old red wheat king and so I put a single .303 round through its head. Part of the skull blew off into the ditch, and one of its antlers spun across the pavement to the shoulder. It was the only humane thing to do. Problem was, I wasn't finished shooting stuff then. I lined up a couple of abandoned televisions that a pawnshop had dumped down by the petrified oyster bed and blew the screens out. The screens imploded with a sucking sound and one of the 1950s style knobs shot into the sky like fireworks. After that, I walked down the street and shot out a few lamp standards and three car windows. A Dodge, a Ford, and a Toyota four-by-four, I think. On the edge of town, I perched myself on a big drumlin so I could get a good view of Main Street. Everything was mine for the taking. I took out a store window with a garden gnome on display and a fourteen-foot plastic Triceratops that floated above one of the department stores. The beast was filled with helium and attached by a long string to a fire hydrant; its green fluorescent body bobbed

slowly in the evening breeze, so basically it was an easy target.
Next, I blew apart the golden symbol of a clown that was
embossed on a mock chapel of a hamburger restaurant and put
a round into the gut of a dead cat that had been lying on the
corner of Main and Second Avenue for three days. Nobody had
bothered to pick it up. As for the ecumenical brass clown, that
thing had always bothered me a lot, and I felt much better after
filling his orange hair with lead. In a few minutes, the sound of
police cars and fire engines filled the streets of our little prairie
town, so I figured it was probably time to start the long walk
back home. Besides that, I was almost out of ammunition.

Half an hour later, when I arrived back at my bungalow in the
middle of a sage field at the bottom of the Red Deer Valley, not
much had changed. My satellite dish in the cottonwoods had
still not been hooked up, a stack of magazines and books still lay
unsorted on the balcony, and on the other side of the field, in
the grey layers of ancient sediment, a thousand prehistoric
beasts still slept silent with their secrets.

I went out into the field and put my rifle in a metal tube, dug
a small trench at least two feet deep, and buried the weapon as per
the instruction in *Soldier of Fortune* magazine. Then I used a rake
and piled some rabbit grass over the hole to make sure everything
looked natural. Off in the distance, the red and blue blinking
lights of emergency vehicles still flashed away in the night like
there was a wedding or Christmas celebration going on, but after
an hour or so, the lights grew distant and then disappeared altogether. I guess the authorities must have caught someone who
they believed was the right person or else just given up.

There was a documentary on channel 273 that looked interesting called *Last Dreams of the Dinosaurs* but as the dish was still

not connected, there was no point in even turning the TV on. Instead, I sat on the back porch with a glass of Canadian Club and read some poetry by Butler and Yeats. From time to time, I wished I had someone there to read it with me. I watched the dead sage roll across the road and dozed off.

Every action has a reaction, and the smart ones have none, so sure as shoot first thing the next morning a police cruiser came rolling up my driveway. There's a plastic dog that sits at the foot of the driveway with a solar panel on his head and a motion detector embedded in his nose, so every time something passes by, the dog barks and his eyes light up bright red like he's possessed, but of course, this didn't scare the police away. I was actually out back washing my hands off with vinegar and baking soda, because this dissolves the cordite on palms in case one is subject to scientific tests. I put all of my things down and went inside to put tea or coffee on as this usually makes the police want to stay and chat for a while and many times they have interesting stories to tell. A few years ago, an elderly corporal named Macnee came investigating some cattle thefts – actual cattle rustling – and stayed for over an hour. Macnee wasn't much into poetry, but he became obsessed with my fossil collection and we spent many weekends scouring the Badlands and drinking Black Label beer looking for some kind of "missing link." Black Label was his favourite. He didn't drink anything but Black Label. Sometimes fifteen or sixteen in a row. We never found the "missing link" or any fossils of much significance, but we had a good time drinking on my front porch and Macnee suggested I get a dog to keep me company. Sadly, he got transferred to Nova Scotia because he had embarrassed himself during a drunken rage at the Bronto Beer Inn, and I never saw him again.

The police car stopped outside. I dried my hands and opened the screen door and wasn't really prepared for what stood in front of me. An Amazon blonde female constable with wisps of yellow hair falling over her forehead and a few dozen freckles spattered over her cheeks leaned against my doorframe and chewed on her pencil eraser. She was about five nine and obviously spent most of her time finding just the right perfume when she wasn't working out in the gym. Her eyes were the same colour as the prairie sky. She looked me over once and the right-hand corner of her mouth curled up just a little. "Hello," she said.

"Hello," I said back.

"Want to know why I'm here?"

"Sure," I said. Any reason would be good enough.

"I'm conducting some neighbourhood inquiries about the shooting last night," she said and pulled out her notebook. She tried to find an address by the door, but of course there wasn't one.

"Shooting?" I said. "What happened?"

She shrugged and pushed a wad of chewing gum between her front teeth. "Someone went crazy with a gun and shot the town up. Probably drunk or totally right wing. Did you see anything?"

I put one hand on the doorframe and leaned forward into the crux of my elbow ostensibly to show some sign of remorse or stupidity, but in effect to get a closer whiff of her perfume. What is that stuff that smells like dust? Patchouli? Petunia? Permian Extinction? "Shoot," I said, and read off her name tag. "Constable Holocene, you know I feel like a total idiot now. I did hear something last night that sounded like shots. I knew I should have called you guys."

"Really. About what time?"

"About seven."

"Seven? Are you sure it was that early?"

"Well, I thought so. Wasn't paying that much attention, really. Sometimes the ranchers shoot at cattle pretty close to here, or anything else that moves."

"Yeah," she cut in. "And they're not supposed to inside city limits. Anyway, how many shots did you hear?"

"Only two or three," I shrugged.

"That's it? Two or three?"

"Were there more?"

"Ah, maybe." She hesitated. "What direction did they come from?"

"From somewhere down the Dinosaur Trail," I said and pointed way to the west of where the White Tail had met its merciful demise. "And then they just got fainter towards town."

"Yep," she said, and scribbled a few lines in her notebook. "That'd be it."

"I feel really bad about not reporting it last night," I said. "It just didn't seem like anything out of the ordinary."

"Oh, this time it was. For this part of the world, anyway." Then she looked at me with those blue summer eyes and said, "Do you keep any firearms in the house?"

"No. Not even a BB gun."

"Mind if I have a look?"

"No, of course not, please come in," I said, because it was a perfunctory question and I am an expert at spotting those. I ask them so often.

I stepped back and begged her inside. The good constable came in and made quick reconnoiter of my cluttered living room. She seemed more interested in the stacks of books and catalogued fossils lying around the floor than any location that might conceal a weapon. "You're into fossils?"

"I'm especially interested in the Juliana deposits," I said.

"And . . ." She picked up a book off a waist-high stack. "Poetry."

"I do reviews. For a living. Sort of."

"Ah, really?" she said. "For a magazine?"

"Yes. For a national magazine."

"For that slightly right-of-centre national magazine or that slightly . . ."

"Yes, that one."

"Good on you," she said.

"Would you like to have a cup of coffee or tea?" I asked. "I actually have both just about on the brew set to go."

She looked me over again, put the book down and smiled. "I'd really love to," she said. "But we have to have a meeting with Staff Sergeant at nine about the 'incident.'" She raised her finger in the air to quote the word.

"Though the leaves are many, the root is one," I said.

"I swayed my leaves and flowers in the sun," she quoted back.

That was really all it took.

If you believe in God, you will do the following things: 1) Attend all public meetings in the local town hall about shootings or acts of national subversion that have occurred recently in your area; 2) Accept the fact that everyone in your hometown either has a gun or wants a gun or wishes they wanted a gun or wants to do something important with a gun, but if you actually do something with a gun, then this is blasphemous; 3) Try not to throw up when everyone at the meeting is really upset about something that has happened and assumes that their elected leaders are doing nothing because they elected them.

I pass on all three. One far right-wing group who named themselves the "White Cattleman's Petroleum Revenge League" had threatened to ask American president George Bush to send in the U.S. Marine Corps if local officials weren't going to act quickly. There was no mention of the White Tail deer that had died so pathetically tripping over a barbed cow fence. I figured it might be fun to watch (the meeting, not the invasion), and besides, somewhere in the middle of the night it had occurred to me that the first round to be dispatched lay somewhere embedded in a Cervidae carcass not too far from my own home and that had to be retrieved. Evidence is evidence, as they say, and this had to be dealt with.

I walked down the Badlands road with the smell of sage and the sound of cicadas heavy in the air. The height of summer shimmered wet off the hot concrete, and I knew this was the only place in the world to be. When I got to the spot where the deer had died, there was not a hide in sight. No bones. No hooves, no tail. This was the right place all right – centre of the road right, third fence post from the creek, directly under the red wheat king that school kids had painted a giant yin and yang sign on. If one looked harder at the cracked wood, one would find even older graffiti that dated back to the fifties and even one curious faded scrawling that read, "D-Day Is Ours." But no deer in sight. For a moment it seemed possible that the police had impounded the entire animal for analysis, for lead content, or maybe they would conduct a polygraph, but a closer inspection revealed the obvious truth. In the right-hand lane, a thin stain of red blood spread out funnel-like westwards on the road. Bits of squished deer fur had been ground into pavement and the piece of antler that had scuttled away from the impact scene lay in the ditch. This being a well-used road, the poor White Tail had been run over dozens, maybe hundreds, of times in the course of the night; the dead furry pancake had been reduced into a red smear toward the western horizon. In a day or two, there would be not a trace left. The chunk of lead would be an indistinguishable metallic shape and the cartridge just another shiny object sinking into the Cretaceous dust of the Badlands.

With some sense of relief, I ventured into the Maple Leaf Grocery Store to buy a strip of beef jerky and a copy of *Prehistoric History Today* before the meeting. The tales of shooting were on everyone's lips and everybody had a theory. Over nine hundred rounds had been discharged. One round penetrated a sensitive geoseismic centre and the oil industry in Alberta would surely be ruined for it. Another round was specifically sent through the theological centre of town in order to demoralize the city's righteous population. The actions were terrorist related, but not politically motivated, and attributable to some non-sectarian cult group. When I was paying for the beef jerky, curiosity got the better of me and I had to ask, "So what happened, anyway?"

"You haven't heard?" the clerk said. "Someone shot up the entire town last night."

"The whole town?"

"All of it. There's a lot of bullets laying in bad places."

"Is there a good place for a bullet to be?"

"Not where these ones are. The whole thing is very weird," she said, and nodded. "What's in that magazine, anyway?"

"You've never read it?"

"No, but we sell a lot of copies. I don't get it."

"There's a lot of pictures. Photos. Of stuff that's relevant."

"That's too weird. I don't know why they put it right up front at the check stand, it doesn't belong there."

I stuck a wad of jerky in my mouth and walked to Main Street. I really shouldn't eat this stuff. It pulls out my fillings and gets stuck between my teeth and then I'm in a bad mood until I can get a toothpick or floss it out. Usually I carry emergency floss with me, but the Cherry-Mint flavour that I buy at Loo's Import Market that comes only from Beijing had not yet arrived that week, so when I went around the corner onto the scene, I was feeling very vulnerable and agitated. The place was still a carnage. Not one piece of damage had been picked up. Instead, every site, hole, and puncture had been cordoned off with yards of yellow police tape and men in suits were doing triangulation with laser theodolites. A few constables leaned against lamp-posts making sure no one crossed the line. The saddest sight of all was the poor green plastic Triceratops that lay deflated in the middle of the sidewalk with the collar and string still tied around his flat neck. The bullet had pierced his heart and had carried on in an unknown direction.

The meeting was housed in the elementary school gymnasium with red and blue lines painted on the floor and the place was packed. They had set out over a hundred metal folding chairs and they were all full, so the next hundred people stood against the walls. A few of them were drinking beer, but no one paid too much attention to that. Lined up against the far wall stood six overweight men in black jeans and black T-shirts. The shirts all had a giant red C printed on the chest with a white skull and crossbones in the centre. They looked very stern and threatening except for their stomachs, which folded in two or three rolls over their belts. They were holding hoods, scrunching them angrily between their fists, which I presume was because the police told them they couldn't wear hoods during public meetings.

Mary Holocene was on duty again and leaned against the back wall under the basketball hoop with an elderly sergeant who looked rather nervous, like maybe he had to give an explanation about all of this. A wisp of hair fell over her forehead; she seemed pained to be there too. Every time one of the Cattlemen tried to slide a hood over his head, or even got it above crotch level, she raised one finger and shook it until he retreated.

Some things reveal themselves quickly about people who you find attractive or interesting and already I had deduced many things about Mary Holocene. She was a non-career officer by choice and no doubt came to the Force through some biographical accident. By looking at her, I could also tell she probably had some dark or at least embarrassing secret in her past that she wanted to forget or bury so deep that not even the earth would know. The best thing about revealing truths about people who you are attracted to or interested in is deducing what their deep and dark secrets are and where they lay. Burying the secrets deeply would be an essential component for Mary to leave her past behind and embark on a life change in a paramilitary organization. She would have to convince the polygraph examiner that either the perturbations didn't exist or else that there was really nothing wrong with them. But what could those acts be? This was the stuff that novels are made of. No doubt Mary as a small girl stole pears, hot-knifed hash oil, and attended "Love-Ins" at Stanley Park (she was brought up on the West Coast), or doused her Barbie with kerosene and lit it afire until it spread to the curtains or carport or perhaps a slumbering cat. But then, every Canadian child does these kinds of things, and this is nothing to be ashamed of. No, I could sense Mary's perversions ran deeper that this. No doubt they were formulated during her adolescent or pubescent years. Perhaps they involved strange interactions with older gentlemen or retired schoolmarms. Candle wax or Catholic school clothing may have been utilized. But even this was not the Elixir. The *event* would come years later. Some archeological ego-versus-id metaphor that her partner could not understand. Frustrated, she left the relationship and then left town, trying to leave the remnants behind in the gathering dust. But this is not an easy thing to do. Mary soon found that she was only attracted to others with a perverse mindset such as her own and constantly had to be leaving affairs and leaving towns for lack of satisfaction and growing security concerns. Then one day in desperation, when towns had run out, she visited a recruiting office, and a few weeks later found herself at the training depot in Regina. These things happen.

The inside of the gymnasium was getting very hot and droplets of clear sweat had spattered on the shiny floor. I wandered down the hall to a pop machine and dropped a loonie in the slot. The coin rattled into the guts of the machine, but nothing came out, so I dropped another inside and the same thing happened. I had a pocketful of change, so I went over to the next machine and tried a third time. Three bucks gone now, never to be returned. There's no point in shaking or kicking these machines so I moved down to the fourth dispenser in the line and gave it one last shot. This time a soda rolled out at the bottom and then two more followed it. I had an idea.

With three tins in hand, I walked back to the gymnasium. Under the basketball hoops, still leaning against the wall, were Mary and her Sergeant. I offered them both unopened tins.

"Thanks," the Sergeant said immediately. "I've got to get up in front of these morons in a minute and tell them everything that I don't know. My throat is bone-dry." He took the tin and swallowed half of it in one gulp.

"You look like you were having problems with the machines there," Mary said and took the second tin from my hand.

"Yeah, you have more patience than I do," the Sergeant added. "I would have shot the damn thing."

The three of us grunted a laugh, but not too loud, because shooting wasn't that funny a topic on this occasion.

Mary told the Sergeant that I did fiction reviews for national magazines.

"Really?" the Sergeant said. He was thinking about his upcoming speech and had the jitters. He played with his tie clip. "Which ones?"

I rambled off a rather long and detailed list.

"Good for you," he said. "I like books. Especially books about fishing."

Mary nodded approvingly and understood the names didn't mean much to the Sergeant. What I said was actually true. I have published reviews in such magazines, but I wasn't going to volunteer the information that my last three publications had been in *Screw Magazine*, *Hustler*, and *The Northern Beaver*.

The meeting got going. I spent most of my time sneaking peeks at Mary's vest-covered breasts and trying to smell her perfume.

The investigators of the incident had determined a number of facts. First, that all of the targets were hit at long range. Second, that the weapon used was probably a .303 with very old ammunition. Perhaps even war ammunition that had been stored well in a cold, dry place. Third, every target had only one bullet in it and no "stray" shots had been found, meaning that either the shooter was an expert marksman or had a scope with remarkable precision. Fourth, that the targets all seemed to be of a "symbolic" nature and the Sergeant appeared pleased with the use of this word, like he had just picked it up in something other than a police manual. Last, that sadly as of yet there were no suspects; although some interesting leads had been uncovered, there was simply nowhere to go. This bought an angry cry from the black-shirted Cattleman's Revenge League who hooted and hollered that the police were in cahoots with Eastern Liberals and that if everyone could carry a gun around with them then the shootist would have been shot dead before he did any more property damage and land-owning people should be entitled to shoot things out as they so wished. Generally, the crowd didn't side with the Cattlemen, and the Sergeant, no greenhorn at dealing with angry people, concluded by adding that this incident *could* have been the work of extremists, which shut the Cattlemen up right quick and made at least half the crowd cast disapproving glances back at the four fat men who now looked rather silly holding black hoods somewhere around crotch level.

Even a small town has its dark side when it comes to humour and our little town is no exception. The community cable channel has a weekly comedy spot that is actually filmed in the storefront window of a woman's dress shop just off Main Street. People stop and watch it being filmed with bundles of hockey sticks or tubs of antifreeze under their arms, not because they think the show is wise or funny, but mostly because they want to catch a glimpse of themselves on television the following Wednesday when the show is aired in case the camera did a live pan of the audience.

This week they had three contestants who insisted that they were the "shootist" and were trying to prove it to the host by answering tricky historical questions. The contestants were Karl Marx, Indira Gandhi, and Ivan the Terrible. Jesus Christ had been pulled at the last minute and so one chair was vacant. One of the producers shook his head as he muttered to his director that this was still a Christian town and Jesus Christ had better not show up on the set if they wanted any funding next year. As I sat inside the store watching the show, it occurred to me that all of these people wanted to be the shootist. The Cattlemen's Petroleum Revenge League wanted to be the shootist. The grocery store clerk wanted to be the shootist. When Ivan the Terrible was asked at the end why he thought the audience should vote for him as the shootist, he replied, "Because then at last everybody would know who I am."

Outside the mall-cum-TV studio, I asked a construction worker, a gas-station attendant, a bus driver, and a very modern nun who wore a blue suit with a red tie who they thought Ivan the Terrible was and none of them knew.

On my way home, I walked by the Animal Shelter and thought I'd better ask one more person to make the study scientific. Inside, a pimply high-school student leaned over an aluminum counter reading a superhero comic book. There was a bucket filled with disinfectant and a mop behind him, but he didn't appear too interested in scrubbing the floor. When I asked him who Ivan the Terrible was, he said, "Didn't he have something to do with the shooting?"

"Shooting?"

"Yeah, shooting. Don't you know? Do you want a dog?" he asked.

"Not really, why?"

"Because this is the pound."

"No thanks," I said.

"Then why did you come in here? Don't you have a job?"

"Yes, I have a job," I said. "I work at home. In the publishing industry, actually. Aren't you going to clean that floor?"

He looked down at the bucket and then back at me. "No. Take a dog, would you, Mister."

"Don't want one."

"Then we have some old dogs that won't live very long. You'd only have to put up with it for a little while before it died so it wouldn't be much of an investment."

"I'm not sure if that's a good deal or not. What would I do with a dog anyway?"

"It'd keep you company when you're lonely," he said.

I thought about it for a moment. "What kinds of dogs do you have?"

"All kinds. Big ones. Black ones. Small ones."

"What would you recommend?"

"Well, personally I'd take one that's been here the longest so it doesn't get put down. That's sometimes very traumatic for them."

"Okay, show me."

The young boy put a tick in the right-hand column of the white folder he had on the counter and took me to the back of the pound, which smelled like dog fur and disinfectant. In the last cage, an ugly black dog cowered in the rear of the run. Long whiskers stuck out of his snout and white froth bubbled around his mouth. He looked like some combination of Heeler and Lab. "I'll throw in a leash for free if you take him," the boy said.

"Free leash?"

"No charge. And a collar, too."

"All right," I said.

The boy did the paperwork then got the black dog from the cage and found a leash and collar. The dog sat there patiently in the front office wondering what kind of unhappiness he'd got himself into this time, but figuring it was better than whatever awaited him in the cage. I clicked the leash onto his collar, and we walked out the front door together. For the first few blocks, the dog was enthusiastic to be outside. He looked from side to side and sniffed at a bunch of rabbit grass and growled at a mailbox like he was looking after me, but after a while he slowed to a geriatric crawl and finally by the bridge that crossed the Red Deer River under the giant green Tyrannosaurus, the dog sat down on the hot sidewalk and would go no further. I picked the animal up, but he was too heavy to carry more than a few steps, and outside the Dixie Queen with yellow Durham husks in the air, we stood with no resolution.

A police car stopped at the corner and Mary rolled down her electric window. "New dog?" she said.

"Well, he's new to me. I just got him and he's too old to make the trip home. I should have brought the car."

Mary bit her lip, adjusted her rearview mirror then popped the electric lock on the passenger side. "Get in," she said.

I sat in the front seat with the dog on my lap. The inside of the car smelled like Iso Gel. Mary started down the country road. She talked as she drove and steered the car with one hand. We bounced over a set of railway ties at 105 kilometres an hour. "Isn't this against policy or something?" I asked.

"Probably," she said, and drove on with her right hand on the emergency brake. "What made you decide to get a dog, anyway?"

"I'm not sure. He was in the cage by himself and looked lonely. Besides, the guy in the pound assured me that he was a good copy editor."

"Hah," she laughed and was going to say something but the dispatcher on the radio called her in a scratchy voice that only police can understand. Apparently, a tractor had overturned on the highway and some pigs were pinned under the rear wheels. "Oh ferfucksakes," Mary muttered and pushed the car up to 130. She slid sideways in a cloud of dust near my driveway and popped up the door locks. "Sorry, got to run," she said.

"Okay." I got out and walked the dog back to the house.

I found a big wicker basket that had been used to store mag-azine reviews, tossed the paper out, and put some blankets inside. The dog curled up and went to sleep. Later that evening, I made hamburgers and the dog ate a whole patty and we sat out on the porch drinking rye, watching the summer sun turn red into twilight.

The top half of the ridge caught fire the next afternoon while the dog and I were down on the back porch dozing. The dog was in his basket curled up like a doughnut and only shifted from side to side as the first particles of soot settled on the unpainted cedar strips around him. One moment the edge of the coulee was brown and still, the next minute it was jumping with bright yellow flames. Thousands of sparks flew into the air as the rabbit grass ignited and then the sky filled with sweet grey smoke as the sage began to burn. It was all very exciting. Reams of smoke rolled down the coulee like waves breaking on a beach and the smell of summer filled the valley bottom. Cacti make these strange popping noises when they burn under very high temperatures and all of the eastern slopes were now bursting like tiny landmines. To add to the excitement, I lit up a Camel cigarette that a friend of a friend had assured me was in the backpack of an actual GI at Que Son during the Vietnam War. The dog rolled over and chewed on a biscuit that had been baked in the oven under very high temperatures and I decided since it was after four o'clock (one minute after, actually), having the first rye of the day would be okay. I have rye with all kinds of things: with ginger ale and rootbeer, with tomato juice and lemon water. Sometimes, I have rye with ice or other sentimental objects melting in the bottom of the glass. A spike taken from the Canadian Pacific Railway. A piece of chopstick from Mrs. Chung's Chinese Restaurant on Fourth Avenue, which serves amazing almond chicken. A shred of the original Canadian Constitution Act that was torn from the Senate Chambers when

Pierre Elliott Trudeau signed it in 1980, or so my source tells me. About the only thing I can't drink rye with is milk, and that's probably got something more to do with the aesthetics of the milk curdling like the satellite photo of the moon than with the actual taste. Today I had it straight though, no mixing necessary, because it's always better to have your alcohol straight when something exciting is happening right outside your back door.

Just to keep things safe, I went down into the basement and got a hundred feet of irrigation tubing that the previous owner had left behind when he'd sold the house. I hooked the hose to the faucet under the bathroom window. The faucet was huge and probably used for farm purposes because a lot of pressure came out the end. I drenched the roof and walls of the house and then dragged the hose as far out back as it would go. The hose and me ended up by a windmill with a rooster on top right near a creek that ran through the back of my property. When I opened the spigot, the water squirted another hundred feet toward the coulee. I watered down the single cottonwood in the backfield and then sprayed the grass that looked sad and droopy in the August sun. It's pretty hard to tell where my property ends and the grazing lands begin. I have ten acres altogether and the cattle fence that was once at the back of the property has long since fallen down. The ranchers never bothered to put it back up again. I'm not sure if that's because the land down here is no good for cattle or whether the ranchers couldn't care less if the cows wandered onto my property. Anyway, it's all flat down here for a thousand feet until the edge of the Badlands rise up steeply toward the prairie. When the sage on the flats started to burn, the smell was bitter like myrrh. The bitterness made me think I was in a tomb, and of course, for many ancient animals it was. I started to think about the seasons changing and layers of time being exposed and yielding up the dead and the next thing you know there's half a dozen fire trucks rolling toward me over the grass with their red and green lights spinning away.

I'm not sure how they got so close without me noticing, but the firemen in their heavy burlap coveralls were very excited and shouted instructions at me as if in semaphore. In a way, I was sorry that they showed up. The burning sage was a perfume – pears and birds with pink feathers and Mary enticing me, grain by grain, to think of the passing of ages. Then, the grass flames were like fireworks, only better, because they raced round in circles and leaped from bush to bush, which is something fireworks can't do.

The fire trucks came to a stop where the playa met the steep cliffs of the Badlands and sprayed everything in sight. They used three hoses held by nine men and they sprayed a dozen bushes at a time with water and white bubbly foam. The foam quickly degraded into a grey sludge that was going to leave a horrible mess all over the bunch grass. One of the firemen even uncoiled a long hose with a filter on the end and ran down to the creek to suck some extra water out. I thought this was uncalled for, because it wasn't really a big fire and I probably could have handled it all myself if the thing hadn't burnt out on its own accord first.

Then the police showed up. Mary and the Sergeant drove right up to my back door and Mary jumped out shouting. I waved to her, but she didn't as much wave back as she motioned frantically for me to come over. At that precise moment, a curl of dried grass caught fire just to the east of the cottonwood tree and two rabbits squirmed between the two fingers of flames.

They ran around and around in circles not going anywhere, so I shut the hose off and walked out through the smoke. The ground must have been hot because even with my rubber boots on the heat came through to my feet and the stench of burnt rubber made me choke. The rabbits were either paralyzed with fear or stunned by the smoke. They just cowered there motionless and I yarded them both up by the scruff of the neck and carried them back to the house. I knew the dog wouldn't chase them because he was still eating biscuits, so I put the rabbits into his basket and covered them up with a red terry cloth.

The fire trucks had driven all over my backfield and drenched everything that moved. They squirted the "Hot Spots" a second time after one of the firemen inspected the ground with infrared glasses and then the "Big Tank" truck drove right up to my house and gave it a precautionary dousing. Problem was, the hose was so strong that it ripped off a dozen shingles and shattered my bathroom window. After they figured they had done enough damage, they gave me a friendly wave and turned the hoses off. The show was over. The fire was out. That's the thing with grass fires. They come and go in an instant and they look worse than they really are.

Mary and the Sergeant stood on my back porch. The Sergeant had picked up one of the rabbits and held it in his arms. Mary was scratching its neck. "Do you mind if I keep them?" the Sergeant asked.

"Sure," I said. I had no idea if he wanted them for his kids or if he was going to cook them up in a stew. They weren't really mine to give away.

"Thanks," he said. He picked the second one up and coddled them like he had a newborn set of twins. The four red eyes of the rabbits disappeared into the chest of his khaki uniform. "Well, I'm out of here, Mary. If you want to take care of the report, fantastic. No Further Action, I think. Glad your house didn't burn down, Mister."

"Me too," I said.

The Sergeant left with the rabbits. Mary and I stood on the porch looking over the flat valley bottom. The flat earth had a dusting of black soot. A stench of burned bush moved in from the south. On the western horizon, a grey thunderhead rose tens of thousands of feet into the sky.

"Good work with the rabbits," Mary said. "The Sergeant loves rabbits."

"I wish they hadn't put all that foam on the ground," I said. "It's going to stink. It looks really ugly and it's going to irritate my asthma."

"Better than a burned-down house," she said.

"Maybe, but it's mostly rock out there. It probably wouldn't have come this far. Besides, grass fires, flash in the pan, so to speak."

"Still, it's a good thing you called."

"Called? I didn't call."

"You didn't?"

"No."

"Why not?"

"I don't have a phone. There's no phone line in here. The phone company wanted a thousand dollars to hook it up. Got something to do with my distance from the road."

"Don't you have a cellphone?"

"Why?"

"So people can get in touch with you. Like, say for example, they want to meet with you sometime in their busy schedule, but can't do it because you're not near a landline, they can get you on your cellphone."

Landline? Cellphone? Did I? Yes I did. The producer of a pornographic film company had once given me a "Cellphone Package Certificate" while drunk one night in a bar after I had written a favourable review of one of his pieces. He must have been desperate. "The battery is dead," I said. Like I would know. I have never received a call on the phone, never received any billing for it, and have never phoned out.

The dog ambled out into the backfield. He was angular as he walked, like maybe his arthritis was giving him problems.

"Let's see it," Mary said.

The cell phone was under a pile of papers beside my desk, which sat by the west-facing picture window in the living room. Who puts a desk in their living room?

"This is ancient," she said and rolled the bulbous chrome body over her palm.

"I'm not one for modern technology."

"How about the modern novel?" Mary pried out the spine of the cell phone and then sniffed the guts. "Yep, this is dead and buried. But I think I may have one that will fit it."

We walked out the back door and around to her squad car. Out to the east, the dog was digging away at a section of land that the firemen had excavated with their hoses.

"What is your dog doing?" she asked.

"He's digging at something."

"Yes, that's apparent. At what?"

"Who knows. Dogs do that kind of thing."

And then, only twenty feet away from us, the dog wrenched out a black tube from the ground and all of the air gushed out of my lungs.

"Is that a hose?" Mary asked.

"No, I don't think so."

"We should check."

"Actually, it's just a piece of tubing. There were farmers here before me."

"Well, you don't want him eating that do you?"

Mary took a step across the driveway. We were close enough so the glue sealing the end of the tube shut could be seen. Apparently, the wrong kind of glue had been used because it was already starting to peel off the tube.

"Actually he does it all the time. It's that non-toxic kind of agricultural tubing that was popular during the sixties. Besides, I just try and let dogs do their dog things, I mean, who are we to intervene?"

"Okay," she said and shrugged.

We went out to her car and in the passenger seat Mary had a big black bag. She had a small plastic case with a dozen batteries in it.

"What do you use all those batteries for?" I asked.

"Hah," she said, selected one and fit it into the back of my cell phone. The digits lit up on the front panel. Mary handed me back the phone and as she did her fingers slipped over my palm. "Here's your phone," she said. "Does it have a number?"

"Yeah. I think I etched in on the back."

"Well, what is it?"

I turned the phone over.

"I'll call you on it," she said.

"Sure."

"Have you got any books you could recommend?" she asked with one hand on the cruiser door. "I guess what I'm asking is could I read one of your reviews?"

"All right," I said. I went back inside the house and scanned the jungle of paper. I selected one from a slightly left-of-centre magazine that had no pornographic reviews that month and took it out to Mary. She held out her hand and accepted the rolled-up paper. "Bon appetit," I said.

"Good work on the rabbits," she said and smiled, and then she kissed the end of the newspaper and reached out and rapped me on the back of the head with it. "I'll call you."

The smell of burned sage folded over the road as Mary's blonde head turned and ducked into the squad car and all of the yellow flowers of the bitter bush and pink prairie cactus opened to the sun even as the dog dug out the last of the tubing and tried to drag it back to the house.

It was true. I had been in love many times but had never been loved back. And so after emptying my pockets in front of those who did not know me, I realized there was nothing left to give. I did what anyone in this small town would do in such an event: I went to the Royal Tyrrell Museum of Paleontological History.

Churches and museums and monuments like Stonehenge and perhaps even pornographic theatres are built for certain reasons and that is because people believe. And here, people really believe. They come loaded down with rosaries, notebooks, diaries, wineries, backpacks, furlongs, condoms, and guidebooks of famous fossils. They mutter on joy and ecstasy and the rustling of golden curtains of wheat that leave their traces by their door. Sometimes, they just try to forget what ails them.

They keep their heads raised, as if to the heavens, admiring varnished skulls and polished vertebrae. They marvel over stuffed flora and petrified fauna. To be certain, there are those who came here by accident or because a tour brochure had said to do so when the golf courses were closed, but they are invisible and pass like ghosts through the tiled walls and well-preserved ancestors.

In the Geological Science Centre that is situated directly before the first huge dinosaur skeleton, I played with the sedimentary marble game where you churn a bunch of balls around and watch them settle according to their colour, so you can see how the past covers things up in a very precise kind of order. Then I learned the difference in leverage between a beak and a jaw by manipulating a set of chrome calipers, and came to understand why some animals once thrived while others perished. But of course this was all foreplay, because the moment I walked around the next corner into a dark amphitheatre, a huge petrified skull gazed down upon me from the top of a twenty-foot frame. The Albertosaurus stretched out his tiny hands and his hollow eye sockets were filled with hunger. And although the beast is long dead, it could still snatch up a victim at any second. At that moment, a young boy of ten or so ran around the corner and shouted aloud, "There HE is. There he *is*!" like this was the one and only Albertosaurus in the world.

The young boy stood by in wonder with his arms raised in supplication and, right then, something rumbled in my pocket. At first, I thought I had backed into a museum display that was shorting out, but nothing was near me. The object vibrated again, and I couldn't remember sticking any battery operated sex toys in my clothes. I suppose it was possible a bee could have come in through the double glass doors and gone down my shirt. The blooming sage out front attracts them by the thousands. Maybe even a giant insect had been resurrected from the Badlands' past through some misdeed of cloning and had found its way into my pocket. I fumbled through my clothes and pulled out the cellphone. It played a little tune and a light went on and the whole body convulsed as if it were having some kind of seizure.

"Aren't you going to answer that?" a woman beside me asked.

I punched a number of buttons on the front and a variety of tones and squeaks came from the machine. Finally it stopped, although I had no idea why, or really what had made it erupt in the first place. No sooner had I put the phone back in my pocket than it started to ring again. A line of sweat broke out across my forehead and then above me, the giant Albertosaurus moved his stone head over, as if he were gazing down in pity on this lost soul, and let his petrified mouth creep up just an inch in irony. I started for the door. I pressed a combination of number signs and red squares on the phone that said, "Omit," "Save," "Return," and just as I got free of the museum, the phone sputtered out and shut up again.

The cacti in the Badlands bit through my shoes and the walls of the coulees grew steep and narrow until the museum vanished into the background. In a while, I was down a small creek bed with only a tiny wedge of flat mud in the bottom. Mosquitoes and blackflies rose from the slough in funnels that looked like tiny tornadoes and soon even the sounds from the highway were gone. Some creosote from an old fence post brushed off my leg and a chunk of petrified wood rolled down the layered walls of the Badlands. My throat became very sore, as if maybe a terrible flu was on the way or someone had strangled me with a leather belt.

Rummaging down there in the Badlands, I found many remnants of the past: a roll of duct tape, mosquito repellant, high-school yearbooks, a tube of lip gloss without a cap, a leather satchel with a soiled magazine inside, a safety pin, and a black wristwatch with one strap missing. Not that it's a junkyard, but rather a cemetery. There was a green datebook and a tie clip, the tip of a fishing rod and a bookmark sticking out of the mud, and an old dog collar, too. Under a chunk of fossilized oyster I found a rusted shell cartridge, probably an old military issue and, at that moment, the phone started going off again.

A rusted spade with a box handle was resting against an abandoned roll of cattle wire beside me. In a moment, the spade was in my hand and I opened a great trench in the soft mud of the August creek. I dropped the ringing phone into the hole and covered the hole up with dirt and cottonwood twigs and sage and grey rocks so the secrets of the Cretacea would stay down in the earth with the ancient beasts who knew them best.

CRAIG BOYKO

THE BABY

Delia was again making noises with her mouth. The noises she was making, with her tongue and her teeth and the selective vibration of the vocal folds of her larynx, were intended to convey to me a message. The substance of that message was that she wanted a baby.

"We don't need a baby," I said with my mouth.

"Nobody *needs* a baby," said Delia with hers. "But I *want* one."

"We already have many nice things. That gyroscope, for example," I said, using my finger to point at the gyroscope, which had been bloody expensive, let me tell you. "Or that astrolabe. You should make more use of the things we already have. We don't need more things."

"A baby is not a thing," said Delia, "but a little person."

"We don't need any more persons in this apartment, either," I said. "We've already got two, between us. Where would the baby sleep?"

"In the bed," said Delia, "with us. Until it got older and needed to strike out on its own."

"Correct me if I'm mistaken," I said, stroking my chin, "but don't babies *poop*?"

Delia blushed. "I guess so," she muttered. "Sometimes. But they come with diapers."

"And who," I asked, "will remove the bepooped diapers from the baby's person?"

"We will teach the baby to change its own diapers," said Delia with a shrug.

"Tell me," I said, trying a different approach, "what is the *point* of a baby?"

"It is a thing – I mean a little person – into which – into *whom* – we can pour all our unused love," said Delia. "All the latent love that needs an object small and cute. All the potential love that we have rotting away inside us, all that derelict love whose expiry date draws rapidly nigh."

"I do not think I want a baby," I said. "Correct me if I'm wrong, but don't babies grow into *children*?"

Delia did not deny that this was the case.

"I do not care for children," I said, in a pensive tone. "They exult in monotony, as Gilbert Keith Chesterton has had occasion to note." (What he had actually written was: "A child kicks his legs rhythmically through excess, not absence, of life. Because children have abounding vitality, because they are in spirit fierce and free, therefore they want things repeated and unchanged. They always say, 'Do it again'; and the grown-up person does it again until he is nearly dead. For grown-up people are not strong enough to *exult in monotony*" (italics added).

Delia said nothing.

"They make me uncomfortable," I went on. "They have a tendency to speak with a certain bluntness. They have a distinct lack of tact. They are, in a word, *indiscreet*."

Again Delia made no reply, and I considered the argument to have been won, beyond possibility of appeal, in my favour.

The next day the baby arrived.

I suggested that we return it as it was obviously defective. Though it seemed, I conceded, to be operating correctly for the time being (in truth I had no idea what functions it was supposed to perform), the harsh noises and sundry smells that issued from it gave me reason to worry that it would soon malfunction. I asked Delia if she'd filled out the warranty card.

"We can't return it," she said. "I love it."

I then gave voice to the suspicion that it was perhaps not the finest specimen of its sort, and that it might be wise to consider upgrading to a superior make or model before we got too attached to it. (Though for my part there seemed little danger of that.)

"It's perfect," Delia assured me. "We're keeping it, and that's that."

Shrugging, I sidled over to our bookshelves and, with the insouciant air of one idly browsing, consulted the *New Family Encyclopedia* (we were a new family now, after all) to see what the average lifespan of a baby was . . .

I offered to take the baby hunting (in truth I wanted to "accidentally" lose it in the wilderness; whether the wolves ate it or raised it was quite frankly of no consequence to me) but Delia put the kibosh on that idea in no uncertain terms:

"Certainly not! It's much too young! Hardly even zero years old yet!"

I argued that if it was true, as the scientists informed us, that ontogeny recapitulated phylogeny (and what cause would they have to lead us astray?), then a child of any age should be quite capable of fending for itself in the wild. For if babies, or baby-like creatures, i.e. our ancestors, had not once been fearsome hunters, how would we have ever evolved to our lofty and majestic stature?

But my arguments fell on deaf ears. For Delia had left the room, leaving behind only her aged aunt Ruthie, who had come to live with us for a few weeks while her sock drawer was being fumigated. I entertained myself for a few moments (but only a few) by applying scabrously pejorative epithets to Ruthie (who, shameful to report, had never learned to read lips), but in a kind and solicitous manner, so that she presumed (presumably) that I was inquiring after her health. This entertainment promptly backfired, however, as Ruthie, with suspicious alacrity, launched into the litany of her many ailments.

Then Delia returned, to my relief, and, to my dismay, resumed our debate: "And when have you ever gone hunting?"

"I killed a deer once."

"You ran over it with the car."

"Well, I did aim for it."

"You wept for days afterwards."

"I am not heartless."

But the hunting trip was a no-go.

Names for the baby were suggested:

Abraham Aloysius Montaigne

Andrew C. Andrews

B.J. "Youdat" Brahtman

Faithful Begg and Strangways Pigg (if the baby had been
   twins)
Fergus McGillicuddy
L. Sanchez Gongoozler, Jr.
Laocoon Applebee Littleton
Mediocrates
Methuselah "Slim" McAvity
Nathan
Nicholas Nym
Numbskull B. Horscheit
Oscar Wilde
Søren Gutbucket Smith
Ulf Battersea
But (perhaps fortunately) none stuck.

To Delia I broached the possibility of giving the baby a tattoo for
Christmas? Something small, tasteful, nowhere conspicuous, on
the ankle perhaps, a plump little red heart with an arrow through
it, say, with the word *Dada* inscribed on a rippling cartouche.

I was overruled. We got the baby a rattle, a crib, and a gross
of diapers.

(That's foreshadowing.)

I read aloud from the *New Family Encyclopedia*'s article on enure-
sis (or bed-wetting):

"The vast majority of cases result *from emotional disturbances.*
Too early or too vigorous toilet training *may produce frustration
and guilt*, and urination may become the focus of *a power struggle between parent and child*. Night control is often unsuccessful
and the child uses bed-wetting *to express his hostility toward his*

parents." (Italics added by inflection.) "What 'emotional disturbances'? That's what I'd like to know! We haven't even *tried*
toilet training the thing yet! So where's it getting all this 'frustration and guilt'? Where'd it get this 'hostility toward [its]
parents'? If it wants a 'power struggle,' it's got one! Let's see how
it likes it when *I* pee all over *our* bed!"

"At this age it's natural," said Delia, making soothing sounds
with her lips (though whether for the baby's benefit or my own
I was not sure).

I stared at her agape. I realized with horror that she was
probably *telling the truth*.

Time passed and, by degrees, I began to warm to the baby. It was
not without its uses. To amuse visitors, I would demonstrate its
remarkably prehensile fists by dangling it from a broom handle
and swinging it around the room. Responses to this spectacle
included (but were not limited to) such exclamations as:

"Astounding!"

"Unutterable!"

"Discombobulating!"

"Beggars description!"

"Inexpressibly *outré*!"

"Gurgle! Goo!" (Thus spake the baby itself.)

It was the middle of the night and again the baby was petition-
ing us stridently and wordlessly for some love, or affection if
love was scarce, or attention if affection was not to be had.
(The baby was not picky.) Unfortunately, we had just that day
depleted the final dregs of our stock of patience, let alone any of

the nobler feelings, and so we simply lay awake waiting impatiently for the baby's cries to cease.

Delia nudged me in the small of my back with her bony kneecap. "Go read it a story."

I pretended to be asleep, seasoning the deception with a life-like snore. Alas the success of my dissimulation was a pyrrhic one; it earned me a vicious slap upon the head and the demand that I awake that very instant. I feigned a yawn and shambled into the baby's bedroom, where it was wont to while away its days and nights in peevish sleeplessness.

"I want a water," it said.

I told it that we were in the midst of a drought and the taps and wells and pipes were dry. (This was, I confess, an untruth. In my defence, it hadn't rained for at least a week.) Without hope I suggested a story instead; to my surprise, the baby accepted this compromise.

I seated myself at the baby's bedside, picked up a nearby colouring book (noticing wearily and despondently that our baby's crayons had wildly transgressed their assigned boundaries, I made a mental vow to discuss with the baby's mother the feasibility of cancelling the baby's university scholarship fund) and pretended to read from it.

"There once was a monkey who danced very well, and he so delighted the other animals with his antics that they appointed him Emperor of Animalia, King of Plantae, Duke of Fungi, President of Protista, and CEO of Monera." I yawned (genuinely this time) and looked at my watch. "The moral of the story is that true talent never goes unrewarded. The end. Good night."

The baby, predictably, remonstrated: "That's not a story!"

This was, I thought, to say the least, disputable. But it would be disingenuous of me to say that I did not capture the drift of the child's objection. It wanted a longer story. So I continued:

"The only animal displeased with this coronation was of course the erstwhile king, the lion, who promptly leapt upon the monkey and devoured him crown and all. The moral of the story is that it is not such a good idea to incite the jealousy of those who have bigger claws and teeth than you, and that the sword will always prevail over the dancing shoe no matter how skilfully plied, and that the dulcet voice of the enlightened majority is forever being drowned out by the shrill roar of the barbarous minority." I looked at the baby meaningfully. "The end, now go to sleep."

The baby's protestations were, I thought, a little less vociferous this time. Encouraged, I carried on:

"The fox, however, was not altogether pleased with this latest turn of events and declared to an *in camera* assembly of the other animals that the lion had relinquished his eligibility for the monarchy when he had besmirched that divine office by committing regicide and since the Emperor was by definition he who wore the crown upon his head he proposed that whoever got the crown out of the lion and onto his head first would be the new king and so the animals in their eagerness to improve their political standing set upon the lion en masse and ripped the poor terrified creature into little strips of steaming still-quivering flesh but alas the animals were all so worn out by the slaughter that the fox who had foxily abstained was able to dash forward and grab the gory crown and the authority it conferred without any difficulty whatsoever."

The baby, shivering now in wide-eyed horror (the youngster's imagination being, or so they say, much more vivid than that of the full-grown adult), asked what the moral of this story was.

I hesitated. "The moral? Why, the moral is look before you leap. Or perhaps it's don't bite off more than you can chew. Or maybe it's don't shit where you eat. Or perchance it's think before you speak. Or mayhap it's don't do something just because everyone else is doing it. Or peradventure it's pay no attention to honey-tongued demagogues for they act only and always in their own interest. All right? Okay? Now good night."

The baby yawned. "Nigh-nigh daddums."

. . . My heart melted.

DAVID WHITTON

THE ECLIPSE

My brother, Anders, had been with us for just two days, but already Larissa was complaining about the smell.

"He smells like a goat," she said. "It's like we're keeping a herd of goats in the living room."

"OK, OK," I said.

"I mean, it's everywhere. The carpets, the curtains. It's seeped into the fabric of the couch."

"I know, I know, I know, I know."

For most of the two days, Anders had perched in a chair at the kitchen table, rolling cigarettes and staring dreamy-eyed into space. He was very quiet. Were it not for the smell, you'd forget he was even there. But Larissa found him unsettling. Part of this, of course, was his appearance. He had confused blue eyes, broken teeth, and drifts and stacks of pale yellow hair; it gave him the look of a demented baby duck. And he rarely slept. At four in the morning you could get up and go to the kitchen for a glass of water and there he'd be – smoking a cigarette and leafing through one of Larissa's *Women's Health & Fitness* magazines.

"Please, Chet. Get him out of the apartment." A lock of

Larissa's hair came loose from her ponytail; it floated above her head like a question mark. "And keep him away until the place has a chance to air out."

"I said OK," I said, hoping that would be the end of it.

I took him to the car wash, the hardware store, the pet-supply store, the electronics superstore, the coffee shop, the library, the movies, and bar after bar.

It was on the patio of the Eclipse that I found out the reason for Anders's visit.

"I'm meeting a woman," he said.

Over in the corner, a chair scraped back, and then another, and then another, as a party of pink-faced businessmen paid their tab and left.

"What kind of woman?" I said.

"Just a regular woman."

"You mean, as in a date?" This was a rare and amazing piece of news.

"I guess you could call it that."

"You're on a date," I said, working the information over in my mind.

Anders lived in a derelict school bus on a scrubby tract of land in the Ottawa Valley. There isn't a whole lot of talent in a place like that. His last girlfriend had been a Wiccan pot farmer who'd led him on just long enough for him to drywall her cabin. But at least she'd been single – the one before that had been fifty-eight years old and long-married. My brother: twenty-eight. When her husband found out about the affair, he paid a visit to Anders's school bus and knocked out two of his teeth with a Coleman flashlight.

"Tell me about this woman," I said. "Where'd you meet her?"

Anders took a sip of beer, wiped the foam from his lip. "Ummm," he said.

"What does 'ummm' mean?"

"It means I don't want you to judge."

"When do I ever judge?"

"You always judge," he said. He looked around to see if anyone was listening, but all the tables were empty. "I met her through the mail."

"This is beginning to make more sense."

"See? You're judging already."

Anders zipped up his jacket and crossed his arms. The day had been partly warm and partly cool. In the shadows you could still feel winter; in the sun it was all bird's nests and crocuses. And the air! The air felt like it had been locked away for months in some dark riverbed. It smelled muddy, fertile. Full of waking things.

"I just think you need to be careful of mail-order brides," I said. "They're mostly Russian hookers trying to get citizenship. You can pick up some vicious fungal infections from Russian hookers."

"She's not a mail-order bride. She's a . . . She's a . . . regular woman. She took out an ad, and I answered. We've been writing back and forth for a year and a bit."

"So she's your pen pal."

"Yeah, sort of, I guess."

"What does your pen pal do?" I said.

"What does she do?"

"For a living."

"Ummm," he said.

I see it in him. I see it in the way he holds his cigarette, the way he sits in chairs, the way he talks: I see me. Because I'm seven years older, and I've had some influence, you know? I see my mother's lunacy, sure, and my father's Nordic solitude, but mostly I see me. It makes me feel responsible. It makes me want to take care of him, because the poor bastard sure can't do it on his own. I throw him some work when I can. In the warm weather he'll come down south for a few days and work on my crew, laying expansion joints, tearing up old parking ramps . . . whatever. In the cold weather he'll spend weeks at a time up north by himself. He'll make beeswax candles to sell to cottagers. He'll get bored and experiment with explosives. And, apparently (this was a new one for me), he'll sit around writing love letters to women he's never met.

"She's currently pursuing some interesting opportunities," Anders said. "Trying to turn her life around, make a fresh start. That sort of thing."

"Uh-huh," I said. "And why's that?"

"Because she . . ." Anders scratched his head, coughed twice, and picked at something on his knee – anything to avoid my eyes. "Because until recently she spent some time in a federal penitentiary."

What could I do but laugh? "And why is that?"

"She stole some money from an old-age home."

"You don't say."

"At knifepoint. But," he added, "she admits her mistake."

I had a swig of my draft, and then another, and lit up a smoke, and considered my fingernails, and stared off at the fragrant, peaceful sky. "Well," I said, "all things considered, she sounds like a step up for you."

"She is. She really is."

A new woman, a new start – it sounded pretty good to me. Someone who'd love you for all the wrong reasons. Someone who wouldn't identify and exploit your every little weakness. It sounded pleasant.

I took a hard look at my brother. He was wearing an old blue plaid shirt and a pair of filthy army pants. His hair was mushed up on one side of his head, and his face was covered with a week's worth of glistening blond stubble.

"You can't go on a date looking like that," I said.

"Why not?"

"Because you look like a felon. Bad analogy. But you see what I'm saying."

"No."

"You look like you've just spent three months in the bush."

"Well, but I have."

A tiny brown sparrow fluttered down to our table, eyeballed me critically, and fluttered off again. "But that's not appropriate in your dating-type scenario," I said. "It's unappealing."

"So what am I supposed to do?"

"Buy a new wardrobe."

Anders slumped in his chair, his face slack with desolation. "Really?"

"A new shirt that's not frayed in the cuffs. A new pair of pants that's not covered with food stains and bloodstains and . . . and whatever that is on your thigh. There's a flower in you, and it's just waiting to burst out."

"Couldn't I just –"

"No. And then you're going to need a shave. Why? Because a good shave sends a signal. It tells the woman you care about your appearance. It lends you the illusion of being further from rock bottom than you really are."

Anders ran a hand across his cheeks. His eyes were red-rimmed and shiny; he looked like he might start to cry.

"And lastly," I said, "and most importantly, you need a bath."

It was like I'd waved a rifle at him. He flinched, raising a hand to his head in a protective gesture. His face was full of pain, defensiveness, and, mostly, panic. If he'd gotten up and run away, I wouldn't have been surprised.

"I just *had* a bath," he said.

"When?"

Anders eyed the front gate, the back gate – all the escape routes. "Why do I need a bath?"

"Have you smelled yourself lately? No woman wants to become intimate with that."

He raised the sleeve of his shirt to his nose and inhaled. "I smell good," he said. "I smell like woodsmoke."

Our waitress came out onto the patio with a fresh ashtray.

"Hannah, Hannah," I said.

Hannah was dark-eyed and almost pretty. She had long brown hair that she wore in fetching arrangements. And although I knew her only in her professional capacity, she seemed like she was a sophisticated and socially adept kind of person who could give us a lot of valuable feedback.

"Yes, darling?" she said, picking up our old ashtray.

"Do me a favour, would you?"

"Anything." She set the new one in front of me.

I pointed at Anders, sitting there with his stunned-deer look. "Smell my brother," I said. "Smell my brother and tell me what you think."

I try to be patient. It's not Anders's fault, the way he is. Defective DNA travels through our family like a bad case of lice.

Our mother, for instance.

Mom was never entirely steadfast and rational, even when we were kids. There were always long summer afternoons in bed with the shades drawn, a damp washcloth on her head, *As the World Turns* on TV. There were always manic cleaning episodes: on her hands and knees, scrubbing floors till her hands turned the colour of raw pork. But, on the bright September day, twenty-odd years ago, that she discovered our father screwing the next-door neighbour, Mrs. Bridges, on our rec-room sofa, something in her head unspooled. It was a memorable day, though I don't remember much of it. I remember the screaming and crying, the slammed doors and thrown porcelain, the phone calls to the police – and then, suddenly, an eerie quiet.

She kicked Dad out, of course, and soon after filed for divorce. The real trouble started a couple of years later, though. The real trouble started when, flush with alimony and a bottomless pool of spite, she decided to realize her life's ambition and become everything my father despised: a dealer of fine collectibles. That was the beginning of the long, slow slide. Because as soon as she got hold of, say, a Victorian watering can or an art deco snuff box or some other piece of dusty, worthless crap at an auction or estate sale, she couldn't bear to let it go. It was too valuable, she said. Too precious to go into the homes of whores and libertines. And so she put it all into cardboard boxes and stowed it away, and the boxes accumulated, and Anders and I watched as our childhood home slowly filled, floor to ceiling, with junk.

"One day I'll pass all of this along to you," she told us.

I had no doubt she'd make good on that threat. All those mouldy old boxes, full of stuff that belonged to someone else . . . It's why I got myself snipped. I was determined not to pass that crap along to my own kid – my own sweet, innocent, the-oretical child, who, had he actually existed, would've never asked to be born.

"You look terrific," I said. "You look like a new man."

It was two days later. Anders was standing in the kitchen, submitting himself to our examination. In two days a miracle had occurred – a miracle of good taste, hard work, and organi-zation. The man in front of us was clean-shaven and freshly bathed, wore a fashionably cut pair of jeans and an expensive blue shirt, and sported a flattering haircut, moderately gelled.

"Who knew?" Larissa said, scratching her cheek.

"Just one more thing," I said, "and the makeover will be complete."

I rushed into the bedroom, grabbed a bottle of cologne, and, before Anders could protest, sprayed some just above his head, so that a fine cloud drifted down on him.

"Why'd you do *that*?" he said.

"Because," I said, "cologne, like a good shave, sends a signal. It tells the party in question that you've taken care to smell nice. And if you've spent all this time trying to smell nice, it means you've probably taken the time to wash out the crack of your ass."

It was twenty minutes to six. Anders had arranged to meet his ex-con at six o'clock. They were having fish and chips at Neptune's Cove, on King Street. I walked him down there in case he needed some last-minute advice.

"Whatever you do," I told him, "don't talk about Mom and Dad."

"Uh-huh," he said.

"And try not to talk about your school bus or anything involving candle-making. Or that incident with the dynamite – that was just embarrassing. And if the subject of ex-girlfriends comes up –"

"Yes, yes, yes."

"But do try to find out about life in prison. I want to hear about that."

It took ten minutes to get downtown. Anders and I walked along in silence, down cracked sidewalks and buckled roads, the last of the sunlight making the sky go pink. Then, a block from the restaurant, he stopped. A warm spring breeze gently raised and lowered the flaps of his shirt pockets. He regarded me with great urgency.

"I don't need you to walk me to the door," he said. "I'm not some fucking baby."

He spun around and walked the final few steps to Neptune's Cove. There was a cockiness to his stride, a vanity to his bearing. And I'm not afraid to say there were tears in my eyes. Every doctor wants his patient to thrive, and I was no different. I'd done the major surgery. The rest was up to him.

To my way of thinking, it's better to indulge your vices and live a short, noteworthy life than to shy away from everything fun and turn into a sickly, neurotic freak like so many of my friends and family. And maybe, yes, you spend too much time at your local pub, drinking with your buddies, and not enough time at home, talking about your feelings with your girlfriend, but if you don't take time to nurture yourself, how can you take care of anyone else?

That's why, after I delivered Anders at the restaurant, I popped in for a quick beer at the Eclipse. Larissa had told me to be home by seven. She wanted us to have a quiet dinner together, just the two of us, and I had every intention of being there, I really did. But Hannah was working that night, and the usual crew was sitting around the bar, and by the time I checked my watch, three hours had gone by.

"Oh shit," I said.

Hannah was at the cash, ringing in someone's tab. "What's up, Chet?"

"I'm two hours late for dinner."

"Shall I ring you out?"

"Nnnn . . . I'd better just stay here till she's gone to bed."

Hannah counted out some bills and laid them on a little plastic tray. "That's a fantastically bad idea."

"On the contrary, I thought it was pretty good."

"Go home," she said. "Take your punishment like a man."

I pretended to consider her advice. "All right. Sure. I'll go home," I said. "Just give me one more pint. For, you know, courage."

Because, after all, what did Hannah really know about my relationship with Larissa? She knew what I told her. She didn't know it had devolved into a state of absolutes, of alwayses and nevers: I *always* left my underwear on the floor; I *never* emptied my ashtray; I *always* left the margarine out; I *never* flushed the toilet. She didn't know about the long silences, the nights on the couch. She didn't know about the screaming fights. I'd changed, Larissa had said. I wasn't the person she'd fallen in love with.

I left the bar around two, profoundly shit-faced, but managed to steer myself home. I stumbled down mucky spring sidewalks, past darkened houses and thrumming electrical boxes. The night sky smelled of birth. The trees were erupting into bloom. I soaked it all in and, for a while, forgot about my troubles. Forgot about Larissa. Forgot about Anders. It wasn't until I reached my front stoop, checked my pockets, and realized I'd left my keys on the kitchen table that the troubles all came flooding back.

"Oh no," I said. "No, no, no, no, no, no." And I kept saying it, over and over and much too loud, until the words resolved themselves into an understanding and, finally, into a plan of action.

The only way in, I realized, was to break in. This made sense at the time. At the time it seemed perfectly correct and reasonable.

I went around back, rifled through the garage, and pulled out the landlord's wobbly aluminum stepladder. We lived on the second floor; if I placed the ladder under our deck and stood on the top rung, I'd be able to grab the top of the deck's railing and pull myself up.

That was the plan, anyway.

I fixed the ladder as soundly as I could and climbed it as carefully as possible. I reached the top rung, yes. But I was drunk, I was very drunk. So, when I reached for the deck, my foot slipped. My foot slipped and then my legs gave out from under me and then I dropped, slow motion, to the driveway, where I heard my right arm make a sound like a snapping branch, and felt the asphalt cool against my skull.

I blinked – twice, three times. Up in the sky I saw clouds, stars, jet trails. People in flight from one place to another. Then the world dropped away and I was swimming, swimming.

"I can't believe we did that," Larissa said, her voice fluttering with excitement. "I think maybe you're the coolest guy I've ever met."

"How many guys have you met?"

"Five. No, sex," she said. Then, catching herself: "I mean *six*."

Larissa buried her face in her hands, her body heaving with laughter. When she took them away, her face was the same shade of red as her lipstick.

"Oh, God, I wish I hadn't just said that."

The train was swaying gently as it shuttled through the darkness. And we were swaying with it, side to side, bumping softly together, our skin sticking whenever we touched. Outside the windows there was nothing but black countryside, our faces reflected against it. The wheels clack-clack-clacked against the track. It was our first date, eighteen years ago. We were on acid and in love.

"Can you imagine what it would feel like to fall all that way?" Larissa said. "The lights of the city spreading out below, and you just, just . . ."

"Bad," I said. "It would feel bad."

"But bad and great at the same time."

An hour before, we'd been at the top of the CN Tower. We'd taken the train to Toronto, taken the elevator up the tower, marvelled for precisely ten minutes at the pretty lights, and rushed back down to take the next train home.

It was a two-hour trip each way, and we laughed the entire time. Some of this was the acid, of course. Some of it was the stupidity of what we were doing. But most of it was relief. Relief because we knew we'd finally found it: a person who'd love us without judgment. A person who'd love us for who we really were.

"Chet?"

"Mmmm."

"Chet? Can you hear me? Are you OK?"

"Ggguuhhh."

"Chet? Chet, baby? Oh, God. Are you, are you –"

"I had the. Best dream . . ."

"What is it, honey? Did you say something?"

"I nnnneed . . ."

"Need? You need something?"

"Just need . . . Just need two wooden spoons . . ."

"Why do you need spoons?"

"Two wooden spoons and. A tea towel. For a. Splint."

"A splint? Is there something wrong with your legs?"

"I think. My arm is. Broken a. Little bit."

"We have to get you to an emergency room."

"I'm OK. I'll. Be OK."

"Really, though. We have to get you to Emergency."

"No. Way. I'll fix it my. Self."

It's interesting – the knowledge that something's gone badly wrong inside you. And it is knowledge – bodily knowledge. It focuses the mind. It amplifies the senses. Wind chimes in the distance, the rustling of leaves far overhead, the squealing of tires down the block – they sound like they're an inch from your ear.

I was in bed. My own bed in my own room. It was morning. I could tell it was morning even though my eyes were closed. I could tell from the sound of birds chirping in the yard and from the light that came in through the windows and turned the backs of my eyelids pink. It was going to be another beautiful day. I could tell that, too.

I opened my eyes and looked down at myself. The sheets were covered in blood. My arm was wrapped in a tea towel, with two blood-soaked wooden spoons sticking out. I gathered that at some point I'd fashioned myself a splint – it seemed like something I might do – but I had no memory of it.

"Larissa?"

The sound of running came from the hall, and soon Larissa entered the room. "You're up," she said.

"Uh-huh."

"Anders is going to drive you to the hospital."

"Yep. Sounds good."

She came over to the bed and sat down. There was a time when I'd looked at her and all I'd seen were sparkles. But now all I saw were puffy eyes, a creased forehead. She looked tired and worried, and I was seized with the profoundest guilt: I hoped I hadn't done this to her.

"I'm sorry," I said. "I'm really sorry."

She seemed to understand what I was trying to tell her. A swirl of hurt and anger passed across her features and, for a second, it looked like she was going to say something – probably something she'd been rehearsing all night. How she'd wasted her youth on me. How I'd jackhammered her life into little bits. Instead, she cupped my cheek in the palm of her hand and kissed me on the forehead. "You piece of shit," she said. "Can you move?"

The answer was: barely. I could move slowly, painfully. I could move even though every movement seemed to damage me a little bit more. And so I travelled from the bed to a nearby chair, from a nearby chair to a kitchen chair, from a kitchen chair to the front door, and, finally, from the front door to the driveway, where Anders sat behind the wheel of my idling pickup.

I slumped in the passenger seat – unwashed, hungover, most likely concussed – and waited anxiously as Anders began to back the truck onto the street.

"Why a ladder?" Anders said. "Why didn't you just knock on the door?"

"There's a car parked behind you."

"I see it, I see it."

He jerked the truck to a halt, then carefully started to back out again.

"I didn't want to wake her," I said.

"Why didn't you call and tell her you'd be late?"

"Please shut up."

It was a short drive to the hospital – but everywhere was a short drive in this little city. On the way I made Anders stop at a variety store for a pack of cigarettes. It was, I surmised, going to be a long wait in Emergency. After that we detoured east, to a Portuguese bakery that sold the most unbelievably airy, buttery crescent rolls I'd ever tasted, and a wide selection of exotic cheeses.

After this second stop, Anders hopped back into the truck, made a theatrical sniffing sound, and said, "You smell like a bar."

"Do I?"

"You should have splashed on some cologne before you left the house."

"You're hilarious."

I cracked the window to let some air in and stared for a few moments at the streets, the sidewalks. Larissa was going to leave me. I could feel it in my stomach, in my balls. She was going to leave me and find someone boring.

"How'd your date go?" I said.

"Not bad."

"What's she like?"

"A lot bigger than in her pictures," he said. "She was, like, a giantess."

"Mmm. Bad genes."

"And she has kind of a gravelly voice and a lot of tattoos."

"She sounds, ummm . . ."

"And she collects dolphin figurines." He thought about this, then shook his head in amazement. "Which I suppose you wouldn't expect."

We motored down Wellington Road. Ugly southwestern Ontario architecture whizzed by on all sides. There was no snow or darkness, unfortunately – nothing to hide under. The sunlight exposed every last brick.

"So do you think you're going to see her again?" I said.

"Maybe tonight."

"Tonight! Wow! Then I guess it went well."

"It went well," he said.

"I guess my advice helped."

"No. It went well in spite of your advice."

One moment you're a successful concrete-protection con-
tractor. Someone whose opinion is sought. A tastemaker, a
counsellor. A man of confidence and dash. The next, you're bat-
tered and fucked and your misfit little brother, a person who's
always depended on you, a person who's missed out on so many
fundamentals, is shepherding you to the hospital, taking care of
your most basic needs. You look like the same guy, but something has changed. The old you has cracked open. Something
new is pushing out.

"Something new," I said.

"What are you talking about?" Anders was smoking while he
drove, eating a crescent roll while he smoked.

"Did I say that out loud?"

"You said something out loud."

"I was just thinking," I said.

"You were gesturing and making faces, too."

"I have some things on my mind."

"You better not do that in the hospital. You'll scare the
nurses."

The nurses, yes. I pictured the nurses: a bunch of huge, tattooed women in white uniforms. They carried stainless-steel
trays covered with drugs and knives. "I wonder if they still give
sponge baths."

"Who?"

"The nurses," I said.

A sponge bath, a shave, a comb through the hair – these were things that told the world you were doing all right. A dab of fragrance, a change of shirt – they made you feel almost halfway normal. Not that there was any hope for me. My problems ran deeper than that. My problems required X-rays and IV drips and titanium rods drilled through bone. And even then: no guarantees. Fixed or broken, I'd be discharged. Spat up and expectorated. I'd be back out here with the rest of the wounded.

NADIA BOZAK

HEAVY METAL HOUSEKEEPING

How is it that the directions on detergent boxes and fabric softener bottles, colour care charts, iron indicators, and the instructions on clothing labels, telling moms how to properly care for cotton, woolens, linens, silks, synthetics, nylon, and sturdy polyester-acrylic blends, say nothing about caring for *metal*?

As in *heavy metal shirts*, hardcore *metallics* like Metallica and Metal Church and Metal Patient, the tender type of laundry that reeks of havoc and nicotine and both kinds of grass, black T-shirts, baseball style with the three-quarter-inch white sleeves. *Master of Puppets*, *Sabbath Bloody Sabbath*, "Die, Die, my Darling," these ostensibly tough items can in fact withstand only a delicate washing-machine cycle. An optimum speed setting would be, depending on your machine, either Extra Delicate or Hand Washables. Rinse Options: One Rinse. Water Temperature: obviously Cold/Cold. Cycle: Short. Use only a quarter of the soap the manufacturer recommends. Buy the expensive liquid soap because cold water often is not enough to dissolve the powdered kind. And never toss a metal T-shirt into the destructive inferno of a dryer; only jeans, sport socks, sweatshirts, and underpants can take the brutality of hot heat and hot and fast and soapy washes.

Become acquainted with what you are washing. Your son's metal T-shirts are mostly those for Metallica. He also wears ones for Anthrax, Megadeth, and Black Sabbath. One Iron Maiden and one Napalm Death, one Misfits. Also, there is a hooded sweatshirt for Rotting Christ buried in his drawer someplace. Know that there are eleven in total, but the four Metallica and the one Misfits are in constant rotation. These are his favourite bands right now, but they are wearing thin as it has been some time since a tour has come around. Though he should have no money, he always finds a ticket and a way to go, catching a ride into the city with someone's older brother: mustachioed, twenty-two and still in high school, who no doubt drives there stoned and drives back drunk. It is always on a school night. But he gets up for class the next morning. Forget academic commitment, he goes just to wear the shirt, to show off his dedication to Metallica or Anthrax, saying how he only slept for, like, four hours, after drinking, like, ten beers. But the girls there in the smoking pit at school don't know that like a baby with its blanket he slept in that concert tee and will sleep in the concert tee for days to come. When you finally fish it out of the laundry hamper, the lettering will still be crisp and will still smell mildly of glue. On the back especially, where there is emblazoned an impressive list of cities included on the tour. World tours always, each city is claimed as a conquest, another victory in metal's tireless bid to take over the world.

You work hard at their preservation and yet still your son's metal T-shirts will become blistered and cracked, ragged with age and constant wear, faded, and soon enough, outdated. He wears his metal tees only and always. No sweaters, no undershirts, no button-downs. Without a heavy metal T-shirt your son is nothing more than a little boy, shivering, head bent, trying so hard not to be naked. He wears a T-shirt at least twice before he'll put it in the laundry hamper that you keep in the bathroom. He puts them there not so much because he's a thoughtful kid, but rather to keep his fucking mother – that's you – from going into his bedroom in search of dirty clothes when you are determined to turn a medium load into a large one. You put your stuff in the hamper too. Your son does not know that in the laundry hamper your intimate smells mingle with his sour ones. Your undies to his metal tees. This is the closest you have had your bodies since he reached adolescence. Before, you used to hold him, hug him; before, when he needed to hear your heartbeat to get to sleep. Always those nightmares when the lights went out, that insecurity, panic, anxiety – the typical manifestations of a shabby and shattered home. A single mom with no man about except her demons. Demons do not good fathers make. Now you wash with love and precision the demons on your son's metal T-shirts.

Stains. There will be stains: blood, booze, barf. Just as long as it is not brains. Stains. It is late, but you are not asleep. He stumbles into your room, falling into bed beside you. You feel him quietly crying, but you leave him be, though you think you ought to maybe reach over and embrace some part of him. He has his runners on and his dirty jacket, and so you think twice about it, touching your son, with his dirty fingernails and the pimpled cheekbones and the shaggy hair. The *Ride the Lightning* metal tee stinking of something from another earth. Then, when he passes out, you lead him back to his bedroom, head lolling, feet dragging, where you take off his shoes and jacket. All the while the glossy overlords of metal leer down at you from the photos plastering the walls. Lay him out in his single boy's bed. In half-light you see the blood on his metal T-shirt. The blood on his chin; crusted blood darkens his nostrils. You pull the soiled T-shirt over his heavy heavy-metal head. There is his pale chest, the nipples still soft pink buttons. You feel sad for him a little. And you feel sad for yourself because your son, like every other man, will not come into your bed unless he is drunk and desperate. Closing the door behind you, you leave him to sleep it off in his lair of heavy metal worship. That blood-stained metal tee goes right down to the laundry room. But stains should not be of such concern to you, for stains are like scars. They complement the metal tee. They are war wounds, proudly decorating the heavy metal army's scrawny soldiers. Blot with bleach if the stain is on the white of a sleeve; soak in vinegar if it is not. Scrub out with a hairbrush, going against the grain. To make up for your deficiencies as a mother, you wash his heavy metal T-shirts with this kind of dedication and precision, for this heavy metal exterior is what fortifies him and makes him strong. Strength is what he needs, for there is so much confusion in the eyes you cannot see, hidden as they are behind the bangs he has grown out so that he can chew on the tips; strength because there is so much pain in the hunched shoulders that are so thin and self-conscious beneath the grotesque metal T-shirts. Grotesque heavy metal T-shirts that spill blood and profess destruction and that you must tend to and care for and caress as if these shirts were your son's flesh and his spirit. They *are* his flesh and his spirit. They are more himself than he is.

Hang them to dry, these heavy metal T-shirts. Not on the line outside, that's for jeans and sport socks and your uniform from the hospital. Hang his shirts to dry in the basement, on plastic hangers suspended from ceiling pipes in the boiler room, along with his smallish boy's underpants and your meagre scraps of lingerie. These are things too secret to show, too proudly personal to go out on the line where bright sun and strange eyes can get at them. Under such glances and glare, be afraid that his black metal T-shirts might fade out, be afraid your greying panties might shrivel and die from embarrassment. So keep the heavy metal T-shirts to dry in the dark. It's like keeping something from dying: a mould, a moss, a mushroom. You will have noticed that the skulls and the blue lightning, the electric chairs and calls for chaos, the most delicate items to care for are also the most violent and aggressive to look upon. These things are fragile and must be treated as such, like polishing knife blades, like how they say the armoured knights of old could not get up off the ground if they happened to fall off their horses. Like how under that inhuman mask, Darth Vader is but a face of delicate spongy flesh, inset with the rotting eyes of a sad and fading man. Swords and sci-fi, medieval lore and martial arts fantasy: these references will become familiar to you, heavy metal moms, for your heavy metal sons are steeped in the fantastic dreams of the awkward and the outcast, the miscreants, the obsessed. The heavy metal fantasy delivers the minds of young boys with dreams of immortality. Doom and despair are their solace. The drive of adrenalin, the rush of metal and machine, horror and hardcore: implicit in heavy metal is an embrace of death and dying, a stubborn determination not to give a flat fuck, and this is to them almost as good as immortality. Immortality, death-drive, driving death: your son is fifteen years old.

And you, you are thirty-four. Your son knows that you are thirty-four but he does not realize how young you are. Before you had him, life was somewhere else, not here, and if you could colour it, it would be blue with white streaks like a spring sky, looking up, up, up, without a horizon to say this is heaven and this is earth. Now it is all earth: all dirt and drudgery and day-in/day-out and getting good at carrying out demands. Laundry is a demand, a chore you must perform. But this careful way you wash your son's metal T-shirts, this is because you love him so. It is being close to him, smelling his smell and touching the fabric that has soaked up all his little boy sweats. Dull like a baby's cloth diaper, but instead of pee and poo there is pimple and pus. Muss, fuss, because you deserve to die for bringing him into this world and forcing him to live this life he does not want and did not ask for. You know this because he said it to your face and it echoes on and on. Allow the churn of the washing machine to drown out the sound of the hate in his voice. Forgive me: these are words neither of you know how to say. So don't say them. Wash his dirty metal tees instead of caressing his face, looking into his eyes. You wash his metal T-shirts and you alone are the only one on earth who touches this smell and loves this smell, or at least tries to. The smell is that of a boy boiling with hormonal rage and a boy grown ugly and deranged by the oppressive confusion of his poor young life. This is the smell of your own and only son. But don't smell his metal tees too closely. Do not attempt to contemplate the source of the odour he bears with him, that sour teenage smell. There is no other smell like it on

earth: the smell of big brother, the smell of adolescent son.
There is also the question of nicotine. This composes part of the
smell of him. He smokes at school. Some nights he smokes in his
room, but only when he knows you are smoking too. Two nega-
tives equal a positive, he will say if you ever confront him. So
don't. Just scrub out the smell, bitter, acrid, putrid, like the poisonous air about him when he is about you.

And finally, confess. As these are the only men that you have
in your life, you, like your son, fantasize about these heavy metal
demigods. Clad in tight leather and torn denim, hairy, spitting
men, men enraged, men engaged, men with tattooed forearms.
Men who've torn the metal tees from their raw and glistening
chests. Voices that are gruff, voices that rev. Eyes blaze, are
crazed with passion. Some of them you recognize. Some of
them look as old as you, they look like they could also be thirty-
four, some even older, these lords of metal that in glossy photos
cut from magazines adorn the walls of the room where your son
sleeps, hallucinates, passes out. Beneath black demonic glances
and postured virility these demigods have gentle hearts, and
these demigods would help to raise your son and teach your son
to feel passion and also fix things, drive a truck, murder an
amplifier with a flying V electric guitar. And one will be your
iron man. And you, his metal woman. Instead of your sensible
hospital whites, you will wear for him nice things, tight things,
always black, like how it was in high school, how you dressed
back then during the lifetime that ended fifteen years ago. But
you do not, you cannot, remember back that far. That part is all
over now. You are responsible now, and so of course you know
that metal gods do not real husbands make. But you can, like
your son, always dream. In the room that smells like his shirts

before they're washed, the metal gods, eyes red, faces bled, watch as you gently lay the pile of cold-washed, drip-dried, department-store-folded heavy metal T-shirts back in your son's drawer. Now. Exit the room that is a shrine to the lords of metal. Put on your fresh, crisp uniform, your hospital whites. Go to work. Try not to imagine what your son is doing all those moments you are struggling to make ends meet. Just as when you are tending to the laundry, you try not to imagine how his metal tees come to smell of damp sewer, his jeans of gasoline.

That's right. Concentrate on other things. Like on getting the smell out, not on how the smell got *in*. Concentrate. Like the soap itself. Like the detergent. Concentrated. Like orange juice. Like prisoners of war. Like your mind on your work. Like your mind on these words. Like the pain in your son's eyes, like the hardness in his smile. Concentrate. And don't forget: Wash those metal tees as if they are a wounded soul, a damaged heart, a blistered brain. Cold – Gentle – Delicate – Slow. Just like your son. Cold – Gentle – Delicate – Slow. Think of it that way and it becomes so easy to remember, so easy never to forget.

DAMIAN TARNOPOLSKY

Sleepy

Perhaps it was my dad who brought me here. He would have stared ahead, hands like bunnies on the steering wheel. He stared ahead in the taxi, he stared ahead on the airplane, he stared ahead in the rental car, he stared ahead as I fetched my tiny turquoise suitcase. Did he look down to find the lever when he popped me the trunk? I don't know. I walked round to the driver's side window, and I gave him a dry kiss on the cheek. He drove away.

Sometimes in my bathroom the tiles jump up to meet me.

This is the story Lennie, a boy here, told me on the smoking patio. Dying I'd been to have a cigarette, this is what happens off Prixamil, and Lennie said "Smoking kills." I didn't know what he meant. The orange glow in your hands is enough for me. He said in his quick brown voice: "This buddy of mine, his girlfriend won't let him smoke in their apartment, okay? Her cat's allergic or something. So every ten minutes he's out on the fire escape to smoke. Sneakers, jacket, snow, he sits on the iron grille, legs poking out between the bars. He sees the backs of houses. Garages, vegetable gardens, the ash drops down between his feet four storeys down into puddles. His landlord's got a friend in the

City, landlord sends this guy a crate of oysters every Christmas; so his landlord doesn't really do much in the way of upkeep, okay? Sometimes the balcony creaks and shakes in the rain. He hears it rattle. But he doesn't think anything of it. Plus he's got to smoke, okay? But one night he's out there and the wind blows and the screws give out and the whole damn thing collapses boom and he falls four storeys and the ironwork falls around him onto him and there you are."

I like oysters.

"Smoking kills."

I asked him, True story?

You open the curtain and pull it back. You fill your hair with conditioner. You wash your top half then your bottom half. Then stand under the water then stand under the water then stand under the water. Watching scenes in the warm water from last night's movie you saw half of. Waking up is a process of asking yourself questions, Dr. Frink says. Sometimes the questions don't come. The water's soft on my forehead, it runs down over my breasts and down over my thighs. A woman is banging on the door. An hour's passed.

Dr. Frink my shrink says I should engage with my surroundings. Otherwise I may persist in this belief that I am the sole moral arbiter of the universe. I don't really believe that, Dr. Frink, I'm pretty sure that you exist; I am just tired occasionally. My surroundings. There is a watercolour painting in my room of a boat tied to a very clean dock with a pebble beach in the background and a clubhouse and in pencil in very thin small caps beneath it is entitled "A Snug Harbour," 121/450, Mary Fitzgerald. I have stared at it for hours trying to work out what

in god's name. The rest of the building, oh, I don't think I have
patience for the rest of the building.

The rest of the building is also like a golf club. My dad would like
it. Fat vertical lines of green and red and cream paper the walls.
The couches are patterned with ducks and the one in the near
social area is the least comfortable. There are corridors between
the two social areas. One of the social areas has a television, the
far one has a pool table. Off the corridors are everyone's rooms.
It doesn't look like a hospital. No, it is not an asylum. There's too
much wood here. But near each social area is a nursing station,
just in case. Sometimes walking down the corridors you find
pieces of medical apparatus that you've seen before but can't
place. The men shuffle and hack. The social areas are very large
like a swimming pool and divided into areas – dominoes, magazines, Monopoly – by wooden slats. Day and night I spend in my
room. All my possessions fit into the top left drawer of the white
dresser. There is an eighteen-inch screen television on it. The
closet is empty. I do not have my own bathroom. I do not have a
window. I feel tired all day and so woozy and I think probably I'll
never have that feeling again of feeling *awake*.

Once in college before I dropped out the first time I was
doing the dishes. I always did: I liked the chocolatey smell of
yellow gloves and I'd put on the radio in the living room loud
enough to hear over the water (Classical 93) and fill the sink. I
liked it because I was washing up but also I was somewhere else,
grocery shopping, talking to my sister Becky, making a list in my
head of the clothes I would buy if I had money. Splooshing the
sponge over the soup bowls, working, thinking of Lena Horne

and my Portuguese chemistry teacher. Then Jennie my roommate was yelling and only when she slapped me I woke up and
the water was overflowing, there was foam all down my front
and worst of all nothing was clean.

Lennie has big huge eyes that sit in wineglasses in his cheeks.
He has dark insect hairs on his cheek but no stubble. He doesn't
know how to laugh only a little; when he laughs he laughs with
his whole chest. I think just possibly I am falling for Lennie.

I got pins and needles all over, I lost the sight in my head. I
almost fainted again, thinking of that.

#24
LENA FEKE
CHECKLIST

Cataplexis (list triggers):	4 (stress etc)
Somnambulism:	2
EDS:	0
Automatic behaviour:	2
Food craving:	5 (olives)
Hallucinations:	0
Nights of whole sleep:	7
Nights of disturbed sleep:	1
Hours of day sleep:	34
Medication missed:	2

Signature: _____

There are beautiful nasturtiums and hortensias in the gardens,
and red walking paths. I'm finding myself there a lot. Also clay

tennis courts. But best of all, towards the wall hedges on the far side of the gardens from the road, someone has built a Japanese garden. There are a thousand white-grey pebbles like the sea as its base. And low bushes growing out of the sea, and larger black rocks like shipwrecks. And I think that the moss growing on these rocks must be wet to the touch, but I don't want to walk out over the perfect engraved lines of the pebbles and ruin them, you great galoot. Actually I took ballet for nine years, I should give myself a little credit. The moss is the same colour almost as the round bushes, from the same square in the palette.

Would you believe that Lennie is a ventriloquist? The second week of October is National Ventriloquism Week. When he says these things, I . . . I don't know. He says that he is, however, an avant-garde ventriloquist. I said it was a lot of big words in a little sentence. It was like he was angry when he told me about his act: "I don't understand why the only art that's stuck in the nineteenth century is mine. It's as if all painters were still doing water lilies. Listen. I do an act with a digital mike that makes you think the girl in the second-last row is crying, okay? Even her mother turns to her. I make bikers sing nursery rhymes and tell me they love me. I do an act with a sex doll: it blows people away. Ventriloquism was originally associated with demonic possession. The only challenge is the illusion of action."

Okay.

All this happened in the medical staff cafeteria. I had never even been there before. I had not been exploring. I ate my bacon and eggs by myself or with Tom and Jerry, sitting in my bed, tray over my knees. My bed! Where else. It is the safest place for me and the warmest. But Lennie took me with him into the main building and down a flight of orange and brown stairs into the light-blue basement ballroom where the doctors ate. He had on a labcoat and on it a blue badge said "ANDERS. VOLUNTEER." He told me he'd borrowed it. I bumped into the steel bars that you're supposed to slide your trays along and almost dropped everything. He had cannelloni stuffed with rabbit, which made me sad; I ate a salade niçoise. After, he played with the plastic tag around my wrist.

"Parts of a dream you remember and parts you don't," I said. Often I feel that when I'm talking in our little interviews it's not me talking but a different girl with my voice.

"What do you think you're getting out of this?"

I find Dr. Frink's beard distracting. It is mostly brown, with grey strands coming out of it. The beard is the dominant feature of his facial anatomy. It is immense, and without it I fear what would become of his physiognomy. If someone were to shave it off in the night.

"You don't have anything to say?"

I usually run out of things to say after about ten minutes. After that I struggle to stay awake. I think that's why he keeps talking, to keep me awake. And he tries to keep me talking. But it doesn't usually work.

"How are you finding the meals now?"

It was like he knew what we'd done.

We are sitting facing each other. Next to his elbow there is a small green sculpture of a polar bear. Behind him I can see a painting of a girl sailing. He's a gentle man, sometimes he puts his pen in his mouth and it disappears into his facial hair. He doesn't breathe, then he takes a big long breath that raises his trunk and shoulders. He pays attention to detail. I don't have to keep reminding him who my sister is when I mention her name.

"You keep a lot to yourself, don't you."

Deep breath.

"I don't lose my keys any more because I don't have keys. I don't crash into things because I can't drive. I'm not fighting with my parents because they're not here. I'm not buying mushrooms because you won't let me leave. I'm not skipping class or sleeping in school because I'm not in school. I'm not forgetting things because I've got nothing to remember. So what do you think?"

Pins and needles in my eyes; I shouldn't let myself yell.

When I get emotional he writes it down on his yellow pad.

"I think you're a smart young woman with a future," he said. "I think you're doing your best to get through this."

No, I thought.

We looked at each other, I heard another office door close.

"What do you want, more than anything else?"

"To stay up all night," I said instantly.

I was thinking of Lennie. He wakes me. Going away together maybe.

Then I yawned. He wrote some more.

"Sometimes people just yawn, you know."

He grinned.

"We're going to have to stop there," he said.

I shrugged.

The other narcoleptics (like when I used to go to camp):

Karryn. Australian, schoolteacher.

Dim, paper merchant. Jet black hair.

Helder: was born in Lebanon. Guileless.

Serena: music journalist.

I take pills from my boot-shaped locket.

You never call a ventriloquist's dummy a dummy. They don't like that; they have names. The word *ventriloquism* comes from the Latin for speaking and belly. Lennie also does magic, and once he performed for Elton John.

We were lying in the long yellow grass off one of the paths. Low behind three maples. People walking by could barely see us, only if they looked. But we could hear them come and go. I felt the warmth rising in me as my skin met his, and the deeper we kissed the less I could feel it: I felt something bubbling inside me and I pulled away. I didn't want to stop. To have to stop made me angry. Then I had to calm down from that too.

"My darling duck," said Lennie, and I kissed him on the arm, breathed.

Then pulled away, out of contact, for the best.

Lennie's the opposite of me.

He said he was doing the study for the money. Dr. Frink had been pestering him for years. He did something with his eyebrows that gave him Dr. Frink's caring bewildered eager gaze. His condition was unique. The study was funded by NASA. The U.S. army was curious too, but Lennie wasn't so into that. He's like some kind of Norwegian, he said: he's awake half the year. Then he sleeps for six months at a time.

"You're more fucked up than I am!" I said delighted.

He pretended to pout and I kissed his dark green T-shirt sleeve.

"I haven't seen winter in eight years," Lennie said like a plantation owner. "That's why you know I've got such a great tan." He does these voices . . .

No work or school to keep us from each other.

Sex is one of my triggers. It does a little too much to me. At least it did: halfway through my one sexual experience, I disappeared. First I couldn't move my left side, and then suddenly I was laughing and I couldn't stop, and the poor boy I was with took it very very badly. "It's not you," I kept saying, coughing and shaking, laughing, wrapping the sheet around me, "it's not you," and soon he was in tears.

We kissed. I stayed longer than I should have. Earth under my jeans, grass against my back, his scratchy face. I drew away and gasped.

"Sorry," said Lennie. He stroked my cheek with his soft knuckles.

On the path two insomniacs walked by with tennis rackets.

"What's it like?"

"Normal for four-five months. Then close to when I go under – I feel it coming – I start to get pretty manic. The way I understand it is it's like I need a break from the world? I start making calls, crazy phone calls, to Steven Spielberg because he should make a movie about me, to the TONY awards, Where's my statuette. I'm learning Italian, I'm writing letters to the *Times*, I'm laughing constantly, okay? I write and rehearse a show in three days and I think it's the best work ever done by man or woman. Spending a lot of time on the subway writing down the numbers of the cars. There's a letter in my back pocket telling people what to do if they find me. Dr. Frink's PalmPilot beeps and he gives me a call, begs me to come in. I start to see this orange glow around the edge of things, the smell of mint. I'm angry. Don't feel like myself any more, my eyes are burning and scratching, not feeling like anything any more. Then boom, in a cab, in the shower, backstage, boom, I'm out. Eventually someone finds me and they take me to hospital and eventually they figure things out and they bring me here, okay? Nice Asian nurses. But it's close now, I'm close to going under. This is the first year I haven't been all crazy."

He reached his arm around me and kissed my head. Our limbs together like putting bikes away in the garage.

"How close?"

"Next week, sweetcheeks."

Me floating in amber.

Then, up on my elbows:

"I always tell people I fight it," I said. "Struggling to stay awake like struggling to stay afloat and I fight it, I spit water out of my mouth. It's true."

I swallowed and looked at how he was looking at me, inches away. "But you know, there's a pleasure in giving up. There's a pleasure in going under. Knowing everything's lost. Sometimes there's a part of you that just wants to give up."

I never told anyone before.

"I'll be dreaming of you the whole time I'm out, baby," he said.

I looked at him with big wet eyes: and he burst out laughing at me.

"You son of a bitch," I said, and I slapped him. And then we were wrestling and laughing.

Before coming here my school sent me to see my GP because I'd got anxious and fainted in a geology exam on question 4 ("Describe the situation of three sedimentary rocks") and they couldn't wake me and they'd carried me out of the gym (I failed). My GP didn't know what to do with me and he sent me to a neurologist. Then I went back to see my GP, and he sent me to a psychiatrist. All these doctors. It didn't work, and I went to see a Chinese naturopath. He gave me some twigs and bark that were ridged and brown like his own skin. I boiled them into a tea that stank up the entire house. I went back to see my GP. He didn't know what to do with me. I was out of school by now. Near my parents there was a community centre, a support group: women in a circle talking about their symptoms as if their symptoms were their children. *My symptoms are developing so quickly – Guess what my symptoms did this week!* Me too. I remember bits and pieces, without them adding up into anything. I was better off in chatrooms, heard a lot about various meds. I spent a lot of time online: no whiny voices. Someone mentioned the clinic. And so.

1. Will you remember me when you wake up?
2. Was it just fun for you?
3. What are you thinking about?
4. Will you wake up even?
5. What did you mean when you said you thought consciousness was overrated?
6. Will we go on the road together or was that just play?
7. Do you understand me, really?
8. What do your parents do? I forgot to ask.
9. Can I buy you a new Cuban shirt?

10. You look like a punk Cary Grant.
11. Are you dreaming of me?
12. I can't wait any longer.

In my dream Lennie was telling me he'd slept with someone else and I was telling him it was okay. Then he had to give a lecture on the spread of plastics after the war (there was a documentary about it), and I was helping him prepare in the big empty theatre. But then I was a waitress and he had gone. I woke up and I knew it was my room because of the crosshatched pattern the light makes on the ceiling coming through the blinds. I wanted to get up, then I wanted to call for help. But I could not move.

I started hoarding my meds.

Then every day I cried for the whole fifty minutes with Dr. Frink. He looked worried and he passed me the box of tissues and I cried. I didn't want to talk about anything. I was crying into one hand the way I always did.

"Do you see how you're sitting?"

I cried.

"You're holding on to the chair arm. In case you black out, isn't it?"

I cried more.

Dr. Frink started talking about chaos. He said, "Complex systems can flip from one mode to another. When inputs grow too great, the system jumps from one equilibrium to a different one. Something like this happens to your friend."

I kept crying. Lennie's spiky thick black hair.

"It may be something similar happens to you," he said. "When your inputs become too much to deal with . . . you shut down. I know it doesn't feel good but do you see it's good that you're crying, talking?"

"I don't want to cry," I said into Kleenex. "I don't want to be here. I don't want to talk."

He looked gently at me, waiting.

Blackouts: 4

These moments of lucidity I can't build into anything.

Nighttime. But I was not sleeping. Like I said, I've been hoarding my meds. I felt tired as a mermaid dredged up from the bottom of the sea.

A change of clothes, a toothbrush, Dr. Frink's Visa card from the top right-hand drawer of his desk.

Sid the night nurse sleeps in front of his monitors and I walk by cool as techno. The wheelchair runs silently on the blue carpet.

You looked different. They'd shaved your head and wired you up. Your shoulders were slack and there was nothing holding together your muscles. The room was full of machines. The two grey hairs sticking out from your undershirt almost made me cry. I kissed you but you didn't wake up.

Pulling the tape off his skin to release the gummy electrodes hurt *me*. I kissed each spot after doing it. He swallowed. I pulled the blue sheet away. He was wearing boxers, and long white gym socks with a red border. I brought the wheelchair close to the bed and pushed it away again, because it was in the way. I stood at the end of the bed and grabbed Lennie's two shins and pulled his legs to the left but he didn't help me out – his top half was still.

"Don't you want to get out of here?"

Problem-solving is the opposite of automatic behaviour.

From the other side of the bed I tried to push him onto his side. There was a pillow. I bunched it under his back so he wouldn't slide down. It didn't work. It struck me: moving an unwilling man around is one of the hardest things you can do.

Suddenly I was exhausted. My head dropped but my neck snapped up and woke me. Moving to the other side of the bed I pulled Lennie's knees up and slid them towards me, then tugged the wheelchair closer with my foot and tried to slide him into it sideways. Gradually his feet and calves came off the bed but I was in the way. I moved round him again and pulled again, but he was too heavy and I pulled again, and he came off the bed and fell onto me and we knocked the wheelchair back into the dresser. I was under him, bruised. I was wrapped up under Lennie in just his underwear. He smelled like soap; they'd been looking after him. I saw then, under the bed, a white crank with a black handle, a tool for raising and lowering the bed, and I kicked at it.

I don't think too long passed. I woke. My toe hurt. Sliding out from under Lennie, I pulled the wheelchair to us, put the brake on this time, and with my legs wide apart lifted him up into sitting. I stood there breathing heavily, sweat on my neck. Wheeling him down the hall I didn't run into anyone.

We took an ambulance from the hospital garage.

At the strip mall I bought sunglasses and lunch meats. If there'd been a medical supply store I could have bought Lennie a new IV, but I wouldn't know what to put in it.

We slept in the parking lot. In each other's arms. I figured they'd be looking for us at the airports and seaports. They have so many ambulances I thought they wouldn't miss one. It was cold but it was a blissful night. I told him that in the morning we'd start for Mexico. I just needed to rest my eyes for a minute.

Sirens woke me, stringy and jumpy and completely exhausted.

Police cars filed into the parking lot in a chain and horse-shoed themselves around us. Followed by fire trucks and other ambulances. The policemen opened their doors and kneeled to aim guns at us. I could see the lake behind them.

"Well, Lennie," I said.

"Sweetheart, I love you for what you've done," said Lennie.

He looked pretty radiant in the black seat next to me, mouth open, sunglasses all askew aimed at the sky, spit crawling down his cheek. I wiped that off on my sleeve.

"Now we'll never be apart," Lennie said.

His voice came out too high, I did it again.

"Now we'll never be apart," Lennie said.

"Lennie," I sighed, "You sound just like Elvis."

"I crack me up," he said in my voice.

I was laughing.

I rolled down the window and stuck my head out.

"What do you want?" I yelled.

No one answered.

A blue Oldsmobile drew up behind the police and out came Dr. Frink. He looked bedraggled and nervous, in wide jeans and a sweater, and when he came to stand next to the bulky black vests of the policemen he looked as light and thin as a locust.

One of them leaned into him urgently. Dr. Frink put his hands up in a No no no kind of way.

In the middle between us there was a control panel with square buttons the size of chunks of chocolate. There were piles of yellow forms and white forms tied with elastic bands and two clipboards, and a box of white gloves. I put a pair on.

Dr. Frink lifted a blue-and-white megaphone to his mouth. The policeman next to him waved three fingers at one of his subordinates. It took Dr. Frink a minute to figure out the buttons. Then, "Hi Lena," came his bass voice, amplified and fuzzy.

I picked up the radio thing and pushed a red button and a yellow one until I heard my voice bounce out above me.

"Dr. Frink," I said. "You look good. You shouldn't always wear a suit to work."

"Thanks, Lena . . . We need to check how Lennie's doing."

"Can you get me some smokes?" I said.

He turned to the policeman next to him, who shook his head.

"You're putting Lennie in danger, Lena. Come out now."

"I took your Visa card. Sorry."

"That's okay, Lena."

"How'd you find us?"

Dr. Frink looked at the policeman again. This time he shrugged.

"There are security cameras all over the clinic. You stole an ambulance. You don't know how to drive."

"I can drive!" I yelled.

I leaned over and pulled Lennie up with me and gave him the CB. "I'm okay," he said. "I'm perfectly happy. Please, all of you, go home."

Dr. Frink dropped the conch to his hip. The tall cop looked at him.

"Let's just talk, Lena."

"Lena's fine too," Lennie said, still eyes closed staring up at the sky. "She's fine. You know, you should just leave us alone. We're in love."

The cop had a bullhorn too.

"Young lady, you're in a lot of trouble. The best thing you can do for your friend is put down the mike, open the door, and come out of the ambulance with your hands in the air."

"You'll never take us alive!" I yelled.

The cops by the nearest car smiled at each other. I'd put the fear of god into them.

Behind the circle of police cars I could see two paramedics in orange clothes chatting beside their ambulance, one of them leaning back against it. They looked relaxed. The lake was like the perfect top of a skipping stone. There was mist, and a low white ball: the sun. I wanted Lennie to be able to see it too so I lowered his window and pushed him with my feet so his head was poking out of the window.

"Beautiful," he said. I pulled him back in. I didn't want them to shoot him.

My breathing was shallow and hurried, and his breaths were long and calm, as if he'd done this a hundred times. I wondered what it would be like to drive into the lake and be submerged together.

"What do you think, Lennie?"

He was still.

"I think it's time to give up, Lena."

I leaned over to kiss him and the stupid awkward dispatching computer dug into my side, and I knocked over an old coffee cup. I opened up his mouth and dabbed away the dry spit. He tasted like him. We kissed for a long time. He was breathing deeply into me now. We kissed and I lifted his tongue and I licked all around and under it and it was almost powdery as we kissed. I felt the thing sweeping up from inside me but I didn't want to stop now; I wanted to be where he was.

I felt tears coming on, and under my closed eyes everything was black and orange. I didn't let go or pull back, I thought perhaps he was waking but no, no. His new stubble felt rough against my cheeks, I put my hand inside the jean jacket, my jean jacket he was wearing and felt the warmth of his chest and his heart beating inside. It all turned white as I fell again and there was nothing to scrabble against or hold on to and that was all.

When I woke up my hand was in his.

No one's going to press charges.

SCOTT RANDALL

LAW SCHOOL

In my third year of law school, I attended four experiments in the psychology department. The first department flyer I happened across by chance; it was taped to a column in the CAW building, overlapping other flyers for an open mike night and a CD launch party. Male smokers between the ages of twenty-five and thirty. The experiment paid ten dollars for an hour and a half, and when I phoned the departmental secretary, he told me I could arrange to come in at my own convenience. With only a week before the Christmas examinations, not too many students had yet signed up.

The study turned out to be thesis research for a Masters project. I was the only subject that day, so the psychology student and I sat alone in a common room attached to the grad student offices while he asked me questions. How old was I? How long had I been smoking? Was I currently in a sexual relationship? Was I currently in a romantic relationship? Twenty-seven. Four months. No. No.

I hadn't been involved in any relationship in some six years, but I didn't mention this. With each of my responses, the tester scribbled on his clipboard and nodded as if he approved of my answers.

Then he changed the paper on the clipboard and handed it to me.

"In a moment, I will leave the room and you will watch a series of slides. On each slide, there will be a picture of a woman whom I would like you to assess according to the following scale." He pointed to the clipboard with his pen and read from the survey. "One, I find this woman extremely attractive. Two, I find this woman somewhat attractive. Three, no opinion. Four, somewhat unattractive. And five, extremely unattractive. Do you understand?"

I said I did.

"Do you have any questions before we proceed?"

I said I didn't.

I'd say the youngest pictured was probably eighteen and the oldest couldn't have been over twenty-two. In the photos, they all stood in the same pose in the same location. Standing in front of a tree, leaning backward slightly. The park was probably right in Windsor, but the background in each photo was unclear and I couldn't place the location.

None of the women was dressed especially provocatively, but none of them was dressed especially conservatively, either, and to be honest, I found all of the women appealing. But I varied my survey responses between extremely, somewhat attractive, and no opinion.

Around the twentieth photo, I noticed some of the women in the photos held a cigarette between their fingers and a thin line of smoke ran up their arm. This was the point of the experiment.

I should have realized this earlier. I was meant to find the smoking women more attractive. Or less attractive. I'm not sure now. For the rest of the photos, I graded the smokers high and the non-smokers low. This is what the tester wanted, I supposed.

When it was over, the experimenter shook my hand and gave me the ten dollars in cash. I was curious about the ultimate purpose of the study, but I left without asking.

I had stopped following the assigned law readings some time in October, and by November, I had stopped going to classes altogether. This happens in law school. Some students don't survive and drift away. Members of my study groups in first and second year had, in fact, shared these stories of danger. Someone misses a few lectures here and there, and then no one even sees him in his library study carrel any more. And then he's just gone. Classes, assignments, and exams just march on without him, and pretty soon his name and face are forgotten. Like all the study partners, I had nodded my head when these stories were shared and told myself I would never let this happen to me.

When this did happen to me, my greatest fear was of bumping into any of the people I had met in law school. Although I had no close friends there, many people in the program knew my face, and I imagined turning a corner among the stacks only to be confronted by a classmate who would ask how my Constitutional Law paper was coming along. And since I lived on campus in a senior student apartment and I took my meals in the student union when I didn't feel like cooking, I was uneasy for about a month. I imagined the details of a family emergency just in case. It was my father. One of his traffic court rulings had been overturned and he'd turned to drink. I had to take a break from my studies to care for him.

Most of my former classmates ventured no farther than their study carrels or the Paul Martin Law Building, though, and I never did have to explain myself.

When the Christmas break came, I took an evening train from Windsor to Toronto to spend the holiday with my father. At the last minute, I put two textbooks in my suitcase, but the pretence wasn't necessary since he was out of the house most of my visit. When he left for work in the morning and I slept late, he probably imagined that I was reading late into the night. Over the entire holiday, he took only three days off from the courts, and the majority of that time he spent stopping in at the homes of family friends. He had bought several identical gift baskets of jams and crackers wrapped in red and green foil that he delivered in person. The friends were all couples he and my mother once spent a lot of time with, and he worked to maintain these connections after her death.

Most days I spent alone in the house, sleeping late in my old room. In the afternoons, I watched television and enjoyed the cable choices my father paid for, the Documentary Film and the History on Film channels that he probably never turned on himself.

Sometimes I walked from room to room just to look around. My mother had never worked outside the house during her life, and she had laboured to keep each room in perfect order. Even the guest and family rooms, which were seldom used, were vacuumed and dusted once a week throughout my childhood.

Although my father didn't help with these chores while she was alive, he had since taken up her cleaning routines, and all of the rooms maintained their quiet order. The carpet in the guest room even had tracks in the pile where he'd vacuumed but no one had walked.

I imagined him coming home from court at the end of the day and setting right into these tasks. He would change out of his pressed slacks and shirt shortly after he came through the door, hanging them neatly in the closet before he put on the grey sweatsuit he wore around the house. Maybe he used the same orange rubber gloves my mother had always worn when she cleaned. He would crouch on his knees and scrub the corners of the kitchen floor where the mop couldn't reach.

Boxing Day was set aside for a dinner with the Wus and Xings, and father spent the day preparing a variety of dishes in that same grey sweatsuit. I came into the kitchen late in the morning, and he had already begun arranging ingredients to cook in the afternoon. Pork and beef were minced in a metal bowl and he rolled balls of the meat into dumpling papers.

"There is tea on the stovetop, Xiaolong."

He was wearing a white apron over his sweatsuit and didn't look up from his work. I sat down across from him at the table and watched as he placed the dumplings in neat rows on a cookie sheet. He frowned in concentration while wrapping each piece. Beside the cookie sheet, there was a bowl of chopped cabbage and tofu that he would encase in spring roll wrappers with equal concentration. I stood to take my tea back to my room, and he reminded me to dress appropriately for company. He had pressed a blue dress shirt that he would like me to wear, he added.

During dinner, I listened as Mrs. Wu and Mrs. Xing talked about their children. The Xings' daughter, Samantha, was finishing studying dentistry at Queen's and the Wus' daughter was engaged to marry in the following fall. It seemed that the more time I spent alone, the less I was able to engage in conversation, as if talking were a habit I'd fallen out of. Still, I nodded and agreed at the points I was expected to do so. Although my father was able to prepare a meal that would remind guests of my mother's meals, he was not as adept at playing host and during dinner he only offered comments to what had already been said. Dentistry was the shrewdest of all medical specializations, my father commented, because the training period is relatively short and the stress was less intense in the long run. And an autumn marriage is best. Summer was much too humid for a proper wedding.

When my mother was alive, holiday gatherings had seemed more boisterous to me. I remember sitting on the floor colouring with Samantha Xing while a number of adult conversations floated about the room above us. But perhaps my childhood perception isn't as accurate as I remember. Maybe conversation had always been as strained as it was on Boxing Day.

As was expected, I excused myself after the meal, but from upstairs I continued to listen to their conversation. My father lied and said that I had helped to prepare the dinner. The eggplant was all my doing and I'd wrapped most of the spring rolls. He wouldn't boast to his company but he said that I was progressing in school. Mrs. Wu expressed her relief and I imagined all of them nodding.

Before law school, I studied history. General European history as an undergrad and mostly medieval European history as a Masters student. It was generally agreed that such pursuits would not lead to a profession, and in private, my mother and father had threatened that they would not pay for tuition indefinitely. Mr. Xing added that at least history was a good preparation for international law, and as a border city, Windsor was probably a good school for such a program.

"Children sometimes have to take an indirect route," Mrs. Xing said.

My father would have turned his face down to the table and remained silent at that point, as I had seen him do before. Although he had been the one to bring up my studies, he would have been embarrassed to continue the topic, and his guests knew enough to move on to other matters.

Although the courts weren't open, my father went into work on New Year's Eve to review cases that were postponed over the holidays, and I took an evening train back to Windsor. Most of the tenants in my building had not returned from the holidays, so the building was quiet. After putting my suitcase on the bed, I flipped through my mail and decided not to stay in.

The Detroit River is a couple of blocks from the campus, and in January it looked frozen over. It wasn't, though. The current moved too quickly to freeze much of the river, and even when there was a crust of ice over its surface and a layer of snow on top of that, there was still the danger of falling through. Although it looked like you could walk on the ice, getting to the States wasn't as easy as hopping over the rail at the bank of the river and walking over. It wasn't as if one could simply walk into an entirely different country and expect to get away unnoticed.

When I first moved to Windsor, I came to the river once a day to run. Although I was never a standout at meets, I'd been in track throughout high school, and I kept up the running through my first six years in university. Once I was in grad school, my classmates would ask how I found the time, but I relaxed when running and often went just before writing term papers. The path from campus extended along the entire length of the city, and I would follow it past downtown, past the river-boat casino, and past the permanent casino once it was built. I turned back once the path started to enter the suburbs, and I'd pick up speed, pushing myself as much as I could. In total, the jog took an hour, and by the time I was back near campus, I would be winded and have to sit down to rest on a bench under-neath the Ambassador Bridge.

If not for the cold, I might have run that night.

I found a second posting for an experiment sometime in the middle of January. By then, my neighbours had all returned to the building and the campus was again busy, so I stayed in my apartment during the day and went out for walks only after dinner. Individual offices closed after five, but I had the run of the hallways and walked through all of the connected depart-ments in Chrysler Hall North and Chrysler Hall South. Of the four ads outside the psychology office, all but one called for female subjects only, and the one study I did qualify for didn't pay cash but promised movie vouchers.

The experiment was once again held in the graduate students' common area, but the woman running the study wasn't ready for me when I arrived. I stood in the door and watched as she moved the extra chairs in the room and rearranged the two tables. She was thin and tall, probably the same age as me. Her hair was long and she wore it pulled back tight in a ponytail that hung down across her face as she stacked the extra chairs against the wall.

"May I help?" I asked.

"No, that's about it. Sit. I have to grab a few things from the other room."

I waited, and when she came out, she was holding a series of file folders jumbled in her arms.

The experiment itself had to do with memory. Using her watch to time herself, she placed a series of cards with unrelated letters in front of me for ten seconds, turned the cards over, and then asked me to list the letters I had seen. Fsut. Trel. Nial. From four letters, we moved to five, six, and then seven letters, each stack of cards from a new folder. Histiel. Bubblew. Ecotrum. As long as I could pronounce the nonsensical words in my head, I had no trouble remembering, but once into ten letters I found myself confused. Bitlerwerq. Tderibophl. Gwilghulte.

I apologized.

"No, no. You're meant to get them wrong after a certain point."

She took some time looking for the movie pass in her office desk, and while I waited I tried to think of a conversation I could start with her. She took so long, though, that I'd talked myself out of the conversation by the time she returned. At home, I put the movie pass in a drawer where I forgot about it until I moved out in May. By then, the pass had expired anyway, and I threw it in the garbage.

At the beginning of February, I started swimming in the after-noons. The Addie Knox pool was far enough from campus that I wasn't likely to meet anyone as long as I left my apartment after morning classes began at nine. The lap swim didn't begin until one, but I would sit in a donut shop drinking coffee and read until then. Because I was swimming in the middle of the day and in the middle of the week, most of the other swimmers there were older men that I imagined were either retired or widowed, perhaps both. There were five or six of them who went regularly, and they all seemed to know one another.

They would stay for the entire two hours of the adult lane swim, half of the time paddling laps and half the time resting against the side of the pool chatting with their elbows propped up on the deck and their chests pushed out. I caught some of their conversations but mostly I swam steadily. I would do forty laps of breaststroke and thirty laps each of sidestroke and backstroke. I had tried front crawl on my first few times in the pool, but I was smoking more and more and found that the front crawl tired me out too quickly. I didn't hurry myself while swimming, and the breaststroke was my favourite. With the breaststroke, most of the time is spent underwater, bobbing up only for air, and I found it much like jogging. I could relax and think of nothing but getting the most distance out of each stroke to propel myself forward at a steady pace. Afterwards in the change room, the widowers and retired men talked and joked with each other, shouting out from the tiled shower room to the benches that ran along the rows of lockers. Although old and sagging, they were as lively as boys in a high-school gym class, and they insulted one another and egged each other into arguments. Their fun made me anxious; if they saw me often enough, they might wonder why I was at the pool in the middle of a weekday, and given time, they might even try to make me part of their sport. They never did though.

Although my father was a widower and would retire in another two years, I couldn't place him in these men's company. From what I remembered, jokes and insults were not his way when he was with his friends. Not that he would have disapproved of such behaviour. I just could not imagine that he would be up for such lightheartedness.

While I was a first-year graduate student in history, there was a student who was attacked in a washroom at the Leddy Library. This grad student was a year ahead of me and wasn't in any of the classes I was taking, so I didn't know him well, but I did remember seeing his face around the department. We probably saw each other dozens of times while checking our mailboxes and walking from office to office.

The day he was attacked, he had been going through microfiche in the bottom floor of the library, printing pages of texts and marking them up much the way I did when it was time for my own thesis project. He'd taken a break from his research, and in the washroom he was struck solidly on the back of the head on his way out of a cubicle. His injuries were severe, and his assailant had most likely kicked him in the head or neck after he hit the floor. The washrooms in the basement of Leddy are out of the way, and as I heard it, nobody found him until the building was closing up for the night.

I signed a card that the history secretary passed around, and she told me that he had regained consciousness after the first uncertain week in the hospital. Later, I learned that he had suffered damage to his short-term memory and would not be able to complete his degree. He joined the military after his partial recovery, and over time, people spoke of him less and less.

Why this memory should have stayed with me as strongly as it did, I am unsure. While the details of his misfortune are violent and unpleasant, there was something in the way that he was able to remake himself entirely that I thought of often. He was able to cease being what he was and become someone unlike his former self.

Around the same time I started to swim, I received a red envelope from my father in the mail. Inside was his usual hundred dollars of lucky money to celebrate the Chinese New Year. He had included a short note to tell me that I should go out for dinner and remember the coming Year of the Horse. He did not mention that this would have been my mother's year and that she would have turned sixty had she lived another three years, and I wondered if he had made the connection. Perhaps he meant for me to think of her while I sat alone in a restaurant. I did not treat myself to a dinner, though, and instead spent the money on a swimming pass for two months.

In truth, the New Year was never a special holiday in our house, any more than Christmas was. On both occasions, I was given an envelope and told that it was money that I wasn't to save. My parents didn't exchange gifts, but they did make a large purchase together to mark occasions. Usually something that they wanted for the house. A large-capacity microwave one year, and a gas snow blower another year. As far as I remember, they didn't even buy each other birthday gifts.

Like Christmas, part of the New Year holiday was dinner at our own house and trips to family friends' homes. I can recall the crowded homes of the Wus and the Xings, but there were probably more that I can no longer remember. The families in these homes included sets of grandparents who lived with their children and increased the size of the parties. The parties were loud, and for the children, there was an excitement in playing games in front of so many admiring faces. I can remember someone's grandmother urgently pulling me away from a game of Risk to ask what I wanted to do with the New Year. At that age, it felt like I was being asked what I wanted to do with my whole life. Her question confused me and she eventually released me to ask other children how they planned to spend the year.

While driving home after these parties, my father would share memories of childhood holidays. Extended families from across three provinces would gather, he said, and they would all celebrate together. There would be red envelopes from all his relatives, even from the far-off relatives whose names he was not sure of. What he seemed to remember most was the food, dozens of courses in succession and meals that would last four and five hours.

"Here," he said, "my own parents do not even live with us. Here, we live with very little connection."

On the day that the New Year came, I sat in the psychology students' common area once again. This was the longest experiment I attended, but the least interesting. First I filled out a seven-page list of foods and indicated how desirable I found each choice. Chocolate cake, four for somewhat appetizing. Corn chips,

three for indifferent. Buttered popcorn, one for wholly unappe-
tizing. A second survey listed the same foods and asked how
often I ate each.

My vices, then as now, were cigarettes and coffee, and I don't
think I was the kind of subject best suited to the study.

At the end, the graduate student stretched a measuring tape
around my waist and recorded the results. Then he asked me to
step on a scale, and I saw that my weight had gone down. I was
fifteen pounds less than my usual body weight. The change
worried me but I attributed it more to the swimming than anything else. He thanked me and gave me twenty dollars.

When reading week came in late February, the school emptied
out, but all of the buildings remained open. It was understood
that I would not return home to Toronto for the break, as it had
been understood throughout my years in university. I was
meant to spend the time off reading ahead or reviewing what
had already been covered in classes. Except I had nothing to
review that year.

During that week, I felt free to move among the university
buildings without worrying about meeting anyone who knew
my face, and I took to reading in the CAW building in the morn-
ings before the afternoon lane swims.

Sitting across from the food court lines, I noticed a street
person who seemed to have the same schedule as me. It was
strange to think that homeless people kept daily routines as
much as anyone else, but for several days running I watched him
pick up a plastic tray and make his way through the food stands
to the cash register. All I ever saw him purchase was a coffee, but

he carried the single coffee on the cafeteria tray and acted out the same ritual of all students in dining halls as if he were not at all out of place.

For the most part, the homeless in Windsor stayed downtown and did not make their way to the campus, but this particular man must have had some connection to the school that had drawn him. Perhaps he studied here decades earlier, or he had estranged children who graduated from here. His face was unshaven but clean.

Once, while reading and waiting for my afternoon swim in the donut shop, I saw a professor's assistant from the law program. She had been a marker in my Property class, a lecture section with over two hundred first-year students. I didn't think she would recognize me even if she happened to look up from her work. With school nearly finished for the spring semester, she was no doubt loaded down with final papers to mark.

She did look my way twice, though, and the second time she smiled and nodded. I nodded in return and went back to my book. The novel could easily have been taken for school reading. Maybe she thought I was cramming for exams. Or she might have thought I'd just finished exams and was treating myself to some pleasure reading. Either way, she couldn't have known I hadn't been to classes in nearly six months.

I thought of a joke I learned before starting school at all. My father was out of the house for long days then, beginning to try cases, and my mother raised me almost entirely by herself. Much of the time, she read to me, and although my parents had moved to Canada some eight years before I was born and had always spoken English in front of me, my mother would still sometimes come across unfamiliar words and phrases in the early readers and picture books.

The passages that gave her the most trouble came from a child's book of humour, and the joke I remember best was about an armless man who lived in a bell tower. This man would toll each hour by running headlong into the town bell, but one day he overshot his mark and fell to his death below. No one in the crowd that gathered around his body could identify the dead man, but one woman was sure that his face rang a bell. My father explained the meaning of this word play to us later at dinner, and I remember that even once she understood, my mother didn't smile or react. It was, she said, a sad joke.

By the time my father telephoned in April, a number of the students were moving out of my building. Exams had ended and many of the apartments were already empty. While we spoke on the phone, I watched a couple move their belongings into a U-Haul trailer at the front of the building. The boyfriend kept disappearing into the building and bringing out boxes for his girlfriend to load into the trailer.

"Did you celebrate the end of the school year?" my father asked.

"Not yet."

"It is still early. Some of your classmates still have late exams, I imagine."

"Yes."

He told me to make sure I celebrated with friends once school was finally over.

"In a few years, you will find that these classmates were an important part of your school days. And they will remember you the same."

He mentioned a few names of friends he had gone through law school with. Some were still lawyers in Toronto and he saw them around the courthouse from time to time. I didn't recognize any of the names.

"I was frankly lost during much of my first year," he said. "I was too new to North American education, and there weren't too many Chinese students in the law school then. Plus I was already married and a few years older than most of my classmates. It was difficult to get to know them well. But as time went on, I found I had more and more connections."

The couple outside my window had finished packing the trailer, and after they closed the back gate, they kissed and walked back into the building together.

I had already given my notice to leave the apartment in Windsor at the end of April, but I had not yet decided how I would tell my father that I wouldn't be returning to the school the next year, and I didn't know what I would do after I told him.

"I look forward to having you at home this summer," my father said.

"Pardon?"

"The house is quiet."

He talked about selling the house in a few years and perhaps moving into a condominium. Something farther out of the city. Maybe north.

"There won't be a reason to stay in the city once I retire."

★

Shortly before he was to retire, my father died in his car on the way home from the courthouse. He was driving alone, and the police said he might have had a slight stroke or heart attack before he went off the road and into a guardrail. After his body was taken away and the car towed, the police had gone to his house but no one came to the door. I was contacted by phone the following afternoon.

By that point, I'd already been living out of the country for over a year. At the end of the conversation, the police officer said he had appeared in my father's courtroom a few times, and the death was a sad loss. They'd not known each other well, he said, but my father had always treated him courteously during trials and had always greeted him when they saw one another in the courthouse.

My wife offered to take time off work and travel to Toronto with me, but I wanted to be alone to make the arrangements by myself. I took a month off teaching and contacted a realtor as soon as I returned to the city. Mr. Xing had passed away earlier in the year, but Mrs. Xing and the Wus came to the funeral and spoke well of my father.

"I hope that you will still keep in contact with us from time to time," Mrs. Wu said.

Although the house was in good condition, I cleaned it thoroughly on the days that it was shown, and it sold after only three weeks.

Before I left Windsor, I attended one more study in the psychology department. The student running the experiment was reading when I went into the graduate common room, and she looked pleased to see me.

"You're Xiaolong?"

I said I was, and asked if this was for thesis research.

"Ph.D. dissertation. I started collecting the data in September, but I had to stop to finish my coursework. I started up again in January but I'm still seriously behind. The year just seems to have gotten away from me."

"Do you have much more to do?"

"I should finish collecting the data this month. It will take me the summer to go through it all. After that, I don't know."

She was wearing jeans and a bulky wool turtleneck that made her look friendly, like a skier just taking a break from the slopes who would be happy to chat over a hot chocolate. She wore a wedding ring and that somehow calmed me.

"Are you a graduate student?" she asked.

"Yes. In history. It's my second year in the Ph.D. program."

I hadn't intended to lie, but such things came out of my mouth when I forced myself to chat. They still do, but less and less.

She talked with me another ten minutes, and even though I had to keep up the lie I had already started, the conversation was pleasant. Unlike the other psychology students I had worked with, she was not in a hurry.

She sat beside me at a desk and put a sheet of paper between us. The results of the study were for research purposes only, and my results would be wholly confidential. My name would never appear in the final dissertation or in any subsequent publications. I signed the disclaimer, and she explained that she would read a group of words and that I was to repeat back as many of the words as I could recall. After she read the list, but before I repeated the items back to her, I would be required to count backwards by three from the number she gave me.

"Do you understand?" she asked.

I told her that I did.

"Zebra, dingo, lion, black bear, gazelle, leopard, lemur, tiger, panda, grizzly bear, eagle, penguin, ferret, kangaroo, polar bear, koala bear, sparrow, mole, gerbil, yak."

She paused and gave me the number eighty-five to count down from. By the time I was at sixty-seven, she stopped me and asked how many of the list I could remember.

"Polar bear, black bear, koala bear."

"Yes."

"Tiger?"

"Yes."

"Lion."

"Yes."

After recalling only five of the first set of words, I concentrated harder when she read the next list.

"Bobsledding, football, javelin, squash, hockey, discus, hurdles, wrestling, rugby, cricket, baseball, fencing, basketball, racquetball, diving, archery, figure skating, pole vault, volleyball, surfing."

This time I was able to recall football, baseball, basketball, volleyball, racquetball, hockey, and squash. I also said swimming but she told me that it wasn't on the original list.

"Sorry."

"Not at all."

She moved a pegboard in between us on the table for the second part of the experiment. The blue board contained about twenty pegs of different sizes arranged in a random pattern. She explained she would touch a series of pegs in a certain order and then I was to repeat the pattern by touching the pegs myself. The patterns would grow more difficult.

Leaning forward in her chair, she touched the tops of the pegs and watched each of my repetitions. Her hair was pulled back but strands that had fallen free hung down over the pegboard. Compared to the first memory task, this was a quiet activity. She would smile after each of my correct responses, and after ten minutes of this, I felt the unspoken movements of our fingers were becoming somewhat intimate. She knew I would fail to repeat the pattern eventually, but each time the pattern became more complex, I felt as if she were daring me. Finally, after a pattern of nine pegs, I was unable to repeat her movements.

She shrugged and explained we would repeat the process, but I was now to repeat the patterns backwards. I concentrated on her hand moving over the pegs, but was once again distracted by the silence in the room and her smiles. The patterns of six defeated me this time.

Afterwards she told me that her dissertation project was on associative memories. With the ability to recall meaningful memories over the ability to recall insignificant details. I nodded as if I understood and no further explanation was necessary. Payment for the experiment was a fifteen-dollar certificate at the school gift shop and bookstore, and I redeemed it before moving back to Toronto.

MELANIE LITTLE

WRESTLING

"Out of the tree of life, I just picked me a plum . . ."

– from Gram's favourite Sinatra song

For Christmas last year, my grandmother gave my mother a T-shirt picturing an impossible poker hand. Five queens, all hearts. She'd hand-written "We're Even Better Than a Full House!" on the back, in glitter glue. My mother was civil about it, stretching her bottom lip into her standard shorthand for near-pleasure (her most blissful state). But Sally, my sister, who snoops around when my mother and I are at work, told me that the T-shirt sits in a folded square at the bottom of our mom's least-used drawer, untouched.

My gram lives with her own mother, my great-grandmother, in three rooms in our basement. They even have their own kitchen. The house has always belonged to us women, according to Gram, and it's been passed down from one to the other – it'll be mine and Sally's next, I guess – though none of the women have ever left it.

The two of them keep that basement so sweltering we don't need to heat the rest of the place except in the very coldest days of January. In their kitchen particularly, the temperature always seems to be at least a hundred degrees and rising. Gram and Great-gram sit there at their table, stewing, slurping at the red tea they sift through the Morning Glory coffee maker from dawn till practically dawn again. We all know, though she pretends to hide it, that Great-gram smokes two-dollar cigars and swigs chasers of sherry from her Santa Claus shot glass. Gram (also known as Gram Gram, when distinction is a problem) prefers to suck candied ladybugs down to nothing and poke away at a never-ending series of needlepoint creations on black velvet backing. The kitchen was converted, at great expense (says my mother), from a bedroom, and the Grams decided that the door should stay. Unless someone knocks – not likely, especially when I'm already in there – their two sets of false teeth sit centrepiecing the table in matching plain water glasses, ones from the hotel with "Topniche" brailled on the bottom. When I'm not at work but my mother is, which means she isn't around to deter me, you'll find me there with my toothless Grams, sweating in between the two of them.

The Grams' kitchen has three separate refrigerators. Maybe this is because the heat would spoil whatever was in the cupboard or the pantry, canned food included. Or maybe canned food can't spoil, and there is another, loopier reason, like occult powders requiring storage below certain temperatures, a secret sperm donor business, preserved corpses of keened-over cats. What do I know? The mysteries belonging to the Grams are kept locked fast in the crazy helix of likemindedness that binds them. The rest of us – well, those of us that care, namely me, I – can only sit there, enchanted and apart.

What I do know is that the first refrigerator – the one that's a normal, eggshell shade, not dark brown like the other, off-limits two – is a culinary Valhalla for a person whose mother's idea of an after-dinner treat is a cup of cottage cheese. Behind Door Number One you'll find every kind of condiment, seasoning, and all-around food accessory imaginable, even by me. Any chance I get sees me at the Grams' table, spooning from a bowl of straight corn syrup, garlic-flavoured breadcrumbs, neon purple plum jelly, or another such food-group-defying delight. My sister, a health-head who spends three hours a day at the gym, stays away.

Sometimes, I'm there when my grandfather comes home. We hear his truck park beside the house and then, seconds later, see his feet pass the one basement window. This is what Gram calls a beeline, and it leads directly to his own little corner of our queendom: the shed. He can't abide heat; ergo, he can't abide the basement, or in fact, any part of the house. When Gram wants to do It, she has to put two coats over her nightie and go out to Granddad among the saws; never believing that children (her word) should be sheltered from These Things, Gram told me that herself. Anyway, it's common knowledge that Gram and Granddad have a Very Healthy Relationship.

Everybody knows that Granddad is Hard, has spent much of his life being a Bad Man – though the exact nature of this badness has never been defined, at least to me. But Gram says that his heart is solid, evidenced by the fact that he loves her. "There are two kinds of men in this world, Muffin," she's often told me. "Don't listen to your Grandmother, she's a sack of wind," my mother will say, but as far as I can tell, Gram is about the only one around who takes me seriously. So I return the courtesy and listen to her like she's the nightly news – as delivered by the Pope. Strapped to a polygraph.

"There are Bad Men, and there are bad men who have fits of wishing they were Good Men. You can sift and sift until your fingers bleed, but I guarantee you won't find any other kinds."

What about men who just Don't Care? I know from rare conversations with my mother that my dad is one of these.

"A Don't Care Man is a lazy idiot," says Gram, "like someone who can't even be bothered to stand up and pull a stray hair out of his arsehole. Heaps more heartache than they're worth, the Don't Cares. Stay away from them." But she knows who I'm talking about. She knows I can't stay away from someone who has himself made staying away into an art, a science, a full-time job.

You may have noticed that I don't ask my gram about wait a minute aren't there any Good Men. I've been working lots of overtime lately and frankly you don't see too many of that type in my line of employment. It's not that our guests are any seedier than most people in most hotels in most armpit places on earth. Middle of the Road in the Middle of Nowhere, that's us to a T, I figure. In fact, I've been trying to sell Topniche head office in the States on the less snarky half of this slogan – maybe *Middle of Your Road* – to go along with my new name: "Crossroads Hotels Incorporated." "Topniche" has got to be just about the feeblest name in the whole world. Nobody can say "niche" without sounding like some kind of hillbilly CEO so everybody ends up calling us "that Top-whatever place." But we're owned by so many different companies now, I can't figure out who it is

I really need to talk to. This is what I do on my breaks when I'm on the night shift. I let myself into the Front Desk Manager's office with my master key and I use her directories to call all the different company managers around North America. I leave messages in their voice mailboxes with these and other observations and ideas, identifying myself as a "freelance marketing consultant." I give my home phone number but since I'm working so much these days, the machine must get their return calls (both my sister, all business, and the Grams, "none of our business," have their own lines). My mother has a habit of picking up our messages from outside when we're both on shift and then erasing them all. Whenever I bump into her in the course of a workday, in one of the hallways or down in the laundry room, she always says "No messages" before I can even say hello. And generally, that's the extent of our conversation. My mom is Head House-keeper – a.k.a. my immediate boss – and when we're at the hotel, she uses this as an excuse not to talk to me, the same way she uses my preference for the Grams when we're at home.

In hotels, the bad things always come when you're least equipped for them. For instance, there was a fire last year during the exact five minutes in which the entire staff had run down to the basement bar to toast a waitress's last day. She'd been at the hotel for twenty years; she deserved at least a drink, you know? The guests were all standing out on the sidewalk, freezing and outraged, when we got back to our posts. Six people were trapped in the elevator, glued somewhere between the sixth and seventh floors. No one was hurt or even canned, because you can't fire an entire staff, but we were all docked a painful chunk of pay at the end of the month. That's just one example.

My mother's best friend from college stayed with us last night, in town for one full day only. When I saw my mom writing a goodbye note to this woman at five o'clock this morning, on flimsy pink paper I'd had no idea she even possessed, I told her to go back to bed, get up at a moderately sane hour, and spend the day with her pal. I expected her to click her tongue and ignore me like she always does when I make a perfectly reasonable suggestion, but this time she came and put her arms around me, the note crumpling softly in her fist. So I've had to clean double the rooms I normally would today, and I haven't eaten a single thing in six hours besides about twenty of the repulsive strawberry soymilk kisses we have to leave on the pillows as our "Goodnight Wish."

When I've finally finished both my floors, I call down to the desk from a Vacant. Just one unplanned Stayover to investigate: not bad. I should be sitting down to a cheeseburger – no mother to order me a salad – in no time. I pound on the door and yell "Housekeeping" in my biggest voice. I do this three times. These people, 317, were due to vacate at noon but they haven't checked out with the front desk and they still owe $33.54 in movie charges (divisible by $11.18, the price of an Adult Movie, hence my from-unfortunate-experience knowledge that it's safest to give *lots* of warning). Most likely they've skipped out without paying but I knock once more just to be sure, then yell "I'm coming in!" as loudly as it is possible to yell while still maintaining the sanctioned Topniche tone of gleeful subservience. I'm out of drinking glasses, which I would normally press my ear to at this stage.

I swipe the key card and push. There's a cold feeling in my hand the second it's in the room, like there are eyes in the pads of my fingertips and they're trying desperately to squeeze themselves shut. A very small female and a very, very large male are on the bed, going at It. At least I think It is what they're at because I don't see clothes and they're in some way wrapped around each other and they're both suddenly screaming like they're in the throes of something pretty extreme. The woman is on top (wisely), and although she doesn't swivel her head to look at me when she yells "Christ! Christ! Christ!" I'm sure I can hear a challenge there. I'm out the door and I'm running and there is laughter chasing me down the hall. I slam past the elevator and into the stairwell, utterly convinced that they are in hot pursuit, closing in, just a room's-length after me.

Down three flights of stairs flying and I'm telling Rosie, at the front desk, all about it. Her eyes go really big, practically eat up her face. "That's her kid," she whispers, her stagy smoker's voice a monster truck trying to sneak along a gravel road. We go into the back to confirm this with the Front Desk Manager, Mrs. Mills. "Three-seventeen? Yup," she says. She hardly bats a lash. "Mother and son. Says here it's a hospital outpatient rate – the mother, I think." This is nothing new; we're the only real hotel close to the only real hospital in the whole area. People get flown in from all over – we hear the Health Ministry's helicopter at all hours of the day and night, and make ready to receive another stricken, bleary-eyed family of the sick.

"They were sitting down here for an hour yesterday while everyone else was on lunch," Mrs. Mills says. "Telling me all about their budding family wrestling empire. I did think it was a little odd they were holding hands – the kid must be what, fourteen? And guess what? I just got off the phone with them. They called down to extend."

"Were they laughing?" It's the most I've ever said to her. I was hoping she'd think I was like the other housekeepers, made mute by fear or language or resentment. If managers figure out you can communicate, for some reason all the panicked pager requests – for extra towels, a kumquat-flavoured tea bag, a cleaner set of curtains, a plunged toilet, a painting above the bed that doesn't contain tulips – start coming to you. She looks at me funny, like she's seeing me for the first time.

"Laughing?"

"I think they might have been playing a joke on me. I mean, on us."

"Really amusing, hunh? Don't worry about it right now, Wilhemina. Are you okay? Do you want a glass of water or something? Want to go lie down in one of the Vacants? Did you tell your mother what happened?"

"It's okay, Mrs. Mills."

Later, after I eat my lunch – proving once and for all that my appetite brooks absolutely no opposition – and once Rosie swears three times on her dead dog's grave that 317 have gone out, that she herself called their lazy asses a taxi to the hospital (it's a block away) – I have to go back up there and clean their room. It's my responsibility, my floor – well, my mom's – and anyway, the other maids have all heard about the whole side-show by now and there's no way any of them will trade with me. And what do you know? The 317s have left me a present. A heart. A gigantic, junior-kindergarten-crude heart, lovingly smeared in fat streaks of brown – two different shades of it – on the wall beside the door. I don't think I have to spell it out any further than to tell you that it wasn't done in finger paint.

I clean it up, yes I do, and I clean the bathroom and vacuum the rug too; but I refuse to even go near the bed. Nor will I, I decide, pick up any of the junk they've got strewn all over the floor; but then I make an exception. There are suitcases, at least eight, lined up along the heart-wall. Full of what? Wrestling costumes? Enema equipment? Porno tapes? Some terrifying combination of all three? I take a case, still zippered, horribly heavy, in both arms and I walk out the sliding doors – wide open, these people's one act of mercy – onto the balcony. The room faces the alley, and there's no one down there but a few demented squirrels. First, I take a gasp of much-needed air and then I start to count to three, for courage. But right after two, I let the suitcase go. I hear the echoing *whap* as I step back in and then I push my cart out of the room, calmly, like I've just finished any normal clean. But I let myself into a Vacant two doors down and I throw up and throw up, and too soon, so it's all over the gleaming bathroom floor. And then I have to clean that up, too.

When I tell Gram this whole story, she says joke or no joke, it sure is a dirty job I have. Or maybe had, because I tell her about the suitcase too. "Don't worry about it," she says. "They're all a bunch of shit-disturbers and motherfuckers at that hotel anyway." I actually have to laugh. That's Gram all over. I wish I could fold her like a piece of tissue, take her in my pocket to work. Gram could ward off anything.

It's the second Sunday of the month, time for my visit with my dad. It's not like it's of incredible urgency that I have him in my life at this point. I'm practically an adult now, almost ready to move on to a whole pageant of Bad Men of my own. What do I need with him? But every second Sunday, we keep trying. Or I do.

This morning, he's the one who calls me. "I'll meet you at Eureka Park, under the big dome," he says. Immediately, this causes me stress. Which big dome? I swear I'm not going to let him elude me this way. Eureka Park is the biggest thing in town. It'll be all too easy for him to say he was lost, to lie that he must have – no, *I* must have – been waiting at the wrong dome. But before I can pin him down, he has to get off the phone. "You'll find it, Baby," he says. "Don't forget to be there," he adds, in what he must think is a teasing, fatherly-admonishing tone, as if I'm the one who's stiffed him the last seven times. And then he hangs up. I try to call him back but the voice says, "The customer you are calling is unavailable."

I wait for two hours at the park, speed-pacing back and forth from one dome to the other, and then I walk back to the hotel. I don't want to go home because I hate the smug hurt on my mother's face whenever I tell her he's stood me up. So before long I'm at the front desk again, keeping Rosie company.

"Heather, I know this is you," Rosie is saying into the phone. Not that I understand what my mom calls the "nuances" of any of the union stuff, but everyone says there's going to be a strike in July, peak month; the managers are getting really nervous and trying, secretly, to recruit scabs. So the girls from the bar and the restaurant have taken to calling up and attempting, very badly, to disguise their voices, asking if there are any jobs coming up. For some reason they think the desk clerks and the management are on the same side, which Rosie says is sheer folly. "This isn't grade one," she tells me. "Just because I'm next-door neighbours with someone doesn't make me their best friend." The managers have their offices right behind the front desk area, and this makes the girls in the restaurant, way at the other end of the hotel, twitchy. You can tell by the way their bodies vibrate when they come behind the desk to punch in, Rosie says. Their shoulders up around their ears. Friendly, but not. I'd like to ask my mom about this, but I know better than to talk work around the house. I even made Gram swear secrecy over the motherfucker thing – especially the part about the suitcase. Mom keeps saying lately that it was a big mistake to bring me in there in the first place.

So what about Bad Women, Gram? I mean, that mother in the room – surely she's one? Are there two categories of woman, too? This is the question I want to ask her, but she's like a cat who'll jump into your lap and stay there for two hours but who hates, refuses, to be picked up: she has to initiate things herself. I'm feasting on one of my favourite dishes: dry-roasted peanuts swimming in red-wine vinegar. It's been an okay day. The Motherfuckers are still around but they kept the Do Not Disturb sign on their door all day, thank something. And no one's said a thing to me about the suitcase, although I have this chilly feeling that everybody knows.

A week later, alas, I'm back on the third floor – another favour for my mother who, though this is a separate story entirely, is not exactly unravelling but definitely shedding a few threads. I'm waiting in vain for the relic of an elevator, more commonly called the Night Bus because of how long it takes to come. I've got the cart, so I'm at its stingy mercy – I can't exactly use the stairs. I jam at the down button for the fifth time and then go over to the window to calm myself. It's good to look out over the city from here; I like to remind myself that there's a semi-normal world out there, people who've never even heard of the freaks in this hotel, people who've never stolen table lamps or asked for seven extra pillows or drawn on walls with excrement in their lives. But there's a huge crack in the window I haven't noticed before, top to bottom, a rip in the uneasy peace I was starting to make with this day.

A voice behind me. "You should have seen the blood," it says.

It's Mr. Big, the hotel's General Manager. A dangerously stupid man, hated and feared by us all.

His voice is oddly relaxed. I try to let his nonchalance infect me, can in fact feel it crawling through the pores in my throat and into my esophagus when I say, "Um, what happened?"

"A maid. Not much older than you. A scab, actually, during the last strike. Nineteen-ninety-six. Something someone out on the line said to her, I guess."

"She –" I don't get it. "What happened?" I ask again.

"She ran into this window. Face-first. A guest coming out of his room saw her do it. Broke her nose in two places. So much blood we had to replace the carpet."

"But not the window," I say. I think I detect a red spot or two on the pane.

"There was a strike on," he grimace-grins.

"But she was okay, then," I say, because much as I want to get away from him, I want to clarify this. "She lived, and all."

"Oh, yeah. Yes, she did. Live. But we had to let her go, of course." Like that was the main thing.

I sneak a look at the elevator; the flickering numbers admit that it is yet again on its way down to Parking. Since Mr. Big shows no sign of leaving his leering post at my side, I go backwards and let myself and my cart into the room I just finished, 322, muttering that I forgot to leave the Wish on the pillow.

The phone rings and I just about paint myself all over the ceiling. "Oh, good, you're still in there," says Rosie. "Got a call for you. Want me to put it through?"

"If it's about three-seventeen, I'm somewhere in the basement," I say. "Or dead."

"It's not. Here you go." A click.

"Baby," says my Dad. I mouth the words along to his next thing: "I am sooo sorry."

I grunt, waiting. Though I really have zero interest in what might come next.

"I was in a car accident."

That would make four, or maybe five, this year. I actually laugh. Well, it's more of a snort than a laugh. But the point is taken.

"I'm not lying, Baby. Aren't you worried about me? Don't you want to know if I'm okay?"

The difference between men and women, Gram has told me, is all in the will. Both have it. But maybe men have too much of it.

"Just a few scratches, that's all."

All this will, she says, it fills and fills up their brains, their balls, their days, so there's not enough room for doing.

"It wasn't me driving, though, my record's still clean, ha ha."

So in the end you can only judge them by their intentions. By whom they love.

"I love you, Baby. Let's do next weekend, okay?"

But I'm not anyone yet, not anything. So loving me doesn't count.

"I should be all healed up by then, I hope," he adds, laying it on real thick.

"I'm not a marathon you have to run."

"Ha, ha, uh – no, I promise, it's next weekend. Tell your mother that I promise, okay? Sally, too. How is she, anyway?"

"A week is forever. It's the same."

"Ha, ha, I know, I miss you, too – OW! Sorry, nothing major, just a muscle spasm. . . ."

"I'm going now."

Below me on the street, the mother-and-son wrestling team is crossing toward the hotel, hand in hand. The boy's eyes are sunk into the mounds of his face; he has to swerve his entire body around just to look beside him. But the mother is focussed. She burns toward the entrance, a taut network of wires and will. I step onto the balcony. For only the third floor, it's surprisingly high. "Hey!" I yell. They both look up, the boy searching, she zooming right in. "I'm gonna jump!"

They keep right on going.

After work I hike over to the Heritage Museum, my secret haunt of haunts. Once, a short-lived boyfriend of my mom's who worked there gave us a behind-the-scenes tour and we got to see the room where they keep what's not out on display: aisles and aisles of ancient and indefinable objects, some damaged or filthy, some unwanted, some just waiting. There was a painting that'd been slashed from one corner of the canvas to the other. "Some angry kid," the friend had said. He moved away, back to Toronto, a year ago.

What I really liked about that room was the shelf crammed with silver: knives, spoons, teapots, cups, steins, and even some religious stuff, like censers and chalices and other things I was sure I'd never even heard the words for. The friend told us that someone goes in there at least once a week and polishes every single silver artifact; there must be at least a hundred. When things get too crazy at the hotel, I close my eyes and I think of this person, alone down in those aisles, the only sound the whispery kiss of her cloth. On its best days, the ones when I can actually get my mind to shut up for a while, my work in the rooms can have moments like that, too. Of that kind of quiet.

When I go to the museum now, I can only see what's out on exhibition, of course, but still I love to press my forehead up against the cool glass and stare. I do this until the security guard, sighing (he knows me), shuffles over and puts his hand on my shoulder. I like even this part, that although this guy is giving me shit, sort of, he has to be polite about it. And he's pretty considerate, too; his voice stays low, despite the fact that, as usual, I'm the only non-staff person in the place.

Today, after I've done my staring, I climb the creaky stairs to the tiny gift shop and I buy a postcard with a silver chalice on it, one that's currently on show. There's something satisfying about being able to hold in your hands even a mere picture of what you've just seen without being able to touch. I stamp it first – I always carry stamps – and then I address it to the post office box my father uses, leaving the message side blank.

Dad needs to see me urgently, he says. His tone suggests that I have been impossible to reach. Whereas I'd bet a cosmic Get Out of Hell Free card that this is only the second time he's called me in the last five years.

I meet him, of course. It's down in the restaurant, between meals. The only person around is the busboy, Jimmy, who never seems to take his chin out from between his pudgy little breasts.

Some of the staff are convinced that his face is joined to his chest by a skein of skin, that he has special holes in the fronts of his shirts to accommodate it. Once, between meals, a bunch of us tried to hold him down and get his shirt off, but Jimmy screamed such bloody murder the guests from the rooms above the kitchen called the front desk in a froth and we had to free him. I think even Mrs. Mills, who came to break things up, had wanted to find out the truth, and secretly wished we'd worked faster.

There is, I am informed, a reason for my dad's urgency. It is, you see, in the direct interest of my apparently incredibly fragile mental health.

I'll come right out and tell this: my father, my own flesh and blood – though by what act of bad timing and judgment on my mother's part *that's* the case I don't like to contemplate – thinks that *I* think he is the earthly incarnation of Jesus. I mean, he is really convinced that I believe this. He says I got the idea when he told me, during one of those sad, excuse-glutted phone conversations, that he turned thirty-three in the year 2000, the very age Christ was when he died, and he regrets telling me because ever since he did I've been obsessed with this idea and in fact that's why he's been avoiding me. I don't know if this all means that he actually thinks he *is* some sort of saviour and is just scared I don't share his opinion, or that he might actually be right – I mean about *me* thinking it – and I'm somehow completely in the dark as to my own sad, sad delusions. "Nobody knows what they really believe." That's a direct quote from Gram Gram.

But come on, I do not. "You do," he says.

"I do bloody well *not*!" He smiles, shakes his head. "Denial is a river in Egypt, right?" he says.

"See!" I yell. "What kind of Jesus would spew sorry-ass clichés like that?"

"Who are you trying to unconvince?"

"Dad, why are you doing this? If you want to break up with us for good, just say so." He is silent, the smile of a melancholy saint tugging at his lips. I shout, "Are you trying to drive me crazy?" I don't care who hears us now.

"You see everything in checkerboard colours of good and evil."

"I don't believe this."

"Oh, you believe in me, that's the whole problem. You believe too much *into* me."

"You're insane!"

"Why did you take my gym towel, then?" He is glowing with righteousness now.

"You mean –"

"Your mother told me, Baby. She sent my agent an email."

"You mean, like you think I think it's the shroud of Turin, or something?" I say. "Hey, good idea! I'm starting to like this idea. Maybe I can take your funky towel, which for your information I took because the goddamn cat missed you, and sell it to the lonely old priests over at Holy Family and make some money off your cheapskate ass for once."

"I can't see you any more, Baby. I love you but I can't. I've been praying on it and I've come to see that it's doing you no good."

"Wait a minute –"

"I know this breaks your heart, but it will be made whole again. The sooner I'm out of your life, the better. I've already mailed a letter to your mother and the courts explaining the situation."

"– you've been *praying* on it?"

"What?"

"Since when do you pray? You said you've been praying on it!"

"I didn't say that, Baby, you see how you've become, you know I've never been religious and you're just projecting your fantasies onto me –"

"Oh my GOD!"

"You see? This is really destructive, Bay –"

"No shit, asshole."

"And now I really do have to go."

"I don't suppose you'll start sending money to Mom or anything."

"I can't perform miracles, Baby." The smile more Cheshire than martyr now.

"Because good. I never want to hear from or about you again. And neither does Sally." As if she ever did.

"You won't. Regardless of what you may want to believe, there will be no recursion, or resurrection, if you prefer – as I'm sure you do – of me into your lives. Please, let's go in peace."

"Okay, stop. This is a ridiculous conversation. It's terrible in every way. I'm embarrassed to be having it with you."

But I wasn't having it, because he was gone.

Jimmy the busboy was there by the entrance, his head lifted up, watching him go.

On the strike line, my mother talks to me like I'm an adult, doesn't tell me what to do or not to do, what factions to associate with or which people not to believe. In fact, on the line, barriers of all kinds seem to fall down: waitresses share smokes with the front desk staff; cooks from different shifts, normally at perpetual war, exchange recipes (though they themselves would never use such a frilly word); housekeepers bend over the daily *Sun* crossword with the big, burly doormen from the bar, tickling the men's bare scalps with their long, bleached-out hairs. Even Jimmy is relaxing into it, took off his shirt one day when it was thirty-five degrees out and everyone else was baking their skins. The hotel is on the sunny side of the street, and Mr. Big had all the awnings removed when the strike started so we wouldn't have any shade to picket in.

The 317s, unfortunately, are still around. Apparently, she has bone cancer, is here for regular treatments, and he has to be with her because the father is not available. It's true that she's looking even more frail of late, as if every night she gets stretched over a longer rack. We have plenty of chances to notice; we see them going in and out of the hotel every day, though unlike most of the guests, they never say hello or give us a thumbs-up.

Mr. Big, with the help of the head accountant (she has five kids to feed), is trying to run the whole hotel himself. At dinnertime Mr. Big leaves in his red convertible – no waving or honking from him, either – and returns an hour later with two girls in jeans and big hair, his daughters. The girls are in there until at least eleven every night, when we're almost done our last line shift. They clean rooms, do laundry, cook and deliver the meals for room service – all this even though they're both in summer school the whole day. We know because the accountant still talks to us, gives us the skinny whenever she comes out to make the bank deposit. This woman used to be famous for her beautiful nails, bitterly ridiculed for it, to be honest. But now her fingers are full of paper cuts, the nails tattered and bitten down, the polish chipped as if nibbled by mice.

When Mr. Big's daughters are finished their work they have to wait for the Night Bus; their dad, who gets up at five to handle the early checkouts, will already be snoring in one of the empty king-sizers. The older girl sometimes comes to the curb and sits with us. Mostly she doesn't say anything, just smokes. But one night a cook slips her a mickey and she opens up, starts telling us how the guests are mostly doing their own laundry now, making their own beds, ordering takeout from the places in the area instead of calling down for food, even though their medical insurance gives them a certain room service allotment per day. "There are some good people in there," she says, narrowing her eyes and looking up at the hotel. Lights are on in most of the windows. It looks just like a fully functioning, unremarkable way station.

The girl takes another swig from the mickey, hands it back to the cook with a nod. "And then there are some real motherfuckers." She tugs her skirt over her knees as she stands up, flagging the approaching bus, her middle finger ever-so-slightly extended. The younger one walks over to meet her, throws us a sympathetic look. They remind me of Gram and Great-gram, united by their quick, cool judgments of others, by the separateness from one another that is real but so superficially slight, its exact code known only to themselves.

MATTHEW RADER

THE LONESOME DEATH OF JOSEPH FEY

Reflection

Seamus and Jacob watch their reflections shiver and blur in the cold mountain water at the bottom of the falls where their brother's body was found early last summer. Fir trees and cedar stretch long shadow-fingers over the pool all morning; mid-afternoon and they're in the fist of the forest. Somehow, over the years, Seamus has grown taller than Jake, and Jake has grown heavier than he imagines himself, his jawline weakened by the flesh of his throat. Above on the cliffs, the call of kids who polish off their Luckys and then step into the air, fall three storeys into the belly of the rock where the river thrashes and turns for a thousand feet before the falls. Hard to imagine what event or conditions of the distant past caused the water to move as it does through stone. Hard too, not to imagine their brother's face there in the pool with their own, his lips turning blue, his eyes wide reflecting the sky as it is said they found him.

Seamus is not a talker, but Jacob can tell by the way he rests his hand on the water and looks aimlessly into the sky that there is something Seamus would like to say. Shirtless and barefoot, Joseph was floating belly-up when a young couple, perhaps descending the steep valley slope to swim naked in the early morning light, emerged from the forest and stood on the rocks overlooking the pool. It is said his long blond hair radiated on the surface of the water like cold sunshine. His sandals were found in the scrub at the edge of the road a mile or so towards town. His shirt was never found, though Jacob has heard rumours, and believes he has seen it pass by him in a crowd. Some say he meant to die, but Seamus has never believed this. Some say he died by accident, but this seems unlikely to Jacob. I've seen him, Seamus says, twice.

Sighting: *Seamus*

Sometimes my eyes won't focus. Like I'm just waking up, only I wasn't asleep. Like when you get up too fast and your head blurs, but in my eyes alone. And it happens, out of the blue: watching the tube, drinking a cup of joe. It's what comes next though, that worries me: I see things. Usually people, but sometimes scenes, brief episodes meant, I believe, to have meaning for me or those I know. Which is what happened the evening Joseph died. I was at home alone, watching the ten o'clock news. Mum was in bed, and Jake wasn't back yet, which was usual, I suppose, for a Friday night. Hudson Mack was on reading his cues and when they broke for commercial, it happened: a spell, of the kind I just described, and when it cleared: a figure standing next to the television set, fully fleshed but with a blue hue that seemed to soften his edges.

To say I recognized him would be untrue, but I knew what he was just the same and so did not panic or try to escape. He's dead, was all the figure said, and was gone in a blink. And I remember thinking he meant Hudson Mack, which I suppose would have been sad, at least for his family, but to me was a perfect way to spook Jake, you know, call Mack's demise that night, and wait for the news to break the next day. Only, Jake didn't come home until very late and I fell asleep on the couch, dreamt Joe and I were playing poker underwater: Two aces, two eights, and a jack, laughed Joe. Now show.

The Passing Stars: *Jacob*

The moment Joseph died, I was sitting in Jackie Clark's kitchen with my back to the wall, which is not quite instinct or habit for me at bars and parties, but acquired skill, akin to riding a bike, which I no longer think much of, but doubt I will ever forget. Three girls and Tommy Jackson playing poker at the kitchen table, people dancing to Friend of the Devil on the back porch. I have never told anyone this before, but there's an overwhelming pleasure I get when around certain people. Strangers or those I know, it's like a wave or force, almost erotic but not. It feels so good at times it hurts. Like a thousand silk butterflies brushing your face and your lungs filling with water at once. And this is how it was just then. My skin burned red like an allergic reaction and the air thickened: fruit flies slowed mid-flight, the smoke from Tommy's cigarette curled like a snake around the lamplight that was stalled just below the ceiling. I cannot explain it, but I wanted to kiss everyone in the room and I knew I had to leave that instant. I couldn't breathe and I stood up so quickly blood rushed from my head and I stumbled blindly to the sink and was sick.

Forgiveness is a bitch, either to give or to get, and to think back on that night is to face a sense of guilt for not knowing what it meant, for not being able to read into the significance of the event. I staggered from the Clarks' into the lush summer dark of the front yard, where moths glowed in the moonlight like tiny ghosts and the only breeze was from the wing of a bat. I passed a couple making love in the back of an Oldsmobile that was parked on the lawn, and I thought I might combust, burn on the spot and be turned to dust. If only I could go back. Could have it to do over again. I think I would understand and be able to act. But that night all I could do was lie in the grass and listen hard: earthworms, root systems, the passing stars.

Faith

A crow shadow skates across the pool and is gone. From here the river rambles through a narrow field of rubble as if what stone was bored from the long channel of rock above was spit out in one colossal and violent event to lie strewn as distant memories at the foot of the falls. Joseph, it was said, was born *en caul*, meaning before his mother's water broke, the amniotic sack torn from his head to let him breathe. Meaning, as some believe, ready to vet messages from the deceased. Seamus, it seems to Jacob, has come to collect whatever evidence Joseph may have left strewn among these rocks, but of this he will not talk.

A sloe-eyed hound appears on the cliff overlooking the pool but does not descend, her long flat muzzle angled up to puzzle whatever scents are borne on the cool valley wind. Somewhere here, Seamus says but does elaborate. He may mean whatever clues swirl in the slow current of the pool: a piece of fabric, a final hair, a rock upturned to indicate something as yet unclear. Or he is talking to himself and is unaware he is even speaking, perhaps rummaging his own rubble-strewn psyche for the precise thought or memory to make sense of or give context to his feelings here. Faith, let it be said, is a sixth sense and like our eyes or ears, easily tricked. As far as Seamus is concerned, Joseph's death was an accident at best, a broken stone or misplaced step, but more likely a deliberate shove from a so-called friend named Travis Dent, a fellow deckhand, and the last man seen with Joseph in the late hours of that evening.

Ocean Voyager: *Seamus*

The year they pushed the road through the top of our hill, Joseph left school and took a job as a deckhand on an old and doomed wooden trawler called *Ocean Voyager II* and so began a short career on the Gulf of Alaska hauling halibut from the floor of the Pacific. At home, I was finishing grade ten and Jacob landed me work on Saturdays framing houses on the newly cleared land where as younger kids we once built an elaborate yurt-like structure deep in the bush with stolen nails and alder poles we chopped by hand. I met Travis Dent for the first time in the fall of that year, when the *Ocean Voyager II* sailed into the harbour and the rich and weary men walked up the hill to spend their money on drink and whatever else they pleased in the slatboard and ramshackle watering-hole known as The Hotel.

It was a grey Saturday afternoon and I was sitting on the front step of the saloon waiting for Jake, who had gone inside to cash our paycheques with a bartender he knew. Though Joseph was just eighteen, the saltwater and Alaska air had put a rough and curly beard on his face and if it weren't for the expectant set of his jaw, lips parted as if something fragile and slightly large for his mouth could slip out at any moment, I might not have recognized him as he crossed the street to greet me. The things ya see when ya don't have a gun, Joseph laughed as he wrapped his arms around me and lifted me off the ground, the scent of sweat in the nape of his neck. Behind him a step, watched a wiry young man in a dark wool cap who Joseph introduced as Travis Dent, a fellow deckhand. I can't say why, perhaps it was the way the fellow grinned, his teeth fitting oddly like water-warped boards between his lips, or the narrow cut of his chin, but at that moment I had a vision of Joseph and this Travis Dent on the edge of a cliff and then Joseph going over into the river.

Truth: *Jacob*

I don't want to make too much of this Travis Dent since I have nothing against the kid and there is no evidence to suggest he did it or that anything was done except that Joseph jumped. But I'll give Seamus this: someone must have driven Joseph out up Forbidden Plateau Road because there's no way he got that far up the mountain on his own. It's twenty miles or more from town before the paving ends and another handful down the logging road to the river trail. When I left Joseph at the Hotel that afternoon, he'd already lost count of the rounds and was losing badly to Travis at pool. Word has it he left with Dent sometime after ten with the intent, as far as the barmaids knew, to head over to Jackie's by taxi. Travis says he left by himself, walked down to the harbour, and fell asleep on the deck of the *Voyager*, which is where the captain woke him the next morning. So there is no proof Dent had anything to do with Joseph's death, at least directly, but then nothing lies like the truth.

Seamus claims he has visions and I'm inclined to believe him. As a kid he'd get sick with these amazing fevers and spout out all this shit about burning towers and cloned babies, which I chalked up to illness and science fiction but freaked me out nonetheless. I hesitate to say Seamus is psychic but something happens to him and I don't know what it is. What I do know though is that I loved Joseph and I cannot bring him back. I guess this is a case of faith making me blind, but I don't really care what happened that night. Joe was my brother and I loved him if he was murdered or if he jumped.

Medicine Bowls

Some events leave a footprint on a time or place, a kind of permanent echo, metaphysical evidence of the past you feel both inside and outside of yourself, a quiver in your cells. And as the planet spins into that date or you find your eyes and feet travelling that same landscape, it is as though you are standing ankle-deep in water that has risen up out of nowhere and may rise higher before it recedes. And that is how it is for Seamus and Jake here at the edge of the river. A year ago today and Jacob would have slept it away had he not heard the pickup's engine turn over early this morning and got up to see what was about. Seamus, it must be said, is obsessed with Joseph's death, and Jake can't blame him, since it seems senseless and unfinished to him as well. But that's just the way it is and more than anything Jacob wants to rest. And still, it doesn't work that way, Jacob has to admit. You can't escape what's inside yourself and to come here on this day with Seamus is a way to remind himself that he is still alive and drawing breath.

The river above them passes through what resembles a series of giant mortars ground into the earth by an ancient water-witch and is known to the locals as the Medicine Bowls. It is into one of these mad pools that Joseph likely fell and was sucked under, perhaps struggled a time for air before being pulled down

and over the falls, where he was found that morning, insects
sewing the sunlight just inches above his head. Jacob would like
to say that this is it, that he has returned to the scene of his
despair and now will put it behind him, draw the curtains, so to
speak, on the whole affair, and get on with things, but he knows
it's not that easy, no matter what he says or what he'd wish. And
he knows too, that even more than himself, Seamus will remain
in this place long after they have left.

Framing: *Seamus*

We were sheeting the east wall of a rancher on the crest of the
hill late last summer, getting ready to quit for the day since it
was dark much earlier by then and we'd already worked through
supper, when the wind picked up and the dust lifted off the
undeveloped lots like a plague of tiny locusts and descended on
our eyes and mouths. Jacob wanted to finish up, so we wrapped
our shirts around our heads and got on with the job, fastened
the last sheet of plywood and got ready to lift. Jake took one end
and I took the other and together we stood it up and fit it on the
house. And just then the dust slacked off and I could see the sun
through the unframed window skewered on the mountaintops
and standing a pace or two from the edge of the lot, Joseph, all
blue hue and ghost.

There are very few people you can tell this kind of thing to,
and I can't say I felt Jake was one of those at that moment. It
seems to me that people reveal themselves to some and not to
others for a reason and it's usually best to respect that decision.
Which is what I did: Jake and I nailed the wall to the frame like
we would any other, and I said nothing about the spectre of our
brother who watched as we put that house together in the dust

of what was once a forest where we played when we were younger. On the horizon the white tooth of the glacier bit into the sunset, and a vulture teetered as if hung by wire over the valley fields. Distance seemed collapsed and I began to wonder what loomed ahead or in the past. Jake took a final nail from his mouth and drove it through the wood in a single blow: the timber quivered, and for a moment I thought the house might not hold, let go of its fastenings and like some long dormant animal unfold on the hilltop before us. To say I was afraid would be untrue but I eyed that creature until it shook itself still and I knew it would stand the way it was built.

Grace: *Jacob*

The rock is black with age and slick with river spray. Seamus goes ahead of me, searching for a hand and foothold to haul himself up on, the echo of the falls like a faint pulse in the folds of the stone. No moss or lichen, no roots grip the rock, so to scale it like we do is treacherous and slow. From below, I watch Seamus move over the cliff at a steady and careful pace, his hands testing each crack and crag before shifting his weight. Moments like these should last forever, but seconds pass faster with each dying day and even grace goes by now in the blink of an eye. Which is a lie I allow myself since it feels right and helps ease the guilt of living out my time.

Already the town kids have slipped back into the timber and the clouds have gathered at the foot of the mountain to await further instructions. There is a sound I have heard all my life when quiet and deep inside myself, like rolling water in a distant hollow, like blood through a narrow channel, and I hear it now, only much louder, rising from the river canyon like mist. For me, this is a kind of silence, a kind of movement before think-ing, before thought. As I near the top of the cliff, Seamus offers his hand and I take it. This is as close as he and I will ever get but it is a strong grip and no words are needed to make the meaning clear. It is possible to explain how a thing happens, the simple mechanics of the action – the lungs fill with water so oxygen cannot be exchanged in the blood, eventually the heart sputters then comes to a stop altogether – but difficult, I have found, to give it meaning beyond *he drowned*. After that it's all speculation and abstracts and what's known is only half as important as what's not. In my eye-corner a flicker strikes across the river like a match. Finally, Seamus says, we are alone.

CRAIG BOYKO

THE BELOVED DEPARTED

"Wretched are the poor in spirit, for under the earth they will be as they are on earth." — BORGES

Claude said: "It's not nostalgia. I'm not stuck in the past. In fact I hardly even think about the times we had together. I don't want to rewind. I want the future to hold her. I just want to see her again. Everything has become tainted with her absence. Everything – a ringing telephone, a lampshade, the economy, lima beans, plumbing, lions, capitalism, Brahms, hydrogen, clairvoyance, grammar, James Joyce, circular logic, shoelaces, Yugoslavia, public transit, algebra, ballet, sodomy, Episcopalianism, architecture, evolution, oakum, loose change, dentistry, taupe, the immune system, hot jazz, cotton, spelling bees – everything is permeated with not-herness. I just want to see her again."

Dr. Mayer-Edelmann said: "The trajectory of your mourning-arc is shallower than I quite frankly would like. Your grief index is falling at what I feel compelled to describe as a less than wholly satisfactory velocity. Your SSHQ – the Stanford Standardized Heartache Questionnaire – scores are manifesting an erraticness that professional propriety demands I consider to be not alto-gether reassuring. But I'll tell you what I'll do. I'm going to refer you to Dr. Grohmuller, a very good oneirologist. She should be able to see you sometime in early autumn."

Dr. Grohmuller said: "Keeping in mind that this is all a gross oversimplification, the neocortex has two distinct modules, which, roughly speaking, are localized in complementary hemi-spheres in the majority of individuals. In general terms, one could say that the first of these modules specializes in what Grohmuller (1989), Grohmuller (1994), and Grohmuller and Kandinsky (1999) have referred to as *narrative* or *seriatim* con-sciousness, while the second module operates in what the same authors have called an *iconic* or *parallel* fashion. Others (Grohmuller & Fitch-Bass, 2003) have posited that the iconic consciousness is, broadly speaking, most intimately involved in the production of the REM dream state. Neurophysiological support for this theory has been steadily accumulating, and it is now believed by many that the recently synthesized chemical berylpotassiumdioxethylmonoamide – or 'Vitamin G2' – is in fact a naturally occurring neurotransmitter that plays a central role in suppressing certain high-level functioning of the narra-tive consciousness at the onset of stage-four sleep (Grohmuller, Davis, Fitch-Bass, Robins, Triptree-Loeb & Caton, in press). So-called G2 Blockers, which are believed to inhibit the re-uptake of Vitamin G2 at dorsal lateral prefrontal cortex receptor sites, have lent support to this theory as a result of their observed effect in clinical trials – namely, the drastically increased trigger-ing of lucid dreaming states."

Claude said: "I think I'm getting déjà vu."

Dr. Grohmuller said: "That's because we've already had this

conversation. It was earlier today. At the end of our consulta-
tion I gave you a prescription for a Vitamin G2 analogue, trade
name Lukoxamine, commonly referred to as simply 'Lukes.' As
I explained to you then, it is my belief that patients demon-
strating irregularities in their bereavement behaviour – or what
Roberts and Reid-Ambrose (1974) have, rather puckishly,
called 'grief paralysis' – may benefit from short-term lucid
dreaming treatment. In short, abreaction may be attainable if
the patient can direct her or his dream toward a reunion with
the beloved departed."

Claude said: "So this is a dream? I'm dreaming right now?
But this looks exactly like your office, your real office."

Dr. Grohmuller said: "What about that penguin?"

Claude said: "You just put that there."

The penguin said: "It's your dream, man."

Claude said: "Then why am I dreaming this? Why aren't I
dreaming of Margaret? If this is my dream, why can't I just make
her appear?"

Dr. Grohmuller said: "The narrative consciousness has vir-
tually no direct authority over the iconic consciousness. To
anyone but a layperson it would be obvious that this arrange-
ment is to the organism's advantage. If the narrative consciousness could interfere with its world-creation, people would sit
around daydreaming instead of getting any work done. They'd
imagine they were well-fed instead of searching for food.
They'd make believe they were good-looking and universally
admired instead of writing scholarly articles for peer-reviewed
journals (Grohmuller & Grohmuller, 2002)."

The penguin said: "Most of the dead *I* know live in the City
of the Dead."

Dr. Grohmuller said: "It's a subterranean city. The dead don't decay as quickly underground."

Claude said: "So I've got to go to this City of the Dead if I want to see my Magpie?"

The penguin said: "Yeah, but they won't let you in unless you've got a pass."

Dr. Grohmuller said: "You can get a pass from your physician. Or your coroner."

Dr. Aloy said: "You look terrible. Lift your shirt. You've put on weight. No, don't say anything, I don't want to hear it. Hold your breath. No, breathe in first. *Now* hold it. Let it out. Just as I thought. You've been smoking again, haven't you? Let's see your tongue. Oh my God. Ever heard of 'halitosis'? Never mind. Hold out your arms. No, to the side. Not been getting any exercise, I see. Does it hurt when I do this? Well it should. How's your diet? No, forget I asked. Look over my shoulder. My *other* shoulder. Can't say I care for the rate of pupil contraction. Follow this pen with your eyes. Without moving your head. Just as I thought. We'd better schedule you for an MRI. I'd tell you not to panic but it might do you some good. I wish you could see yourself. If my patients could see what I see, they'd take my advice instead of turning themselves into walking pastries. Here, feel this. Hard as a rock, isn't it? That's called a latissimus dorsi muscle. But then you wouldn't know anything about that, would you? It breaks my heart to look at you. Or it would, if I didn't run eight miles a day. I've got a heart like a freight engine. Put on this stethoscope. In your *ears*. You hear that? That's not just pumping blood, that's blasting it into orbit. Now listen to yours. It's squeezing that blood out like a little girl handling somebody's used hankie. It brings tears to my eyes. Tears as clean and clear as mountain spring water."

Claude said: "I need a pass to the City of the Dead."

Dr. Aloy said: "Can't do it. You're not dead. You *look* dead but you're not. Not quite. What's the hurry? You're headed there soon enough."

Claude said: "My girlfriend is there. I want to see her."

Dr. Aloy said: "Sorry to hear that. But I could lose my licence. You come back to me when you're dead and I'll see what I can do."

Claude said: "This is all just a dream of mine anyway. Can't you break the rules?"

Dr. Aloy said: "Now let me give you a piece of advice, free of charge. Don't go around saying that this is all just a dream of yours, okay? People don't like being told they're a figment of somebody else's imagination. Now, if you're serious about this pass, you go out there and get yourself killed, come on back and I'll get you straightened away. Of course that's not my *professional* advice. Excuse me. Hello? Oh. It's for you."

Dr. Grohmuller said: "I wouldn't jump out Dr. Aloy's window if I were you. The fall might frighten you and the fear might wake you."

Claude said: "I wasn't going to jump. I have no desire to die in public. Of course I don't exactly want Gary or Lila to see my brains dripping down the bathroom walls or Helen slipping in a pool of my blood, either. Not that I own a gun. And I don't know anything about poison. I guess enough of anything toxic would do the trick, but I don't really relish the idea of writhing around in agony while bleach eats away my innards – even if this is just a dream. I've always thought freezing to death, curling up drunk in some snowbank, would be best. But of course it's summer. I suppose I could hang myself. There's that oak in our backyard. The kids won't be home from school for a few hours yet."

Lila said: "Mom, Dad's stuck in the tree out back."

Helen said: "Mommy knows, dear. Finish your roast beef and you can call the ambulance."

The ambulance driver said: "Stop your squirming back there or I'll have my partner strap you down until the trial."

Claude said: "What trial?"

The ambulance driver said: "You think with that welt around your neck they're not going to know it was suicide?"

Claude said: "Since when is suicide a crime?"

The ambulance driver said: "It's always been a crime. It's the one thing the living can't abide. You kill someone else, that shows a healthy respect for life. Shows you think it's the most valuable possession you can take away from them. But you off yourself? Oh boy. That's like being invited to a sumptuous banquet and shitting in the pâté de foie gras. You leave a note?"

Claude said: "I couldn't think of anything to say."

The ambulance driver said: "That's in your favour."

Claude said: "Anyway I didn't really hang myself. I'm just trying to get a pass to visit my girlfriend in the City of the Dead."

The coroner said: "I can give you one just as soon as we're done with the autopsy. Can you hold on to this for a second?"

Claude said: "What is it?"

The coroner said: "Your stomach. Oh, that's just great. Right on the floor. Last time I ask you to hold anything. That reminds me. Did you fill out your organ donor card?"

Claude said: "It's in my wallet."

The coroner said: "Won't be needing this back then, will you? Or this. Or this. Or this."

Claude said: "What do you need that for?"

The coroner said: "A colleague of mine is writing a dissertation on the effects of defenestration on the exsanguinated human kidney."

Claude said: "What are you going to do with *that*?"

The coroner said: "My brother's a chef. All right, here's your pass. Take that to your funeral director. And here's a sewing kit. Good luck."

The funeral director said: "Dear friends and family of the dearly departed Claude R. Talleurien. I'm not sure what the 'R' stands for but it is always a sad occasion when someone we know dies. It is less sad for those of us – such as myself today – who did not know the dead person in question. But it is still sad. It is always sad. For whom the bell tolls and all that. The fact of the matter is, no one knows a whole hell of a lot about it. Death, I mean. I can't possibly imagine what it's like, and neither can you. Oh, you've got your ideas, and so have I. For me, I suppose it's a sort of infinite succession of intense and always novel joys; an endless concatenation of unbearable euphorias, each one obliterating the last with its impossible brilliance, until my soul is suffused with a pure and unadulterated beatitude that would make falling in love or heroin high or being fellated by a circle of dancing pixies for all eternity seem like excruciating agony in comparison. But maybe that's just me. Now, since we're running a bit late, I will limit myself to only one or two items of parish business. As many of you know, we usually hold a Bingo for Charity night on Fridays at seven, but for reasons that I will not elaborate upon at the moment, because I do not know what they are, that function has been moved ahead an hour, to 6 p.m. If you would like to write that down, here is a pen that I will pass around, starting at this end and proceeding counter-clockwise. If you do not have a piece of paper, you might want to write on the back of your hand, assuming of course that you are not allergic to blue ink. Now, would anyone like to stand up and say a few words by which to remember our dear friend and father and brother and son and nephew and co-worker, Claude?"

Claude's father said: "Truth to tell, I never really wanted no kids. Guessat's why I up'n left town when Claude here was borned. Came back for a visit once. Claude here wanted to know where I'd been at all them years, kept askin' why I wasn't around when he was a-growin' up. 'Well hell,' I says, 'fair is fair. You wasn't around when *I* was a kid, was you?' Left town again pretty soon after that. Couldn't hack it, I guess. Some just isn't cut out to be dads is all. Ain't nobody's fault."

Wendy said: "I didn't know Claude very well, but what I did know of him I liked a lot. I don't know what kind of a father he was, or husband, or friend, or employee, but he used to come into the store maybe once or twice a week and I could tell he was an alright person. He was always polite. One thing I remember is he often had exact change. He may not have done anything noteworthy or particularly memorable but I will always remember him. And so, in a small way I guess he'll live on in my memory. And maybe someday I'll tell my children, if I ever have children, though God knows the way things are going . . . Or I'll tell someone else about him, and then he'll live on a little bit in their memory, but not very much, I guess, because I probably won't be able to explain what it was about Claude that made him special or unique or whatever. But at least I will remember him, and so he'll live on, at least until I die. And then Claude will die too. But if you look at it another way he's already dead, so what's the difference."

Jack said: "Claude was a valuable asset around the office. Now that he's dead I've got Collier breathing down my neck for his Moss-Maple folio, plus the Werner-Fellinger article that Claude was supposed to have on Gernwald's desk Monday has fallen into my lap, and my guys are doing the work on the Horace-Witt summary that his guys were supposed to be doing for the big Thurington-Levy merger presentation on Friday but none of them can do anything without that Kimberley-Woodrow file that Claude was appending to Jenkins's Ruprecht-Smith file but no one knows where it is and his office is a disaster area let me tell you and we were a man short for the interoffice league game last night and that's our third forfeit and one more and we're out of the semis so yeah, he'll be missed."

Helen said: "Claude was a good father, I guess. But he always left the discipline to me, so I always ended up looking like the bad guy. And he was an alright husband. Neither the best nor the worst I've had. As for performance in bed, I'd say he was somewhere in the thirtieth, thirty-fifth percentile. Also while we're here I might as well announce that Jack and I were having an affair and now that Claude is dead we can get married and you're all invited to the wedding, which is tomorrow, and as far as gifts go, considering the short notice, cash is just super."

Gary said: "He was a nice dud. I mean dead. I mean dad. But he never let us stay up late or watch rated-R movies. I hated him."

The gravedigger said: "How you doing down there? Need anything? Hungry? Thirsty? How's your bladder? Any last words? No? Here we go then. Hope you aren't claustrophobic. That's a little joke."

Claude's Uncle Wilbert said: "And this is the fourth circle, where the people who left refrigerator doors open stay. And this is the fifth circle, where the people who amended STOP signs with the word *Driving* stay."

Claude said: "That doesn't seem so bad."

Claude's Uncle Wilbert said: "It's ambiguous. Is their purpose politico-environmental – do they want you to start biking to work? – or are they just being waggishly pedantic? And this is the sixth circle, where Larry stays. Larry was the guy who called escalators 'escalators,' even though they also go down. Hi Larry."

Larry said: "What was I supposed to call them, 'de-escalators?'"

Claude's Uncle Wilbert said: "And this is the seventh circle, where Hank stays. Hi, Hank."

Hank said: "What was I supposed to call them, 'de-elevators?'"

Claude's Uncle Wilbert said: "And this is the eighth circle, where the people who ran crooked lemonade stands stay. Hi there, Gwenda."

Claude said: "Well aren't you adorable. How much is lemonade?"

Gwenda said: "For a quarter you get one chance to win a glass, or three chances for fifty cents."

Claude said: "Here's a quarter."

Gwenda said: "Sorry. Please try again."

Claude said: "I didn't win?"

Gwenda said: "Sorry. Please try again."

Claude said: "Here's a dollar."

Gwenda said: "Sorry. Sorry. Sorry. Sorry. Sorry. Please try again."

Claude said: "That's only five."

Gwenda said: "You win!"

Claude said: "I won a lemonade?"

Gwenda said: "You won a free play!"

Claude said: "Well, did that one win?"

Gwenda said: "Sorry. Please try again."

Claude's Uncle Wilbert said: "And this is the ninth circle, where all the people who make things worse by trying to make them better stay. And this is the gate to the City of the Dead, where everyone else stays. You've got your pass, right?"

Claude said: "Where's Maggie?"

Claude's Uncle Wilbert said: "Check the telephone directory."

Claude said: "She's not in it."

Claude's Uncle Wilbert said: "Then she's not here."

Claude said: "But she's dead."

Claude's Uncle Wilbert said: "You should talk to Mr. Rogobo. He's the mayor."

Mr. Rogobo said: "She's not here."

Claude said: "But she's dead."

Mr. Rogobo said: "She's not on the books. If she's not on the books, she's not dead."

Claude said: "The books must be wrong. I went to her funeral. I watched them lower her coffin into the ground."

Mr. Rogobo said: "The books are not wrong. The books are never wrong. At least the books are *very, very rarely* wrong. To my knowledge, and my knowledge is comprehensive, the books have only been wrong on seven occasions. But the bookkeepers learn from these errors. So, as you can imagine, the art of keeping the books is much more advanced now than it was in the golden age of bookkeeping, before the books ever went wrong, so that now the books are, in effect, never wrong. For all intents and purposes, the books are perfectly all right."

Claude said: "But the books were wrong seven times in the past. Maybe they're wrong now."

Mr. Rogobo said: "No. With each new error the books become ever more right. With each wrongness the overall right-ness becomes more certain. So the chances of the books being wrong are infinitesimal. Ergo, your girlfriend is not dead."

Claude said: "Then where is she?"

Mr. Rogobo said: "Still above-ground, I'd imagine. But no one is ever allowed to go back above-ground. Never has anyone gone back. At least *almost never ever* has anyone gone back. To my knowledge only six people have ever gone back and in all of those cases with the exception of one it was due to errors of bookkeeping and as you know that never happens. The other I permitted to go back because he thought his girlfriend had died and so he killed himself but it turned out that she was living after all and the guy felt like a real schmuck as you can imagine so I let him go back but only on the condition that he would never be allowed to return to the City of the Dead again unless he brought his girlfriend with him. Now before you go I'll need to take that pass back."

The bailiff said: "All rise. The Honourable Sharon T. Smith presiding, in case number FDS-276-5854, The People *v.* Claude R. Talleurien, alleged suicide and revenant. Court is now in session."

The People said: "We are born with brains not yet wired for memory. None of us remembers being a baby being born, coming into existence. Each of us finds himself *in media res*, an amnesiac, an unmoved mover. We therefore possess at every age a full sense of a past, one which seems all the richer for fading gradually into obscurity. Whether eight or eighty, we feel ourselves to be without origin. And from this feeling we fashion, when we are young, the complementary one: that we must surely live forever. But as we age, and watch others cease to exist, we arrive at the inevitable induction: all men are mortal. And though we still feel every bit as beginningless as we did when children, we become disabused of the notion of our endlessness. Life, as a result, seems tragically short. And yet death is, at least, democratic. In depriving us not of a spectral and uncertain future but of an unfathomable past, it takes from each of us the same priceless possession, a treasure that is literally invaluable, because none of us can know its scope. Death takes from us our story. Claude Talleurien has, in trying to write the conclusion to his own story, acted as death's accomplice. What is worse, he has, in returning to this world, blurred the boundary between life and death. We put people in the ground to forget about them – to forget, to the best of our ability, about death itself. What else do we put in the ground? Garbage. And if garbage were to one day emerge from its appointed resting place, we would not hesitate to rise up in retaliation, to crush it beneath the full weight of our legal system, to send it back to hell where it belongs. Let us show no more pity for this man."

The inexpensive lawyer said: "Good gosh, that was nice. I don't know how I'm going to follow that. I guess I could call somebody to the what's it called, the *stand* – incidentally, why is it called that, I wonder, if you *sit* in it? I would like to call to the stand, well, basically anyone who might be able to say something nice about my client, the guy defending himself, Mr. . . . this guy here that I'm pointing at. Anybody? Your Honour, I would like to request a recess on the grounds that I am having a panic attack. I left my medication in my locker at the Y. Oh God, I'm seeing lights."

The expensive lawyer said: "Mr. Talleurien? I saw you on television and you look much more emaciated in person. I'd like to represent you but unfortunately I'm very expensive and you don't look like someone who can afford me. However your case is getting a lot of media attention and my heart goes out to you so I'll tell you what I'll do. For five thousand dollars down I'll give you financing on my legal services at only 11.9 per cent interest compounded biweekly with minimum monthly payments of let's say one thousand one hundred and fifty-five dollars."

The private investigator said: "Sure, I can find her. I can find anyone. I once found a man who'd done a runner on his wife. He took his kids, their kids, *and* her kids from a previous marriage. There were seventeen of them altogether, ages from two-and-a-half to thirty-one years old, sleeping in a six-by-ten-foot roach-infested motel room in Yagé, Mexico. The thirty-one-year-old was a podiatrist in Baltimore. He'd never even met his stepfather. Figured he was being held for some kind of ransom. So he called his mom and asked her what the hell was going on and what did she do? She sent me down there to ship them all home. Another time I found a woman who'd skipped out on her husband twenty years before. They were still married. She still had the ring somewhere, she said. So while she slept I crept into the next room and called one of my assistants at directory assistance and in no time flat I'd tracked down the phone number of the husband. Once the old guy figured out who I was talking about, he *claimed* he wasn't even looking for her, but I was able to convince him to buy her latest address and phone number for twenty bucks. Not that the cheque ever came through, mind you, but you know what the postal service is like. So yeah, I can find your girlie. I'll need about eleven hunnies up front for my day-to-day expenses."

Jack said: "You can't stay here. We're on our honeymoon."

Helen said: "Go away. We're in love."

The landlady said: "I hope you don't have any heart or respiratory problems because this mould you see all over the walls and ceiling and along the floor there, it's called *stachybotrys atra* and it's toxic as hell, that's why I've got this breathing apparatus on, though to be honest I sometimes wear it around just for fun, but if you haven't got like TB or Fragile Lung Syndrome it shouldn't pose too much of a problem, at least not in the short term, that reminds me, how long are you planning on staying, because I'll require an eighteen-month lease and six months rent up front plus of course the damage deposit and the security deposit and a lease-processing fee and a lease-processing-fee fee which is non-refundable, I see you jumping out of the way of that caravan of bugs there, that's good to see, those are the bad bugs, you want to keep your distance from those suckers, but these ones over here, these are the good bugs, they're ugly as sin but they eat the bad bugs so I feed them chocolate and coffee to keep them vicious, but it also keeps them awake all night, so I'd recommend earplugs and maybe some kind of mosquito netting over your bed, not that that will keep them out if they have half a mind to get in but it might give them pause, now you've got four appliances and two of them still work, the padlock on the fridge was put there by the municipal health authority so I don't have a key for that, and these bars on the windows are for your own protection, unless we're talking about a fire, in which case you're pretty much shit O.L., if you know what I mean, and this here is Saul, Saul this is the guy who might be moving in, Saul's all right, as long as he gets fed he's happy, his favourite foods are Cheerios and tuna, but I'd recommend you just buy the Discount Honey-Nut O's that now come with U's and C's, the other day I was almost able to spell *couch*, and instead of tuna I'd recommend you just get the Flakes of Negative Entropy in a Can, Saul can't tell the difference, he won't give you any trouble, he just sits there and watches TV, you might have to help him to the toilet a couple times a week, that's what this trolley here is for, the back wheel squeaks like crazy but basically it's structurally sound, I know you were looking for a suite to yourself but technically speaking he's not really a roommate since he's not paying rent, the fact is that after his lease ran out we couldn't get him out through the door, so I'll need you to provide me with post-dated certified cheques for the duration of your lease, and the rent before utilities comes to eleven hundred and change which I know sounds like a lot considering the neighbourhood and the size and condition of the place and the mould and the bugs and Saul here but I'll be honest with you since you seem like a nice guy, I'm gouging you unmercifully because you're dead and you'll never find a landlord in this city who'd do any different and that's a fact. So what do you say?"

The prosecutor said: "Objection, Your Honour. The defence is stroking your hand in what I can only describe as a lascivious manner, and furthermore I can only speculate as to what is going on behind the bench where my vision cannot penetrate."

The expensive lawyer said: "Counter-objection, Your Honour. Firstly I am stroking your hand – as you yourself could attest, if you were not nibbling on the fingers of my other hand – in an expression of strictly professional admiration for your renowned jurisprudence; and secondly, what goes on behind this or any other bench between the lower moieties of two consenting adults is nobody's business but their own. Now, if that is the end of the prosecution's fatuous maunderings and pettifogging quibblings, I am prepared to outline the arguments I will present over the course of this trial; arguments which will prove, beyond a penumbra of a shadow of a doubt, my client's innocence of the outrageous charges laid against him."

The private investigator said: "Well, I could tell you where she's *not*. She's not in the cafeteria downstairs. She's not in the third stall from the left in the men's washroom on the fourth floor. She's not in the lobby of my apartment building. She's not in the coffee shop across the street. She's not in the bar down the street from my ex-wife's place. She's not hiding behind the dumpster in the back alley outside my ex-girlfriend's place. She's not in the waiting room of the VD clinic. She's not on the number twenty-eight bus. She's not at my mechanic's. She's not under my desk. She's not in Baltimore. Okay, all right, she *might* be in Baltimore. I confess, I haven't had a chance to look into Baltimore yet, but I'll get on it right away. I've got a wedding to attend there this weekend anyway. So I'll need another thousand bucks for expenses. And I should probably give the newlyweds a little something, a card and maybe a hundred clams should do it. Will you need a receipt? There's a receipt fee of fifty-five bucks."

The expensive lawyer said: "Even if my client *did* kill himself, which I am by no means admitting, he cannot be held responsible for that or any other misdeed, however despicable, however heinous. Because whether our characters are the result of our experiences, our environment, our upbringing, or our genes, whether we are shaped by nature, nurture, or some combination of both, the fact remains that *we ourselves* do not choose what we become. Whether my client was abused as a child, mocked as a teenager, or simply inherited a wonky strand of DNA, he can no more be blamed for who he is, for what he has become, than the sun can be held accountable for shining or the river for flowing."

The woman on the phone said: "Hello, I'm calling on behalf of the local chapter of Mothers Against Death. You may have seen our commercial: 'We're MAD and we're not going to take it any more?' I must say, Mr. Talleurien, that MAD strongly disapproves of the cavalier manner in which you have returned to the land of the living from that of the dead. We have taken pains over the millennia to impress upon the younger generation that death is a very serious business indeed, not something to be experimented with, and we cannot help but feel that the message you are implicitly sending our children is that death is not so bad after all. Why, just the other day one of our members found her thirteen-year-old son chewing razorblades. His excuse was that supposedly no one at school liked him. But I think you and I both know the real reason for his deplorable behaviour: the glamorization of death by the liberal media today! And, Mr. Talleurien, we at MAD consider you to be one of the principal offenders. You serve, perhaps inadvertently, perhaps unwittingly, as a role model for all the impressionable children out there who don't know any better. That thirteen-year-old boy chewing razorblades looks *up to you*, Mr. Talleurien, even if he himself doesn't realize it, even if he claims to be unaware of your existence. It is our opinion that only you can undo the damage you have done, Mr. Talleurien. We think it would be in every-one's best interest if you were to visit the Moribund Ward at St. Anthony's this afternoon and say a few words to the children, a little something to restore their natural and healthy fear of that damnable scourge of precious human life, death."

Claude said: "What I don't like about death is not that it ends life, but spoils it. I'm not talking about awareness of your own mortality or the anxiety that causes. I'm talking about what being mortal does to what you do and who you are. The fact that you're born to die makes patience impossible, desire unquench-able, joy fleeting, creeping boredom the only status quo. Because you must die, you must hurry, must fight tooth and nail, must forever ask yourself, 'What now? What next?' Even at my hap-piest, in those tranquil moments alone with Maggie, I was rest-less. If it was morning, I was thinking about what we'd do that afternoon; if it was afternoon, I'd be thinking about that evening. I was always looking forward to the *next* happiness, as though simply lying there, watching the heart-pulse in her warm neck, was a sort of sentence, something to be waited out, lived *through* instead of *in*. When you get on an elevator, it feels, after you've moved a floor or two, like you're already slowing down; the end of the *increase* in velocity feels like a stop. We need to go faster and faster to not feel like we're standing still. Immortality would be insufferable as we are. But if we were immortal, we would not be as we are."

The MAD woman said: "Something a little more . . . con-crete, perhaps, for the children."

Claude said: "Death seems to be a lot like living, only there's less candy."

The children said: "I don't want to die! I don't want to die!"

The private investigator said: "Well, she's not in a jail cell in a little backwater town outside of Atlantic City, I can tell you that much. How close are you to a Western Union?"

Saul said: "Somebody called for you. They said it was important and that you should call them back. They left their number but I wrote it on my hand and it came off when I was masturbating. They left their name but I forget what it was. I think they called a couple of days ago. Maybe Tuesday. The day had a Tuesday feel about it. Anyway, you should probably give them a ring."

The expensive lawyer said: "And finally, Your Honour, I maintain that 'Claude Talleurien' cannot be punished for a crime that 'he' allegedly committed because 'he' does not exist – the concept of selfhood, personality, or individual identity being a pernicious myth perpetuated by lassitude, fuzzy thinking, habit, arrogance, and in the furtherance of inequality, discrimination, and organized team sport."

Gary's kindergarten teacher said: "Once upon a time, an unhappy man tied a rope around his neck. The other end he tied to the branch of a tree in his backyard. Then he knocked over the chair he was standing on. The man was unhappy because his girlfriend had died and he would never get to see her again. When people die, we usually put them in boxes called coffins and lower them down into holes dug in the ground. Then we cover them up with dirt and grass and try to forget about them. Sometimes when people die we burn them up in a hot furnace until they are nothing more than cinders and ashes. Then, after the ashes have cooled, we put them inside an urn. Sometimes we take the urn full of ashes and scatter the ashes in a scenic location

– the seashore, for example, or the heart of the forest. No one knows why we do these things. Sometimes we don't burn or bury a person at all. Sometimes we freeze them so that far in the future, when we believe we will know more than we do today, we (or whoever comes along to replace us) might be able to bring them back to life. Sometimes we give them to scientists who take them apart to try to understand how their bodies work. (This isn't often helpful because one thing that dead bodies don't do is work.) And sometimes we just let them rot. We only do this to people we dislike or disapprove of. You see, we consider burning, freezing, burial, and dissection to be signs of respect. The unhappy man had not turned his girlfriend into ashes. He had buried her beneath the ground. His girlfriend, whose name was Margaret, had died in a car crash. The back of her head had been crushed and her face had been torn by glass shards. It had cost the unhappy man $1,155 to have his girlfriend's head and face fixed so that he could look at her one last time before putting her in the ground. His friends clasped his shoulder and said things like: Time heals all wounds, and This too shall pass. But the unhappy man did not want this too to pass. He did not want time to heal his wound. His grief was all that remained to remind him of Margaret, and losing it would feel like losing her all over again. For three months and three weeks he held on to his pain. In the fourth week of the third month after his girlfriend's death he went to a rather silly movie. He enjoyed himself. He laughed. And when he came out of the theatre, he felt awful. He felt as though he had laughed at his girlfriend's death. He felt that he had joined the conspiracy to forget her. He realized that life is nothing but a protracted death, a plodding procession of little cessations. Maggie had died, and now his grief was dying too. Nothing, not even misery, was immortal. That's why he decided to get it over with. That's why he decided to get all his dying out of the way in one sweep."

Dr. Mayer-Edelmann said: "You feel guilty. That's not unusual. But Margaret's death was not your fault. Or wait. Yes it was. Sorry, wrong file."

The judge said: "Has the jury reached a verdict?"

The jury said: "We have, Your Honour. For the crimes of dying, of self-murder, of belated burial, of reckless resurrection, of polluting the minds of the youth, of egregious failure to pay his legal bills, of grief paralysis, of putrescence, of ingratitude, of boundary dissolution, of failure to achieve abreaction, of sluggish pupil dilation, of weakness of character, of –"

The prosecutor said: "One moment, Your Honour. I would like to call to the stand one Margaret Reynolds."

Margaret said: "Claude was driving but it wasn't his fault. It was raining. It was early in the morning. We'd been on the road all night. I asked if he wanted to rest. I should have insisted. I'm sure he only closed his eyes for a moment or two. There were no other vehicles. I think the car flipped six times but I'm not sure. My spine was broken in two places. My skull was crushed. It didn't hurt. I continued to breathe for three or four minutes. No one came along the road for half an hour. He had a concussion and a sprained wrist. He was conscious but his mind wasn't working. He was confused. It was raining lightly. The rain fell on his face through the shattered windshield. He felt free, light, unencumbered. He was thinking, for the first time in many months, nothing more than how good it felt to be alive. I think he forgot that I was in the car next to him. I'm sure it was delayed shock. I don't blame him. It wasn't his fault. I only wanted him to say my name. I wished he would say my name, just once, before I had to go."

Claude said: "Margaret! Margaret! Margaret! Margaret! Margaret! Margaret!"

Dr. Mayer-Edelmann said: "I cannot without qualm say that I'm altogether in love with your mourning-arc. Though it pains me, I have no choice but to say that your latest grief index results show no trends that I can consider to be promising. And your SSHQ scores are giving me what I think, in the name of scientific precision, I have no choice but to call the willies. But I'll tell you what I'll do."

CLEA YOUNG

SPLIT

Alannah and Case have a one-year-old and insist that Tova and Jed be their guests so the baby will have its toys and comforts on hand should he grow fussy. *Fine, sure,* Tova agrees, though the baby is a messy one and, consequently, its house is too. Tova knows they will end up eating from plates in their laps. *Sure, fine.* Though her Saturday-night-self prefers a candle-lit table and a good red in a globular wineglass. There is also Case and Alannah's dog, Sadie, a standard poodle. She is dreadlocked and smart. And though it hasn't always been this way, much of an evening with Alannah and Case is spent discussing genius – the baby's and Sadie's – and sending Sadie outside so she will ring the doorbell and wipe her paws upon reentering. Tova can never get it straight: talk at one, walk at two? Alannah and Case are always saying things like, "You should get yourselves one." Meaning a baby.

Tova lies back in the tub, a wet face cloth covering her breasts. It's something she remembers her mother doing and so it has become one of those inexplicable habits carried on. Tova remembers, too – it wasn't so long ago – when she and Jed were inexperienced climbers in one another's arms. How even amid their ungainly groping, Tova managed to hide from Jed her split left nipple; whenever her shirt came off, her hand became a shell to cup her breast. Tova peels the waterlogged cloth from her chest and regards her anomaly. She's unsure if *split* is the correct word. Perhaps *inverted*. Maybe *mutant*. Her nipple has since become a joke she and Jed share; when it's soft, it looks like a mouth with no teeth. Yes, they laugh about it now. Privately though, Tova wonders if it will cause problems if, or when, she has a child and wants to breastfeed. What if the nipple doesn't work? What if the breast becomes full but the baby cannot drink from it and it grows painful and huge and must be punctured so that the trapped milk (might it sour inside her?) can flow?

Tova lets the water from the tub. She smears cream on her legs and rubs the excess into her elbows. Even though her mother offered her no counsel on the matter, Tova is sure Jed is her first and last husband. The same way she's sure that when she over-turns a rock at a certain beach she'll find a crab snapping its pincers. It was strange, though, for her mother to have kept silent. Unnerving after so many years of advice, wanted or not, to abandon Tova to her own shaky will at the point of such a crucial decision. She's sure she made the right decision marry-ing Jed. Feels empowered having come to it on her own. Maybe this was what her mother wanted for her. Tova calls Jed her tan-gible man. In the kitchen, she hears the spinner as he whirs dry lettuce for a salad they will bring to dinner. He sings "Piece of My Heart" in his scratchiest, most rock-and-roll voice, which is gentle, barely audible above the watery flush of the spinner.

Tova leans against the kitchen door-jamb wrapped in a towel. With his back to her, Jed slides a disc of flour-dusted pastry into a pie dish and then slops in diced apples. Cinnamon. Jed is a culinary whiz. And so relaxed as he moves from cupboard to stove to fridge. He can carry on a conversation as he cooks, add ingredients that aren't called for in a recipe but which, in turn, improve on it. Tova is spastic around vegetables and knives and pots of boiling water. Everything burning or wilting. Jed has tried to teach her some tricks: mince, don't press garlic, to avoid bruising the juices. But Tova is too impatient to learn. Instead of cooking together, she and Jed jolt about from counters and cutting boards and into each other. Inevitably, Tova grows angry with Jed's precision. "You're so anal," she always says and ends up where she is now, standing in the doorway.

"What are you making?" Tova asks.

"Hey, babe." Jed doesn't turn or look up.

"Alannah said to just bring salad," Tova continues.

"I know. It's for the little guy." Jed shapes the excess pastry into strips and arranges them in letters on top of the pie.

"Tiger?" Tova asks.

"That's what Case calls him." Jed squeezes in an exclamation point so it's *Tiger!*

"The baby can't eat solids yet," Tova says and adjusts her towel. Sweating with the steam from the bathroom only a minute ago, goosebumps now pucker along her arms.

"You're missing the point, babe," Jed says. "It's for Case and Alannah. To show them that we like, I mean we *care* about their baby."

"Well, they'd have to be idiots to think we didn't." Tova

turns toward the bedroom. "The way you goo-goo-gah-gah all over it."

Jed would like to have children and Tova would like him to have them. His arms are made to rock babies, to swing them dangerously high and catch them just in time. Only Tova hasn't yet fallen under that maternal spell she's heard women speak of so rapturously. And so she must wait either until she falls or is pushed head-first into its deep, embryonic darkness. Until then, she will use Alannah's baby as a gauge. Tonight Alannah will offer her the baby and Tova will receive it with tentative arms, note her pulse as she jigs the squirming bundle. She doubts anything will have changed. When Tova held the baby as a newborn, her mouth dried up and she began to sweat. The baby, who weighed nothing, almost broke Tova's back. It wailed bloody murder. How could a rag-doll floppy-neck channel such a sound?

"Those were good apples. I wish you hadn't used them in a pie." Tova has dressed in a pair of old jeans, a sweater, and pulled her hair into a high ponytail so the baby won't unexpectedly, or expectedly, depending who you are, tangle his fists in it. "Not all apples are good for eating. Those ones were tart and crisp. The kind I like."

"I'll buy more tomorrow," Jed says.

"Some apples are grainy and soft, like the fibres or the cellular structure have already started to decompose. I'm just saying, those are the kind to cook with."

"Leave it alone," Jed says. Tova realizes she's picking at a pimple on her chin and has drawn blood. The spot was barely visible until she discovered it in the bathroom mirror a few minutes ago and squeezed and poked in an attempt to extract some impurity from the dark pore. She does this, blotches up her face before she has to be somewhere. It isn't entirely unconscious, but she can't help herself. Self-mutilation, her mother accused her of. Only a mother could say such a thing.

"Case got called in," Alannah says when she opens the door, baby on her hip. "He's got to learn to say no." The baby wriggles in her arms.

"No big deal," Jed says.

"That's too bad," Tova says.

Alannah's house smells like a million things. Like meat. Like garlic. Like diapers. Like dog.

"Hey, Tiger," Jed says and widens his eyes. Alannah sets the baby on the floor, and he weaves dangerously, unsteadily through her legs.

"Have you seen him do this?" she asks. "It's been a while."

Jed crouches and the baby teeters toward him. Walk at one talk at two, walk at one talk at two, Tova repeats to herself.

"I don't think so," she says.

"No," Jed says. "We definitely have not."

The first time Alannah met Jed, she turned to Tova and whispered, "You've mined a gem from the Arctic-fucking-Circle; looks like he'll be a demon in the sack." Tova had never been one for searching out those kinds of men. For over a year she'd pined after her aerobics instructor despite his being openly gay. Twice a week she placed her mat at the back of a gymnasium and admired his toned arms and synchronization from afar. Jed was luck. Jed was selecting oranges at her neighbourhood grocer. When she tells the story of how they met over a bin of Ecuadorian navel oranges, Tova emphasizes *navel*, and thinks of a kumquat protruding from her belly button. Alannah was right, at first there was no need for costumes or gadgets. The organic track of Jed's tongue like snail-glue over her body was enough.

Alannah wears the earrings Case made her for her birthday, hoops with progressively smaller ones toward the centre, a map's topographical representation of a mountain. From the earrings Tova guesses Alannah must have decided, before Case was called away, that it was her night to have a few drinks. Though with Jed here neither Alannah nor Tova will have to lift a finger for the baby. Jed will be down on his hands and knees for hours, for however long the baby can keep its eyes open, playing with blocks and balls. Or he will sit the baby on his knee, hold on to its fragile upper body and give it gentle, crazy-horse rides. The baby will go mental with excitement and they will all laugh and admire its simple baby glee. And then they will admire Jed's way, Jed's natural way with the little guy, as he gives it a bottle and rocks it in his arms, his perfect cradle musculature.

"I just thought it felt like one of those nights," Alannah says, pushing a wooden spoon in a pot of ground beef and carrots and onions. Potatoes boil on another burner; the starchy water steams the black windows. "It just felt like a shepherd's-pie night. Soul food, you know? It's still blustery out there, isn't it?"

"Power's out in a bunch of places," Jed says.

Soul food? Blustery?

"Everything's changed so fast. At the park today, these leaves were coming down, honestly these yellow leaves were . . . I could cover my entire face with one, which he loved." Alannah nods at the baby, who sits in the middle of the kitchen looking up, a string of drool connecting his chin to the grimy linoleum. "What kind of tree would that be, anyway?"

"Couldn't say," Jed offers.

"Do you want a beer?" Alannah asks. "There's wine, too."

"Wine for me," Tova says.

Jed says, "I'll drive."

"I didn't say I was going to drink the bottle." Every time she has a drink Jed assumes, or Tova assumes Jed assumes, that's the end of her. Blotto for the night. Practically passed out and puking. That's how it makes her feel when he pulls out his "I'll drive" line so early in the evening.

"Red or white?" Alannah asks.

"Whatever's open," Tova says. "Just whatever."

Tova has known Alannah since before the baby, since before Case, when, independently, they found work during their first year of college at an Italian deli in a neighbourhood shopping plaza. It strikes Tova as impossible that the Alannah before her now, grating cheese onto a shepherd's pie, is the same girl with whom she deftly crushed boxes beside a dumpster. Cigarettes hanging between their lips as they stomped and sliced at packing tape. Nothing pretty about it. Hungover, gulls bitching overhead, the cemetery across the street, the guy who said he put on a condom and didn't. But it was real – the heat of that deli kitchen, the line of workers over from the grocery store wanting their lunch, and fast – and this, this humid home cloistered in black night, it feels otherwise. And Alannah seems otherwise – restrained, hunched, and without her old grace.

"Sometimes I want dirty. Sometimes I want to be goddamn spanked," Alannah said one night when she and Tova went for drinks, before the baby, just the two of them. They sat tucked in a horseshoe booth at a high table. Tova loved the way Alannah swore, without drawing attention to the corrupt sounds, so effortlessly. She loved when Alannah reached across the table and grabbed her wrist, for emphasis.

"He's not taking risks, what does that say this early in a relationship?"

"Jed bites sometimes," Tova offered.

"Bites? Where?"

"Once he bit my ass."

"God, if only." Alannah sighed and relaxed into the cushiony velvet. Tova remembers that night Alannah wore pink fishnet stockings. That when she took Tova's hand and raked it up her leg to demonstrate just how Italian, how taut the threads, Tova felt it was her own leg she was touching.

Tova eyes the baby where he stands on shaky legs, holding on to the lip of the coffee table. Jed sits behind him, spotting as though from the edge of a trampoline. He has just changed the baby and now it wobbles about wearing only a diaper. Tova thinks she can appreciate how soft the baby looks. She's heard, at this stage, they're practically all organs. That would explain the baby's stomach starting beneath his chin and puffing down into his diaper. Tova imagines an adult-sized heart beneath the baby's roundness, the person he will become, dormant in that pumping muscle. She looks for the "cuteness" she thinks she should see, the pitter-patter her own heart should feel when he releases an impromptu smile. She feels slightly reassured that her own mother never cared much for other people's children. It wasn't until she had Tova that she understood all the fuss.

Alannah drops cushions around the coffee table and spreads a spattered dish-rag where she sets the shepherd's pie. The baby, swaying at the table's edge, reaches for the hot pan. Even though there's no way his stubby arm could touch it, Jed takes the baby's little balled fist in his own and pulls it gently back. The baby grunts and swivels his head to look at Jed. Jed beams down at him.

"Oh, candles," Alannah says and disappears into the kitchen. When she returns with two tea lights, Tova says, "How romantic." Jed looks at her sideways.

"Dig in," Alannah says and scoops up her baby. She settles on a cushion, lays the baby across her lap and lifts her shirt. Tova is still surprised by the brown smear Alannah's nipple has become, no longer the tight star she remembers from sunbathing. The baby's mouth tugs and tugs. Jed glances from the hockey game, announcing quietly in the corner, to the baby.

"Hungry guy," he says and Alannah smiles in response. A smile of contentment or complacency; either way, Tova hates it. Alannah's bobbed hair swings forward as she looks down at the baby sucking the life out of her. Sitting like this, long legs folded beneath her, sinewy arms curled around the baby, it's obvious Alannah still has the body of a ballerina, only one that's injured.

"This is good," Tova says. "Really great."

Tova's mother never dropped her on her head. She sent Tova to her room only once. Her mother is affectionate; when she visits, she kisses Tova's head and pauses a moment to nuzzle her hair, breathe in the familiar smell of her as she did when Tova was a girl. But her mother has never been one to address the female body's more intricate functions. In her youth, Tova had friends whose mothers took them for lunch or bought them gifts when they started menstruating. And even though Tova scoffed at such ritual, she remembers feeling slightly cheated by her own mother's indifference to her coming of age. In fairness, though, her mother wasn't entirely oblivious; when Tova finally got her period at fifteen, a box of Kotex magically appeared in her room. Initially, she was grateful to her mother for sparing them the awkward words, but now Tova thinks her body's vocabulary is coming up short. Tova looks at the baby sprawled on Alannah's lap and he is every fleshy noun and dimpled instinct she lacks.

Alannah takes Tova's wrist and pulls her onto the porch. Alannah's is a familiar grip, guiding Tova in and out of nightclubs, nudging her through a day at work. In the bed below, sunflowers metronome in the wind on decomposing stalks. No petals, just mushy heads. Sadie has followed them out. She snaps her jaws at each blast of cold air.

"God I need a smoke," Alannah says, then qualifies, "only when I drink, though." Alannah sips her first glass of wine.

"Sure," Tova says. She watches Alannah struggle with the lighter behind her cupped hands.

"Want one? They're kind of stale."

"No thanks," Tova says, for no reason other than to deny Alannah's offer.

"So how are you and Jed?" Alannah asks. "You guys seem good."

"Yeah, we are." Tova can't bring herself to confide in Alannah. To tell her about yesterday when she got her period after a week thinking it might not come. About her elation as she sat on the toilet and laughed aloud. She withholds the part about Jed's hands on her, how she can predict their patchwork movement up her thighs toward her breasts even before he's walked through the door.

"You guys are good, that's obvious enough," Tova says and reaches for Alannah's cigarette. She doesn't want the inhale; she wants the place where Alannah's lips have touched to touch her own. Tova watches Alannah as though from a great distance, then her perspective shifts and she sees Alannah as a strange creature at a rare closeness.

"A baby doesn't make it better, though." The words whip from Alannah's mouth and are gone. "I'm sure you can see that for yourself. And the power you have, so suddenly, it's frightening. Sometimes, when I'm holding him I think, 'I could roll him down the stairs. I could just open a window and toss him out.'" Alannah looks to Tova for a response. Tova watches one of Alannah's hoops, circles inside circles, each on its own orbit. She thinks of the last time they went out, just the two of them, and sat tucked in the horseshoe booth. Alannah may have been pregnant that night. But unaware of the rosy bean in her womb, she spoke too loudly and drank too much. Finger-combed her blonde hair and released the loose strands onto the floor without discretion. That night, too, Alannah declared she was so highly sexed, all she had to do was cross her legs and she would orgasm. And she did, right there in front of Tova, the tables around them full, a line of waiting customers huddled inside the restaurant entrance.

"Obviously I'd never do it," Alannah says. "But just the fact that I could." Tova can tell Alannah's needed to say this for a while. She knows, too, that she should comfort Alannah, open her arms when Alannah asks, "Do other mothers feel like this?"

Instead, Tova says, "I wouldn't know." She only knows who Alannah was before: a girl who didn't wash her makeup off before falling asleep, who didn't need sleep, who climbed a cinder-block wall to skinny dip in an apartment complex's private pool. A girl who told another girl, hesitant to take off her clothes, worried about flashlights and angry residents, to stop being so scared and enjoy it for what it was: water on every inch of her skin.

"You should call me when you feel like that," Tova says. She thinks Alannah must hear the flat-line in her voice. Alannah shouldn't call her. Ever.

Jed appears in the kitchen window with the baby. He rubs a hole in the steamy glass, holds up the baby's fist and makes him wave. The baby doesn't see them, he looks blankly and with lovely ambivalence at nothing. And then they are gone. The baby and Jed disappear. Lights snap off inside the house and the houses all around. There is only the wind as it touches down in backyards and retreats. There is only the wind trying to force the trees into each other. Tova looks up to where wisps of cloud cruise steadily and without obstruction. Sadie rings the doorbell and there is a small shriek from inside.

"Luke," Alannah says and rushes toward the door. She flings the cherry of her smoke off the porch and for an instant it is the sun, or some fiery planet going down.

HEATHER BIRRELL

BRIANNASUSANNAALANA

At the top of the street where Brianna, Susanna, and Alana lived was a parkette in the form of a teardrop turned sideways. The parkette had a slide, two sets of swings (one for babies and one for big kids), and a climbing frame in the form of a rocket-ship. Brianna, at six, was not a baby, but still gave the big kid swings the respect they deserved. Susanna, at ten, loved the big kid swings, and had the soar-and-smash scars to prove it. Alana, at nearly-thirteen, was *so* over swings of any kind.

Just above the parkette was a used car lot, and next to that, an apartment parking lot, and next to that the apartment building itself, a brownstone of moderate proportions. Surrounding the brownstone was a well-manicured lawn that had been sectioned off in the northwest corner by yellow police tape. The police tape had been there for eight days and now appeared slack in places, fatigued.

From the observation pod at the top of the rocketship, Susanna had a good view of the goings-on around and inside the police tape. She observed, then reported her findings in urgent bulletins to Brianna and Alana. The former received these bulletins eagerly, if indiscriminately, jumping up and down below the pod, while the latter sat on one of the rungs of the slide yawning and peeling back the petals of skin around her fingernails. Still, whatever Susanna could tell them could not in any significant way diminish or augment what they already knew. The reason for the police tape was that somebody had been murdered.

"I think," Susanna said, lifting and twisting her chin with what she imagined was authority, "we should all think back to what we were doing the day of the murder."

"Whatever," said Alana.

"Two, four, six, eight," called Brianna, still jumping.

"There's a cardinal," said Susanna, pointing to the tip-top branches of a tall spruce across the street.

"Not a clue," said Alana. "Not a clue." She stood up, climbed to the top of the ladder, and sat down on the platform.

Alana

Alana had been walking home with her friend Zoe when three boys they did not recognize slouched out from behind a parked car.

"Hey," said one, and hiked up his pants, "my friend wants to do you bitches hard and anal."

Zoe turned to Alana, giggling. "What should I say?"

Alana shrugged. She liked the look of one of the boys, his half-up, half-down mouth and red Nike jacket. He sucked his teeth at her, eyed her chest.

"What should I *say*?" Zoe hissed.

Alana shook her head.

So they did not say anything, but let two of the boys follow them to a nearby Starbucks, where they bought chai lattes and sat down to sip at the foam. Two tables over, the boys lounged with their knees akimbo, flicking sugar packets at each other.

Alana and Zoe began a conversation that required them to laugh and twirl their hair. They pretended they knew what they were talking about.

Dialogue, thought Alana. We're doing *dialogue*.

When one of the boys got up and began walking toward them, they leaned in across the table so that their foreheads almost touched. They smiled at each other.

The boy pulled up a chair. "Hey," he said. It was not Alana's boy.

"Hey," said Zoe.

"Me and my boys're going to the ravine. Catch fish or somethin'."

"Yeah," said Alana's boy, now standing behind the first boy. "Or somethin'." He pinched his fingers together, drew deeply on an invisible joint.

"Cool," said Zoe to the first boy. "What's your name?"

"I'm Darryl." He looked for a green moment as though he might have said the wrong thing.

Alana opened her eyes wide because she knew she could appear almost Chinese if she relaxed and was not careful. And because some part of her felt more alert.

"And this is Jordan," said Darryl.

"Cool," said Zoe again.

The boys sat down and pulled more sugar packets from their pockets.

Susanna

Susanna could not remember the day of the murder, nor could she invent it (although she cast mightily back into her mind).

This was bizarre, since memories – their particular bents and textures – were usually her strong suit. At home they didn't really talk about it. *In our own backyards*, she heard her mother say on the phone. *Your friends and neighbours*, her father sighed to himself over the headlines. The problem with the mystery, in Susanna's view, was that the most pressing W questions (Who, What, Where, When) had already been answered. The criminal had been caught. The only leftover was Why. And finding Why after the death, after the arrest, was a problem. How did you dig up the clues that led deep into people's brains? The Motive, that's what Susanna was looking for.

What Susanna did remember was an afternoon two days *after* the murder, walking home by herself, thinking about the Motive and the Concept of Evolution. She knew that sometimes ideas in books that had nothing to do with the mystery at hand could loop you back toward a solution. There was a book she was reading now, one of her mother's, a science book about the origins of the human race. She didn't understand most of it, just read the words like a robot when she wanted to relax. But there were a few pages that had stuck with her, a section explaining our ancestry, way back before kings and queens and ancient castles. It was about chimpanzees, apes and humans, mothers all holding hands with their children around the entire earth – as if the earth were time, the distance years – then turning to face each other as cousins, as relations. What the author was trying to show was that blood and time could not really separate us from the animals we were and always had been. What it meant was that we were *actually* animals. But animals who could write books about how we are actually animals. Animals who murdered for complicated reasons. This was confusing in the best kind of way. She liked it when she had to fight to keep things straight.

There were lots of leaves on the streets, but rain had clumped them up with mud and pollution. Even so, Susanna dragged her feet through the gutters happily. When she got home she would have the entire house to herself. Alana was at piano and Brianna had playgroup. On Wednesdays Susanna was The Latch Key Kid.

Brianna

The day of the murder Brianna hid behind her favourite tree in the schoolyard at pickup time. She watched her teacher, Ms. Sawchuk, talking to her babysitter, Frances, who nodded then shifted her shoulders up and down quickly. Then she saw Caroline – a fat, wily, lively girl from the grade two class – skip up to the two grown-ups and point toward the tree. Brianna pressed her cheek hard into the bark. She turned her face and kissed the trunk with all the tenderness she could muster. "Goodbye, friend," she said. Then Frances hauled her out and pulled her towards the car, which was a modern station wagon named Saturn.

"That was very naughty," said Frances, once belted in. She turned the key in the ignition and the car roared to life. "I was so worried."

"Hello Saturn," Brianna called from the back seat.

Alana

Outside the coffee shop, the light had begun to dim. Alana loved fall; it made her so sleepy and willing. She watched an old man on the sidewalk clutch his hat to his head, railing against the wind like something from a movie. Darryl and Jordan were still there, telling stories involving lockers and basements and cops. From the stories, Zoe and Alana understood the boys were from the high school. The girls, who were not from the high school, didn't tell many stories, unless they were about TV shows.

"We gotta split soon," said Jordan. "You wanna come?"

"Mmm," said Zoe. "Just let me consult with my girl." She tugged on Alana's sleeve and jerked her head towards the washrooms.

The women's washroom was a single, large and harshly lit, with metal bars on the walls for the disabled. Zoe looped her purse over one of the bars, and shimmied her jeans down her hips. Alana looked in the mirror. She was happy with the way her hair was falling in a smooth curtain down her cheek, but above her left eyebrow was the small rosy swell of a blemish.

"Undergrounder," she said to Zoe, tapping at the spot.

"Do you wanna go with them?" said Zoe, standing up. She bounced twice to ease her jeans back in place.

"Sure," said Alana, because she really did.

But Darryl and Jordan were not back at the table. Alana looked out the window and spotted them climbing on a parking metre outside.

"Coupla monkeys," said Zoe, smiling.

On the street they paired up. Jordan asked Alana what kind of shit she was into, and she had no idea. Then he pointed to the earphones dangling like oversized question marks from behind his ears.

"Music," he said. "What do you like?"

"Oh," said Alana. She liked her parents' old cassettes from the eighties and soft rock stations that played people singing about love over mild-mannered saxophones. "Some old school, sometimes pop, you know."

"Cool," said Jordan.

Alana wished he would plug in the earphones so they could just walk. "Yeah," she said. She focused on Jordan's gait; it was purposeful and lopsided, his hip dipped and his arm swung like a creature who had chosen – righteously – to remain less evolved. His hair – jagged at the nape – had been dyed recently; there was a laissez-faire brown crop circle at the crown. Her cellphone began to bleat softly, rhythmically, from her coat pocket. She cherished the phone, its sleekness and weight in her hand, the flutter in her gut when she saw she had messages waiting. She flipped it open, pressed a key.

"H'lo."

It was Frances, the babysitter. Alana was overdue at home. Brianna was waiting. They were both waiting. Alana thought about Brianna. She was twice the age and twice the size of her little sister. If she were a fish in a pond, she would eat her, chomp, just like that. She closed the phone and slid it back into her pocket.

Zoe, who had seen the whole thing, tugged at Alana's sleeve. "What?" she said then clenched her teeth together.

"Gotta go get my sister."

"Lame," said Zoe. She spat into the gutter and looked over at Darryl.

Alana began to walk away, then stopped, turned around, and sidled up to Jordan. "Meet me later," she said, and brought her lips close to one of the headphones. She whispered instructions. He nodded and snaked his hand up under her shirt, brushed his fingers against the skin above her belt.

"Bye," she said.

Susanna

"Hel-*lo* Sunny!" shouted Susanna, as she pushed open the door.
"I'm home! Susanna's home!"

Oh yes, Sunny barked, skittering on the smooth floor of the
hallway, *Oh yes, you are!*

Susanna stroked Sunny madly behind his ears, then slapped
his belly when he rolled over for more. "C'mere, you old mutt,"
she said like a pro, then reached for his paws, holding them up
in the air so he could dance, his legs splayed, the tender flesh of
his underside and the nubs of his groin exposed. "Do you know
the way to San José?" she sang, but he didn't like it, didn't even
look at her. "Not so good on the old hind legs, eh, Sun?"

This was another thing that made humans different from
animals: language. Not only our big brains, but also our breathing patterns – the ability and anatomy to walk and talk at the
same time – made us what we are today. Sunny might be able to
help Susanna with some aspects of the investigation – his nose,
for example, was invaluable – but in the end, the human brain
would prevail.

At school, news of the murder was passed around like an
amulet; it was both excruciating and propitious to give it up to
someone else. What they knew for certain was that the victim was
the murderer's mother, an old lady who once baked carrot
muffins for her neighbours in 3F. Plus, one night about three
months ago, someone had overheard the killer – a quiet man who
wore his salt and pepper hair army short and drove a red Ford
pickup – shouting the questions, "Why?" and "Do you think he
ever really loved me?" in a choked, anguished voice. It was
assumed he was drunk. There were rumours that a reward was
being offered for more information that could, in the words of Jill

Nelson, "really nail the guy." The culprit, according to Jill, was a part-time plumber. "He only did a few jobs here and there," she said, stooped over Susanna outside the gym doors. "He was, like, a temp worker," she added, in a tone that suggested her father worked at a job distinctly full-time, professional, and non-plumber. "They should lock him up and throw away the key."

Susanna nodded. She had no choice; while you were within her range, Jill Nelson's proclamations were indelible. But when Jill was gone, Susanna wondered. Even the dog, who was now blinking up at her lovingly, divined things the rest of them couldn't, despite their big brains. For instance when Brianna had her *petit mals*, Sunny *predicted* them. Susanna had seen him doing precisely the same panicked prance around her sister's feet every time Brianna's eyes pinwheeled back into her head. She had read that some dogs would go further for their epileptic owners: lapping urgently at their faces, pushing them with careful snouts into soft chairs, positioning their bodies in the paths of their falls. That was Love. Or else a Survival Mechanism. Too bad the dead woman didn't have a dog like that. "Loyalty," said Susanna to Sunny, "that's what's missing in Today's Crazy World."

Yes, science could offer some answers, but there were phenomena you smelled without realizing, situations you simply absorbed through your very pores. I went to the University of Life, Susanna once heard her father say. She had filed this away, along with, That's Life in the Big City, and You Can't Always Get What You Want. In the schoolyard, Susanna kept quiet throughout much of the speculation, but in her heart she knew *she* would be the one to finally, glamorously, dig up some obscure, invaluable piece of evidence. What she had was good instinct.

In fact, there were already clever life things she was learning to do, secretly. That very lunchtime, Jill Nelson had followed her into the bathroom, and Susanna had dropped her knapsack in the school toilet by mistake, right down there into the pee. It didn't matter that she rescued it quickly, it was still dripping. It would smell. Jill called in to her, "Are you okay?" But Susanna did not panic. "I'm okay," she called back, "out in a minute. You go ahead." She stayed calm and used her head, reasoned it out, quickly flushing, then waiting for the tank to fill before she pressed the lever again and dunked the bag into the clean second swirl. Outside of the stall, she clicked the hand dryer on, allowed it to fill her head with its heat and noise. She held the bag up to the nozzle until it was dry.

Brianna

Once home, Brianna helped Frances make cookies – there was some bother with a plastic measuring cup whose lines had worn away, but Frances had a feel for ingredients and quantities, and, in this regard, Brianna trusted her – then she went to her play-room to tell stories to her dolls.

She sat down on the floor and surveyed the setup. Her dolls were piled in a heap on an old plastic serving tray her mother had given her, and she had arranged her racing cars in the form of a flower directly opposite the tray. The cars looked like humped metallic insects waiting for something exciting to happen. Something exciting *would* happen. World Creation. She picked out two of the dolls, laid them out before her, stripped off their clothes, and pushed them down, squashing the soft plastic of their tummies.

"You are now part of the earth," she said. Then she scrabbled them up out of the soil, blew on them two times each. "Out of thin air," she said. "Man and woman." They began to stir and come to life, pushing their limbs out, yawning excitedly. Then the girl doll walked over to the racing car/insects and woke them up with a wave of her hand. But next to the racing cars was a flying spindle that sprung up and pricked the girl doll's palms.

"Help," said the girl doll weakly, "I'm bleeding."

"We will have to hang you up on the cross," said the boy doll. "You are a sacrifice. Sorry."

"I don't think so," said the girl doll.

"It doesn't matter what you *think*," said the boy doll.

The girl doll whistled and a silver pony came galloping in from the hinterlands.

"We have not yet created ponies," said the boy doll.

"I don't give a care," said the girl doll, and when she touched the pony with her palms her wounds healed and the pony whispered he would hide her at the top of the CN Tower.

"Goodbye!" called the girl doll.

"You can't leave," said the boy doll.

"You better believe I can," said the girl doll.

Then the boy doll got very angry and said he would punch her in the vagina.

"BE QUIET OR I WILL PUNCH YOU IN THE VAGINA!" Brianna shouted.

And then there was Frances, her face gathering force in the doorway like a thundercloud. "*What* did you say?"

"Sorry," said Brianna, because sometimes saying sorry got people to stay quiet and smile with their lips closed.

"Well," said Frances. "Watch your tongue." She picked up one of the racing cars and turned it over carefully in her hand. Then she looked at her watch. "Where's that sister of yours?"

Alana

Alana took her sister Brianna to the park, their fingers inter-laced in a kind of lock.

"We're trying the big kid swings today, whether you like it or not."

"Not," said Brianna, and Alana looked at her, impressed, but still hoisted her up onto the black rubber band and gave a tiny push.

"Too scary," Brianna whispered, her voice stolen by the sen-sation of so much wind whooshing around her midsection.

"Okay," said Alana. "Corkscrew, then." She began to twist the chains of the swings together. Brianna was silent, holding on.

Alana looked around. Where there had been only fall – trees all lacy with leaves, the night creeping in with the cold, Zoe shifting from foot-to-foot in her miniskirt, cursing September – there was now something else. He would come, she thought. It was like fate, or, again, a movie. Or he would not come, but only because his mother was sick, or he'd been hit by a car. Then she would help him, be his one and only helper. They would maybe go on a trip together – somewhere with a desert and strange mounded homes. But then she remembered his hand on her skin. She was not skinny. If he'd noticed? Put a little pressure on the pudginess there? Fat was bad.

Brianna looked small, all wound up in there. It didn't seem so long ago she was a baby, feet curled into themselves like little mini crullers. She was so easy to love then. There was some-thing about smallness. Even today in homeroom Alana had slipped into a daze at the sight of Zoe's box of mini butterfly clamps. She found she could not stop staring into their tiny, shiny maws, flapping their metal wings back and forth, squeezing to feel the built-in resistance. What it did – playing with small things – was make you feel like a god.

"Ready, Freddy?"

"Not Freddy," Brianna mumbled, hunched over under the chains.

"I'm letting go."

"'Kay."

It was always super slow, the initial unwinding, then there was a moment where the momentum took over, and – voilà! – you were out of it, free, listing lazily in the other direction. Brianna looked like she might puke.

"Again," she said.

Alana began to twist, but then she noticed something at the periphery. A flash of red near the fence, rounding the corner. She turned her head quickly to make sure.

"Don't stop twisting, 'Lana."

"Rocket pod time, Brianna. One small step for man, a giant step for girls like you." Alana grabbed Brianna under the arms so she had no choice but to cling like an orangutan.

"I need you to stay here, in the pod, and be on lookout duty." Alana had secured her inside the bars of the small dome. Brianna was sitting with her knees drawn up, face blanched. "Don't be scared. Maybe one day you'll be an astronaut. You could be that you know. You could be anything in the world."

"Not an armadillo," said Brianna, and Alana knew she was off the hook.

"See you later, armadillo."

Jordan was right there, near the swings, fiddling with an unlit cigarette, waiting for her. He looked good, better than before, away from the street, away from the others. She had forgotten how tall he was, how his hazel eyes darted and understood.

"Can we go somewhere to talk?" he said, and Alana was amazed. She showed him how to scale the aluminum siding that bordered the car lot and they wandered amidst the cars, thumping them insolently with their open hands. On the border between the car lot and the parking lot someone had planted some overgrown shrubbery and two spindly trees and dragged a small picnic table into the patchy shade. When they sat down the picnic table rocked over the uneven ground like a tugboat. They kissed. Jordan pushed his hand under Alana's shirt, and she let him. He kissed her neck behind her ear, and slid his fingers under her thin bra. Alana felt worried. How to reciprocate? Under his shirt was flat and uninteresting. He pushed her hand downward. She unzipped.

They kissed and kissed, slackening their jaws, using tongues. Then Jordan bent her head so she could see exactly what he had below. She kneeled on the ground in front of him. There was a Mars bar wrapper under the picnic table, and some pine needles, which was peculiar, since there were no pines nearby. Jordan took off his jacket, then draped it over Alana's head and shoulders and his poked-out penis. It was the beginnings of a puppet show. His T-shirt was bunched up under his arms. Above Jordan's belt were two long muscular indents, as if he were made of smooth clay and someone had picked him up carefully by his hip bones. The indents ran on either side of a trail of small black downy hairs. But Alana could not see where the hair led; the trail was obscured by white boxers that puffed out of the fly of his jeans like Kleenex. She touched one of the indents with her fingers and her heart began to beat between her legs. The skin was so soft and tight! Jordan made a sound, and Alana understood. She put her lips around his penis then worked them down so that her mouth was full. She did this several times – up and down, trying not to let her teeth get in the way. Jordan placed his hand on her head and made another sound that was almost a word. Jordan's whole body shook. Alana gagged. Alana swallowed.

Then it was over, and the thing itself – the lovely indents, her migratory heart, and the almost-word – was gone, shoved down into the deepest drawer of her self, but the story of it, *this* Alana had already trapped and tidied in her head thousands of times. There was an unstated currency in these happenings; the value would be in the timing of the revelation, the payoff would be in the exact spin she put on the thing.

Susanna

In order to find all the pertinent information, Susanna knew it would be necessary to return to the scene of the crime. "The Return," she said to Sunny, who licked her wrist. She decided to take the dog with her for protection. It could be the murderer had an accomplice, lurking. She gathered some supplies: a magnifying glass from her science set, a plastic bag to collect evidence, an apple for provisions, another plastic bag for Sunny's poop. Then she hooked the dog onto his leash, closed and locked the front door with her key, and began to walk up the street, stopping to let Sunny sniff and snoop in other people's gardens. Susanna recognized the shape of each fading flowerbed, the particular means the cracks in the sidewalk had for accommodating crab grass and dandelions.

It was strange how well she knew her way around here, how everything came to her automatically, like her heart knowing how to pump, and when. It was a kind of memory, she thought, like the monarch's. Monarchs, who flitted around in the backyard in August, settling on blossoms to feed, then swooping and flirting, better than a whole circus. But this was not the most amazing thing. What was mind-blowing was what they did next. When it was time – how did they know? – the whole lot of them began a journey south, across the border, through the States, alighting on a few mountaintops in Mexico. There, masses of them bent boughs with their weight. It took a long time, months, for them to get there, surfing updrafts of warm air, but if they got tired and died, it didn't matter, their sons and daughters had the maps in their minds' eyes; it was a memory that was inherited. Susanna has seen pictures of them clustered around Mexican tree trunks. This was all it took – one giant flapping, delicate creature – to prove how very little we know of the world. And if whole troops of scientists could not solve the mystery of the monarch, how could Susanna discover the depths of a stranger's soul?

What would ever make you so angry you'd want to kill your very own mother? "Your own flesh and blood!" she said, then pinched some skin on her forearm to reinforce the idea. Monarchs could avoid most predators because of a poison in their bodies that birds and frogs, animals with backbones, could not stomach – cardiac glycosides. People were not always so lucky.

Sunny began to pull at his leash. *Squirrels*, he barked. They had reached the park's outer edge, and he wanted to run. But Susanna had other plans. "C'mon, Sunny," she said, "we're going to check out the Makeshift Grave." She tugged him gently. But then something stopped her; when she considered the grave, the thud as the body fell, all her objectivity was supplanted by a terrible billowing sensation in her chest. It was as if her breath had lost its way, as though everything her body ever knew had evaporated. She cut through the parking lot and spotted an old picnic table next to some bushes. "I think we need to sit down," she said to Sunny, who didn't agree, but was beholden. Seated, she bent over and put her head between her knees. Under the bench was a Mars bar wrapper and some pine needles, which was peculiar, since there were no pine trees nearby. Susanna sighed. Then she noticed one of the pine needles was moving. An ant was carrying it! The source of the pine needles was metres away, but the ants were determined to make a nest here, under the table. Incredible!

She remembered something then, from the day in question, although it would not be worth any reward. It was her mother's voice. (Then the three of them *had* been at the park. Curious!)

"BriannaSusannaAlana!" her mother had called. "Don't make me send your father up there!"

Why not, Susanna wondered, and it was a credit to her innocence and her father's oblivious, kindly nature that she honestly could not imagine the answer to this question.

Brianna

Brianna opened and closed her eyes rapidly, and swivelled her head around. This was called Taking Snapshots. In this way she didn't have to see it all – the whole world – at once. She was very frightened. There was no climbing down from the pod. When she looked down at the patch of gravelly ground below she realized what had happened. The pony had succeeded. But where was he now?

"Tallest free-standing structure in the world," she said wistfully. It was likely she would be here for a few days, with no food or water, and wild animals pawing at the dirt, their teeth aglow. She didn't mind raccoons so much, but squirrels were dishonest, and there were certain birds whose long beaks made their eyes appear smaller, like cruel glass beads. Maybe she could escape. What was it Alana had said? *You could be anything in the world.* She let go of the bar nearest her and extended one of her arms out, into the atmosphere. It was not so bad. She brought her arm in again, then dangled one leg down, swung it back and forth. But the actual means of escape confounded her; there was too much space between her body and the ground, too much room for disaster.

She felt cold and hungry. She wanted her mother. She wriggled around and felt in her coat pocket. There were some crispy bits of something! Chips? No, old tangerine rinds dried to hard shards. She took them out, sniffed them, then placed them in her mouth experimentally. She would put the moisture back in with her tongue. But it didn't work at all. It was a bit like the sign for the store called the Bay at the mall, with its large, strange symbol that meant B, but looked nothing like a B at all. Why did they have to do that? Make the connections so odd and tattered? She hated the not-B of the Bay with all her heart. She concentrated on this – hating the B – until there was a noise from overhead, flapping and throat-clearing. A crow landed over near the slide. It had come to keep her company. Or to peck at her head. Brianna began to search for her sisters.

There they were – up near the apartment building, talking to a man with a shovel. Alana seemed to be yelling, and the man was bowing his head. Alana was getting the man in trouble! Or maybe the man was saying a prayer. "Our father," said Brianna, "who art in heaven, howled be thy name. Thy kingdom come, thy will be done, on earth as it is in heaven." What was it like in heaven? Lime Popsicles, Brianna thought. Kindhearted wolves and old men with moustaches who were gods and angels. A few ladies with big skirts and kittens. All of them floating around howling and humming the songs that were the earth people's lives. And if they stopped humming? Thy will be done. She held tightly to the bars.

Whoopsy-daisy, she thought, and the world wrestled her down.

It was the first time she had woken from an absence by herself, without the wild-eyed faces – of her parents, her sisters, Frances – glistening down at her. She was completely alone, up in the rocket pod, and she had come back. It came as a swift, welcome shock to her that she could do it; she could exist without them.

Down on the ground, the crow was showing off, walking in wide circles around a pile of twigs and dog poo. Brianna could hear her mother striding up the street, calling out. She would be rescued soon. She realized she didn't want to be rescued. Brianna, her father once said to her, you're the kind of girl who Turns on a Dime, aren't you? She wasn't sure what he meant, but she thought she was doing it now, Turning on a Dime.

All of a sudden something occurred to Brianna – a historical person from a poster at school. She liked the sound of the name; it reminded her of someone old-fashioned, raw-faced and strong, a washerwoman from a fairy tale.

"Nellie McClung," she said to the crow, who cocked its head as if irked, "the first woman to get the vote."

Alana

Jordan reached into his backpack and pulled out a bottle of water.

"Want?" he said, after he'd swigged some.

She nodded, lifted the bottle to her lips, and felt traces of his very self slide down her throat as she rinsed her mouth clean. There seemed very little left to do. Still, Jordan picked up her hand, released it onto the bench, then placed his own hand overtop of it.

"Your hand's so small," he said.

Alana looked for her hand and could not find it, so she looked out into the evening, which was darkening, the whole sky shuddering with reds. Then she looked for her sisters.

Brianna was still sequestered in the rocket pod, and now she could see her other sister, talking to a man with a shovel, a gardener, maybe, over near the apartment building. Would it always be like this – the three of them linked like points of light in a lopsided constellation? Susanna was laughing at something the man had said, and he was leaning down to pat her shoulder, like they were in cahoots. That was the last thing Alana needed, for her sister to hook up with some old pervert in a granddad sweater. When they were younger they had played a game called

Disappear, designed so that Alana could get some peace. But it was not long before Susanna and Brianna caught on, came blundering in to whatever cocoon Alana had spun for herself, casting off their small squeals and powdery smells, convinced they had won something fantastic. It struck Alana that, of the three of them, she was the only one who truly understood the way things were, and she was overcome by an arrogant upswell of love for her sisters.

Jordan had removed his hand from hers to root around in his knapsack. He hooked a wire and plugged up the ear closest to her, then held up the other earphone by its lead so it swayed in the air between them. "Want?" he said again.

"Sure." They sat there listening. Traffic surging and surrendering up on the main street; P. Diddy doing his thing; Canada geese honking their way to some sunshiny shore. Alana felt something like happiness, but rougher. She could not be happy; she was alive, with tomorrows prickling up the back of her neck. On the hill, Susanna was still talking to the man with the shovel. She had pulled a notebook from her bag and was showing him something. Jesus, *her homework*? Alana could hear her mother's voice soaring through the twilight.

"Who's that?" said Jordan, jerking the earphones away. "Holy shit. That's not your mother, is it? God, how old *are* you, anyway? She's not coming up here is she?"

Alana shrugged. *Of course.* But she knew this first call was only a warning; there would be others, there were always others.

"Fuck, bitch, are you even, like, listening to me?"

Alana stood up on the picnic table to get a better view of the pervert. He was bending down, gesturing towards something bunched at his feet. It was a bag of dry leaves. No, a sleeping bag made of plastic. He pulled the bag closer to where Susanna was standing. The bag was heavy – there must be rocks or tools inside. Then the man tried to show Susanna what was in the bag, and it could be that Susanna *saw*.

"I'm outta here," Jordan said, and shouldered his knapsack. And Alana ran. She zipped like a cursor between a row of gleaming parked cars, skirted the apartment building, came up over the crest of the lawn, and lunged for Susanna. Then she clamped her sister's head hard into her soft tummy, saying, "It's okay." And, "You're *okay*." What Alana meant by this was something akin to what her father told her when she regaled him with her schoolgirl sorrows and grazed knees, before she started curling her eyelashes and carrying tampons like switchblades in her back pocket. What she meant by this was: Buck Up Kid. This is Only the Beginning.

HEATHER BIRRELL is the author of the short story collection *I know you are but what am I?*, published by Coach House Books. Her fiction has appeared in numerous publications, including *The New Quarterly*, *PRISM international*, and *Descant*, and the anthologies *She Writes* and *The Journey Prize Stories 13*. "BriannaSusannaAlana" also received an honourable mention at the National Magazine Awards. Birrell lives with her partner, Charles Checketts, in Toronto, where she is at work on a novel and another collection of stories.

BRIANNASUSANNAALANA

When I was eight or nine years old, and no doubt studying for some form of Canadian history test, my sister and I invented a song. The sole lyrics to this mostly tuneless ditty went as follows: "Nellie McClung, the first woman to get the vote, Nellie McClung." We would march around the house repeating this chant in a kind of joyful militaristic fashion for what seemed like hours. We found the whole enterprise both intensely compelling and frequently hilarious. The rhythm and refrain of this particular "song" and all it evoked (and still evokes) became the seed of "BriannaSusannaAlana."

Of course, the story is *about* a lot of things – sexual precocity, evolution and our relationship to animals, sisterhood, the pitfalls and pratfalls of growing up, how we learn to protect ourselves and our kin from danger . . . But to me, a successful story hangs on something much more mysterious than its various thematic concerns – it has a core bursting with the type of meaning that resists explanation. The Nellie McClung song was the core around which this story grew.

CRAIG BOYKO was born in Saskatchewan and now lives in Calgary. His short fiction has appeared in *filling Station*, *Queen's Quarterly*, *The Malahat Review*, *The New Quarterly*, PRISM *international*, *Descant*, *OnSpec*, and *Grain*. He is currently at work on two collections of short stories, one silly, one sad. He is not working on a novel.

THE BABY

"The Baby" was written while I was still labouring under the intoxicating influence of Donald Barthelme. (Indeed, I'm almost convinced that "The next day the baby arrived" is a direct transposition from one of his stories. I'm afraid to look.) If this piece has one merit, I guess it is the image of dangling a baby from a broom handle and swinging it around to "demonstrate its remarkably prehensile fists." I remember saving that up for a long time, and probably could not have used it anywhere but in a story as goofy as this one.

An earlier draft included the following paragraph, which I almost regret snipping: "Rousseau had written that babies entered this world 'trailing the vapours of their divine origin.' In my opinion this mawkish epigram suffered from inexactitude. Babies did not come trailing vapors so much as emanating or radiating them. And these vapours were not of a heavenly but decidedly chthonic provenance. 'Clearly,' I said, 'Rousseau was a damn fool.'"

THE BELOVED DEPARTED

"The Beloved Departed" began its life years ago as a twenty-thousand-word novella called, simply and rather overweeningly, "The Dead," which arose from the not-very-deep thought: wouldn't life be terrible if you were dead? (Or: wouldn't death be terrible if you were alive?) I must have sensed the shallowness early on, for I see in that early draft that I tried to ennoble the silliness of the proceedings – Claude's children thrash his corpse with sticks, dogs nibble at his appendages, a mob beats the stuffing (and teeth) out of him in a park, whereafter he speaks with a lisp for the rest of the story – with philosophical discursions and quotations from Milton ("Yet one doubt pursues me still – lest all I cannot die; lest that pure breath of life, the Spirit of Man which God inspired, cannot together perish with this corporeal clod; then, in the grave, or in some other dismal place, who knows but if I shall die a living death?"). "The Beloved Departed," of course, still retains some of the original's silliness, incidental ruminations, as well as an epigraph by Borges; but it does enjoy the distinction of being about one-third as long. I hope it also achieves something resembling psychological depth through the ambiguity as to whether Claude's experience is of a "living death" or just a guilty fever-dream.

And one or two lines still make me giggle.

NADIA BOZAK is a Ph.D. candidate in Comparative Literature at the University of Toronto. Her short stories have appeared in *subTerrain*, *lichen*, and *The Shore*, and an essay on filmmaker Werner Herzog was recently featured in *Cineaction*. Her first novel, *Orphan Love*, will be published by Key Porter in

February 2007. She is currently at work on a second novel, *The Black Tide*, also to be published by Key Porter.

HEAVY METAL HOUSEKEEPING

"Heavy Metal Housekeeping" is part of a series of experiments in second-person narration. Dominating multiple fields within all our daily lives, this "you" form of address has particular potency for girls and women. Standard convention in cookbooks, advertisements, love songs, fashion magazines, and homemaking guides, the second-person pronoun is inherently conflicted; both insidious and comforting, it harbours a sense of isolation and loneliness despite intentions to be communal and inclusive.

Originally inspired by the teenage moms I have known, this story finally surfaced during one of my stints as a live-in domestic worker. Socially and emotionally distanced from those whose dirt I was banishing, whose stains I was removing, I found solace and suffocation in the removed subjectivity of being both everyone and no one, in the plural singularity of "you."

Exercising the possible tensions created by the second person, I wanted to both reflect and negotiate the friction of growing up alongside one's children by means of an equally conflicted narrative system. Caught within the intersecting lexicons of pop, consumer, and, of course, heavy metal culture, the mother and, more implicitly, the son, are constructed by the voices in their heads, the resonating "you" that appears on soap boxes, in heavy metal songs, and within the story itself. And so there is another layer at work here: by espousing the story's second-person voice, the reader is, by extension, drawn into the paradox of being no one else but all of us, alone in the mass that is "you."

LEE HENDERSON is the author of the award-winning short story collection *The Broken Record Technique* and the forthcoming novel *The Man Game*, both published by Penguin Canada. Raised in Calgary and Saskatoon, he moved to Vancouver in 1994. He is a contributing editor and writer for *Border Crossings* and *Contemporary* magazine.

CONJUGATION

A few years ago, it occurred to me that there had been a lot of stories told from a child's point of view in an adult world, but no stories told from the point of view of an adult living in a child's world, or none that I knew of or could recall. I thought that for an adult to see children from within their culture, the story should be a metamorphosis. I thought I knew why the narrator had been sent back to grade four, and wrote the story of what he did to pass this grade again as if for the first time. It became a coming-of-age story in reverse. It also seems to me that it's not entirely absurd to imagine that one day employers will see the benefit of retraining themselves and their staff in the most elementary lessons of social skills.

MELANIE LITTLE's fiction has been published in *PRISM international*, *Event*, *subTerrain*, *The Fiddlehead*, *Ottawa Magazine*, and *Prairie Fire*. Her first book, the story collection *Confidence*, published by Thomas Allen, was a *Globe and Mail* Best Book of 2003 and was shortlisted for the Danuta Gleed Award. She was the 2005–2006 Markin-Flanagan Writer in Residence at the University of Calgary. She is at work on a novel, a second collection of stories, and a verse novel for young adults.

WRESTLING

I believe the most astute compliment – I *think* it was a compliment – I've ever been given about my writing is that I have a "composting" imagination. It's true that for me, writing is often not composition so much as *de*composition. I've given up trying to write to a specific conclusion or even effect. I try to leave myself open to all manner and measure of influences, and then let the various microbes embedded in my brain and in the words do the dirty work.

I like "Wrestling" because I always wanted to get my maternal grandmother into my fiction. She's there, though the fictional Gram is a rather reined-in version. My real Grandma Major was the person who made me mad for storytelling. Sadly, almost all of her stories involved feces or flatulence, and I blame the tragic fact that I rarely get invited to book clubs on her.

The story about the mother and son in Room 317 was something I heard when I was working at a mid-size Vancouver hotel, a place I found alternately homey and harrowing. The *belle phrase* Gram supplies when Wilhemina tells the 317 story is courtesy of my husband, Peter Norman, who replied to *my* telling of it in just that way.

The rest is microbes.

MATTHEW RADER is the author of the book of poems *Miraculous Hours*. His poems and fiction have appeared in journals and anthologies across Canada. He is currently a Graduate Teaching Fellow at the University of Oregon. He lives in Eugene, with his wife and daughter.

THE LONESOME DEATH OF JOSEPH FEY

Shortly after the 2003 spring solstice, a dear friend of mine passed away in Vancouver General Hospital after a brief, but debilitating, struggle with mental illness. At the approximate time of her death, a vision not unlike the one that appears to Seamus on the night of Joseph's death appeared to my youngest brother (I am the oldest of three), who was a few hundred kilometres away on Vancouver Island. Despite my desire to support and understand (in whatever weak and nebulous way I could) my brother and his experience, and to leave my heart open to my friend, I found these èvents very difficult to accept.

Later that summer, I made a visit to a part of the Brown's River in the Comox Valley on Vancouver Island known as the Medicine Bowls. The Brown's River runs right out of the high mountains and is by far the coldest of the three major rivers that feed into Comox Harbour. Many times, when we were younger, my brothers and I went swimming there in the early morning while the sun still shone on the last pool of the falls. That was back when we were immortal, and jumping from the cliffs into the freezing water was no more than a thing to do on a summer day. When I went home, I wrote the story that appears in this book.

SCOTT RANDALL has published fiction in such journals as *The Antigonish Review*, *The Dalhousie Review*, *Event*, and *The New Quarterly*. His first short story collection, *Last Chance to Renew*, has just been published by Signature Editions. He currently teaches at Concordia University in Montreal.

LAW SCHOOL

I had wanted to use the punch line "but his face rings a bell" in a piece of fiction for a while before I decided to build a story around a series of Psychology experiments.

The experiments described in "Law School" are based upon ones I did participate in; my first-year Introduction to Psychology professor made a certain number of subject hours compulsory as part of the required coursework. Because the studies usually paid in movie vouchers, however, I continued to volunteer as a subject even after I wasn't required to do so. In total, I probably participated in two dozen studies and during them all, I was preoccupied with figuring out each test's real purpose. I imagine most subjects did the same.

In addition to the experiments, I suppose what holds the story together is the narrator's increasing sense of anonymity, a common enough fear. By the end, he has gotten past this fear, providing the story with a resolution of sorts.

SARAH SELECKY grew up in Hanmer, Ontario. She is now living and writing in Toronto.

THROWING COTTON

I wanted to write a funny story about a character who dropped mangled idioms into conversations, thinking he sounded wise. "Throwing cotton to the wind" was the best one I'd heard. It's an obvious mistake, but there is so much sweetness in the error. This became the essence of Sanderson.

Meanwhile, I was writing a separate story about a neurotic character who wanted to be pregnant because she needed to do something with her life. I'd witnessed several pregnancies that had resulted from questionable impulses – loneliness, ennui, fear – and I wanted to explore my own discomfort with this by trying to imagine myself in the same situation. I think that's why Anne's story is written in the first person.

I wrote most of this story at a friend's cottage. It was a gloomy but magically productive Victoria Day weekend. I started picturing Sanderson and Anne together, and there was some weird chemistry that worked. So I wrote Sanderson into Anne's story. For three days I would wake up, drink tea, write, break for dinner, then watch rented movies at night. No phone, no email. I wish I could recreate that weekend – the writing was actually pleasurable, and I don't remember any anxiety at all (rare for me).

Flip appeared out of nowhere. His name was important. When I found his name, I knew everything about him. I developed a big crush on him. I wrote an alternate ending that was quite extensive and erotic, but, unfortunately, I deleted it.

DAMIAN TARNOPOLSKY was born in London, England, and now lives in Toronto. He studied literature at Oxford University and writing with Mavis Gallant at the Humber School for Writers. His first book, *Lanzmann and Other Stories*, was published in 2006, and he is currently at work on a novel. "Sleepy" appeared in *Exile* and was his first published short story.

SLEEPY

As sometimes happens, "Sleepy" began with other writers, other stories, as much as feelings and experiences of my own. Before starting it I'd been reading a lot of fiction written in what one might call deeply uncertain voices, and found myself getting infected by them. Also, I'd just written a story in an aggressive, hyper-masculine, arrogant tone, and wanted to get as far away from that as possible. I had to do some research into the subject and talk to a few people and sit and think for a while about who Lena was, but writing the story was all about getting her voice right. Once I started really hearing it (as sometimes happens), "Sleepy" became a matter of following her as best I could.

MARTIN WEST has been published in *Grain*, *filling Station*, and *PRISM international*. He spends many days scouring the Badlands for fossils and anything else he can dig up.

CRETACEA
Making a likeable character do a rotten thing has its up- and downside. The upside is that the story writes itself, the downside is that it's hard to do again. I personally have never shot a town to pieces, although I did break a television screen once as a child and I have spent most of my life looking for fossils in the Alberta Badlands. The landscape there is the most sublime and lonely I have ever experienced and I think after a time it makes one off-centred, which might account for the story. For those who are considering it, avoid dating PWs as they can be trouble.

DAVID WHITTON lives in Toronto with Brenda and Millie. His fiction has appeared in *Taddle Creek*, *The New Quarterly*, *The*

Dalhousie Review, and *05: Best Canadian Stories*. He is currently working on a novel and a book of short stories.

THE ECLIPSE

I wrote "The Eclipse" over a series of drab, overcast afternoons in March, a time of year when my neighbourhood, stripped of leaves and flowers, looks like some sort of enormous Soviet-bloc housing complex: nothing but concrete and overcoats and downcast eyes. My routine was pretty much the same every day. I'd watch television, write, walk to the library, write some more, wander over to the electronics superstore, browse, go to a coffee shop, edit, go back to the library, write. A few months earlier I'd written a scene, based on a real incident, in which a clueless guy gives dating advice to his even more clueless brother, but it had seemed pointless and anecdotal, so I'd dumped it. Now though, at some gummy kiosk or coffee counter, I forget which, I got the idea of grafting that scene onto another story I'd had kicking around, about a guy who slips off a ladder and, on the way to Emergency, stops for smokes and pastries. I'd always liked stories that took a big swing in direction, either tonally or narratively; I figured this might be a chance to do something along those lines. So I squeezed out a first draft. Among the wreckage of that draft I could see Chet's and Anders' faint outlines: encouragement to keep digging. And I needed the encouragement because, as everybody knows, writing is hard and there's always something good on TV.

CLEA YOUNG recently completed her MFA in creative writing at the University of British Columbia. Her poetry and short fiction have appeared in *Arc, Event, The Malahat Review, Other Voices, Prairie Fire, Room of One's Own,* and *subTerrain.* She lives with her husband in Vancouver, British Columbia.

SPLIT

I wrote "Split" around the time my peers were beginning to have babies. I was interested in the ways that parenthood divides friends who, only nine months earlier, had everything in common. Writing from the point of view of Tova allowed me to explore the alienating and conflicted feelings of a woman left out of the motherhood club. Tova confronts pressures similar to those I faced – from society, from friends – to start a family. I was in a committed relationship, I was the right age, what was stopping me? I just wasn't ready. And my lack of maternal instinct sometimes made me feel selfish, other times guilty. Although I am not Tova, I certainly instilled in her some of my own doubts about becoming a mother. I have known other women to feel this way, and in writing "Split" I wanted to say something about rites of passage, about misgivings toward motherhood being as common as the role itself.

In my experience, a character's voice usually arrives as if through garbled frequency and must be honed over many drafts. I felt lucky to hear Tova so distinctly and immediately; she stayed with me long enough to write this story down.

ABOUT THE CONTRIBUTING JOURNALS

For more information about all the journals that submitted stories to this year's anthology, please consult *The Journey Prize Stories* website: www.mcclelland.com/jps

Border Crossings is an award-winning magazine edited by Meeka Walsh. In its twenty-five years of uninterrupted publishing, the Winnipeg-based arts and culture quarterly has received 140 nominations at the National and Western Magazine Awards competitions, winning fifty-eight gold and silver medals. In 2004, *Border Crossings* was awarded the President's Medal at the National Magazine Awards in Toronto, and the "Magazine of the Year" award at the Westerns in Vancouver, an unprecedented event in Canadian magazine publishing history. *Border Crossings*'s breadth, which stretches from the local to the international, has earned it the respect of readers and critics around the world. Editor: Meeka Walsh. Submissions and correspondence: *Border Crossings*, 500-70 Arthur Street, Winnipeg, Manitoba, R3B 1G7. Email: bordercrossings@mts.net
Website: www.bordercrossingsmag.com

The Dalhousie Review has been in operation since 1921 and aspires to be a forum in which seriousness of purpose and playfulness of mind can coexist in meaningful dialogue. The journal publishes new fiction and poetry in every issue and welcomes submissions from authors around the world. Editor: Robert M. Martin. Submissions and correspondence: *The Dalhousie Review*,

Dalhousie University, Halifax, Nova Scotia, B3H 4R2. Email: dalhousie.review@dal.ca Website: dalhousiereview.dal.ca

Descant is a quarterly journal, now in its third decade, publishing poetry, prose, fiction, interviews, travel pieces, letters, literary criticism, and visual art by new and established contemporary writers and artists from Canada and around the world. Editor: Karen Mulhallen. Managing Editor: Mark Laliberte. Submissions and correspondence: *Descant*, P.O. Box 314, Station P, Toronto, Ontario, M5S 2S8. Email: info@descant.on.ca Website: www.descant.on.ca

Exile: The Literary Quarterly is a distinctive journal that has published over one hundred issues during the thirty-plus years since it began in 1972. In those three decades, it has become recognized, and respected, as a forum that always presents an impressive selection of new and established authors and artists – soon to reach one thousand contributors. We draw our material (literature, poetry, drama, work in translation, and the fine arts) from French and English Canada, as well as from Britain, Europe, Latin America, the Middle East, and Asia. And, because *Exile*'s history of publishing is so uniquely appreciated, it now acts like an antenna, locating and attracting many diverse voices, searching out and encouraging the most distinctive new writing at home and abroad. Publisher: Michael Callaghan. Editor: Barry Callaghan. Submissions and correspondence: Exile/Excelsior Publishing Inc., 134 Eastbourne Avenue, Toronto, Ontario, M5P 2G6. Email (queries only): exq@exilequarterly.com Website: www.ExileQuarterly.com

Grain Magazine provides readers with fine, fresh writing by new and established writers of poetry and prose four times a year. Published by the Saskatchewan Writers Guild, *Grain* has earned national and international recognition for its distinctive literary content. Editor: Kent Bruyneel. Fiction Editor: David Carpenter. Poetry Editor: Gerald Hill. Submissions and correspondence: *Grain Magazine*, P.O. Box 67, Saskatoon, Saskatchewan, S7K 3K1. Email: grainmag@sasktel.net
Website: www.grainmagazine.ca

The Malahat Review is a quarterly journal of contemporary poetry and fiction by both new and celebrated writers. Summer issues feature the winners of *Malahat*'s Novella and Long Poem prizes, held in alternate years; all issues feature covers by noted Canadian visual artists and include reviews of Canadian books. Editor: John Barton. Assistant Editor: Rhonda Batchelor. Submissions and correspondence: *The Malahat Review*, University of Victoria, P.O. Box 1700, Station CSC, Victoria, British Columbia, V8W 2Y2. Website: www.malahatreview.ca

The New Quarterly is an award-winning literary magazine publishing fiction, poetry, interviews, and essays on writing. Now in its twenty-sixth year, the magazine prides itself on its independent take on the Canadian literary scene. Recent issues have been devoted to comedy, genre writing, and occasional verse. Best known for our fiction, we also publish a series on the intersection of word & image and on the seductions of verse. Editor: Kim Jernigan. Submissions and correspondence: *The New Quarterly*, c/o St. Jerome's University, 290 Westmount Road North,

Waterloo, Ontario, N2L 3G3. Email: editor@tnq.ca Website: www.tnq.ca

Prairie Fire is a quarterly magazine of contemporary Canadian writing which publishes stories, poems, and literary non-fiction by both emerging and established writers. *Prairie Fire*'s editorial mix also occasionally features critical or personal essays and interviews with authors. Stories published in *Prairie Fire* have won awards at the National and the Western Magazine Awards. *Prairie Fire* publishes writing from, and has readers in, all parts of Canada. Editor: Andris Taskans. Fiction Editors: Warren Cariou and Heidi Harms. Submissions and correspondence: *Prairie Fire*, Room 423–100 Arthur Street, Winnipeg, Manitoba, R3B 1H3. Email: prfire@mts.net Website: www.prairiefire.ca

PRISM international, the oldest literary magazine in Western Canada, was established in 1959 by a group of Vancouver writers. Published four times a year, *PRISM* features short fiction, poetry, drama, creative non-fiction, and translations by both new and established writers from Canada and around the world. The only criteria are originality and quality. *PRISM* holds three exemplary competitions: the Short Fiction Contest, the Literary Non-fiction Contest, and the Earle Birney Prize for Poetry. Executive Editors: Carla Elm Clement and Regan Taylor. Fiction Editor: Ben Hart. Poetry Editor: Bren Simmers. Submissions and correspondence: *PRISM international*, Creative Writing Program, The University of British Columbia, Buchanan E-462, 1866 Main Mall, Vancouver, British Columbia, V6T 1Z1. Email (for queries only): prism@interchange.ubc.ca Website: www.prism.arts.ubc.ca

subTerrain Magazine publishes contemporary and sometimes controversial Canadian fiction, poetry, non-fiction, and visual art. Every issue features interviews, timely commentary, and small-press book reviews. Praised by both writers and readers for featuring work that might not find a home in more conservative periodicals, *subTerrain* seeks to expand the definition of Canadian literary and artistic culture by showcasing the best in progressive writing and ideas. Please visit our website for more information on upcoming theme issues, our annual Lush Triumphant contest, general submission guidelines, and subscription information. Submissions and correspondence: *subTerrain Magazine*, P.O. Box 3008, MPO, Vancouver, British Columbia, V6B 3X5. Website: www.subterrain.ca

Every six months, **Taddle Creek** restores the sanctity of the literary magazine, fusing traditional editorial and design values with non-ephemeral, modern-day urban fiction and poetry by Toronto-based writers to create a product unassociated with any one literary movement. Works found in *Taddle Creek* are not easily categorized: intelligent yet stylish, sensitive yet cavalierly violent, self-absorbed yet socially aware, humorous yet disturbing. In short, *Taddle Creek* is the literary magazine for those who have come to detest everything the literary magazine has become in the twenty-first century. Editor-in-Chief/Publisher: Conan Tobias. Submissions and correspondence: *Taddle Creek*, P.O. Box 611, Station P, Toronto, Ontario, M5S 2Y4. Email: editor@taddlecreekmag.com
Website: www.taddlecreekmag.com

Submissions were also received from the following journals:

The Antigonish Review
(Antigonish, N.S.)

Ars Medica
(Toronto, Ont.)

Broken Pencil
(Toronto, Ont.)

The Claremont Review
(Victoria, B.C.)

Event
(New Westminster, B.C.)

The Fiddlehead
(Fredericton, N.B.)

Geist
(Vancouver, B.C.)

Kiss Machine
(Toronto, Ont.)

lichen
(Whitby, Ont.)

Maisonneuve Magazine
(Montreal, Que.)

Matrix
(Montreal, Que.)

The New Orphic Review
(Nelson, B.C.)

On Spec
(Edmonton, Alta.)

Parchment
(Toronto, Ont.)

Prairie Journal
(Calgary, Alta.)

Queen's Quarterly
(Kingston, Ont.)

Room of One's Own
(Vancouver, B.C.)

Storyteller
(Ottawa, Ont.)

This Magazine
(Toronto, Ont.)

PREVIOUS CONTRIBUTING AUTHORS

* Winners of the $10,000 Journey Prize

** Co-winners of the $10,000 Journey Prize

1

1989

SELECTED WITH ALISTAIR MacLEOD

Ven Begamudré, "Word Games"

David Bergen, "Where You're From"

Lois Braun, "The Pumpkin-Eaters"

Constance Buchanan, "Man with Flying Genitals"

Ann Copeland, "Obedience"

Marion Douglas, "Flags"

Frances Itani, "An Evening in the Café"

Diane Keating, "The Crying Out"

Thomas King, "One Good Story, That One"

Holley Rubinsky, "Rapid Transits"*

Jean Rysstad, "Winter Baby"

Kevin Van Tighem, "Whoopers"

M.G. Vassanji, "In the Quiet of a Sunday Afternoon"

Bronwen Wallace, "Chicken 'N' Ribs"

Armin Wiebe, "Mouse Lake"

Budge Wilson, "Waiting"

2

1990

SELECTED WITH LEON ROOKE; GUY VANDERHAEGHE

André Alexis, "Despair: Five Stories of Ottawa"

Glen Allen, "The Hua Guofeng Memorial Warehouse"

Marusia Bociurkiw, "Mama, Donya"

Virgil Burnett, "Billfrith the Dreamer"

Margaret Dyment, "Sacred Trust"

Cynthia Flood, "My Father Took a Cake to France"*

Douglas Glover, "Story Carved in Stone"

Terry Griggs, "Man with the Axe"

Rick Hillis, "Limbo River"

Thomas King, "The Dog I Wish I Had, I Would Call It Helen"

K.D. Miller, "Sunrise Till Dark"

Jennifer Mitton, "Let Them Say"

Lawrence O'Toole, "Goin' to Town with Katie Ann"

Kenneth Radu, "A Change of Heart"

Jenifer Sutherland, "Table Talk"

Wayne Tefs, "Red Rock and After"

3

1991

SELECTED WITH JANE URQUHART

Donald Aker, "The Invitation"

Anton Baer, "Yukon"

Allan Barr, "A Visit from Lloyd"

David Bergen, "The Fall"

Rai Berzins, "Common Sense"

Diana Hartog, "Theories of Grief"

Diane Keating, "The Salem Letters"

Yann Martel, "The Facts Behind the Helsinki Roccamatios"*

Jennifer Mitton, "Polaroid"

Sheldon Oberman, "This Business with Elijah"

Lynn Podgurny, "Till Tomorrow, Maple Leaf Mills"

James Riseborough, "She Is Not His Mother"

Patricia Stone, "Living on the Lake"

4

1992

SELECTED WITH SANDRA BIRDSELL

David Bergen, "The Bottom of the Glass"

Maria A. Billion, "No Miracles Sweet Jesus"

Judith Cowan, "By the Big River"

Steven Heighton, "A Man Away from Home Has No Neighbours"

Steven Heighton, "How Beautiful upon the Mountains"

L. Rex Kay, "Travelling"

Rozena Maart, "No Rosa, No District Six"*

Guy Malet De Carteret, "Rainy Day"

Carmelita McGrath, "Silence"

Michael Mirolla, "A Theory of Discontinuous Existence"

Diane Juttner Perreault, "Bella's Story"

Eden Robinson, "Traplines"

5

1993

SELECTED WITH GUY VANDERHAEGHE

Caroline Adderson, "Oil and Dread"

David Bergen, "La Rue Prevette"

Marina Endicott, "With the Band"

Dayv James-French, "Cervine"

Michael Kenyon, "Durable Tumblers"

K.D. Miller, "A Litany in Time of Plague"

Robert Mullen, "Flotsam"

Gayla Reid, "Sister Doyle's Men"*

Oakland Ross, "Bang-bang"

Robert Sherrin, "Technical Battle for Trial Machine"

Carol Windley, "The Etruscans"

6

1994

SELECTED WITH DOUGLAS GLOVER;

JUDITH CHANT (CHAPTERS)

Anne Carson, "Water Margins: An Essay on Swimming by
My Brother"

Richard Cumyn, "The Sound He Made"

Genni Gunn, "Versions"

Melissa Hardy, "Long Man the River"*

Robert Mullen, "Anomie"

Vivian Payne, "Free Falls"

Jim Reil, "Dry"

Robyn Sarah, "Accept My Story"

Joan Skogan, "Landfall"

Dorothy Speak, "Relatives in Florida"

Alison Wearing, "Notes from Under Water"

7

1995

SELECTED WITH M.G. VASSANJI;

RICHARD BACHMANN (A DIFFERENT DRUMMER BOOKS)

Michelle Alfano, "Opera"

Mary Borsky, "Maps of the Known World"

Gabriella Goliger, "Song of Ascent"

Elizabeth Hay, "Hand Games"

Shaena Lambert, "The Falling Woman"

Elise Levine, "Boy"

Roger Burford Mason, "The Rat-Catcher's Kiss"

Antanas Sileika, "Going Native"

Kathryn Woodward, "Of Marranos and Gilded Angels"*

8

1996

SELECTED WITH OLIVE SENIOR;

BEN McNALLY (NICHOLAS HOARE LTD.)

Rick Bowers, "Dental Bytes"

David Elias, "How I Crossed Over"

Elyse Gasco, "Can You Wave Bye Bye, Baby?"*

Danuta Gleed, "Bones"

Elizabeth Hay, "The Friend"

Linda Holeman, "Turning the Worm"

Elaine Littman, "The Winner's Circle"

Murray Logan, "Steam"

Rick Maddocks, "Lessons from the Sputnik Diner"

K.D. Miller, "Egypt Land"

Gregor Robinson, "Monster Gaps"

Alma Subasic, "Dust"

9

1997

SELECTED WITH NINO RICCI;

NICHOLAS PASHLEY (UNIVERSITY OF TORONTO BOOKSTORE)

Brian Bartlett, "Thomas, Naked"

Dennis Bock, "Olympia"

Kristen den Hartog, "Wave"

Gabriella Goliger, "Maladies of the Inner Ear"**

Terry Griggs, "Momma Had a Baby"

Mark Anthony Jarman, "Righteous Speedboat"

Judith Kalman, "Not for Me a Crown of Thorns"

Andrew Mullins, "The World of Science"

Sasenarine Persaud, "Canada Geese and Apple Chatney"

Anne Simpson, "Dreaming Snow"**

Sarah Withrow, "Ollie"

Terence Young, "The Berlin Wall"

10

1998

SELECTED BY PETER BUITENHUIS; HOLLEY RUBINSKY;

CELIA DUTHIE (DUTHIE BOOKS LTD.)

John Brooke, "The Finer Points of Apples"*

Ian Colford, "The Reason for the Dream"

Libby Creelman, "Cruelty"

Michael Crummey, "Serendipity"

Stephen Guppy, "Downwind"

Jane Eaton Hamilton, "Graduation"

Elise Levine, "You Are You Because Your Little Dog Loves You"

Jean McNeil, "Bethlehem"

Liz Moore, "Eight-Day Clock"

Edward O'Connor, "The Beatrice of Victoria College"

Tim Rogers, "Scars and Other Presents"

Denise Ryan, "Marginals, Vivisections, and Dreams"

Madeleine Thien, "Simple Recipes"

Cheryl Tibbetts, "Flowers of Africville"

11

1999

SELECTED BY LESLEY CHOYCE; SHELDON CURRIE;

MARY-JO ANDERSON (FROG HOLLOW BOOKS)

Mike Barnes, "In Florida"

Libby Creelman, "Sunken Island"

Mike Finigan, "Passion Sunday"

Jane Eaton Hamilton, "Territory"

Mark Anthony Jarman, "Travels into Several Remote Nations of
   the World"

Barbara Lambert, "Where the Bodies Are Kept"

Linda Little, "The Still"

Larry Lynch, "The Sitter"

Sandra Sabatini, "The One With the News"

Sharon Steams, "Brothers"

Mary Walters, "Show Jumping"

Alissa York, "The Back of the Bear's Mouth"*

12

2000

SELECTED BY CATHERINE BUSH; HAL NIEDZVIECKI;

MARC GLASSMAN (PAGES BOOKS AND MAGAZINES)

Andrew Gray, "The Heart of the Land"

Lee Henderson, "Sheep Dub"

Jessica Johnson, "We Move Slowly"

John Lavery, "The Premier's New Pyjamas"

J.A. McCormack, "Hearsay"

Nancy Richler, "Your Mouth Is Lovely"

Andrew Smith, "Sightseeing"

Karen Solie, "Onion Calendar"

Timothy Taylor, "Doves of Townsend"*

Timothy Taylor, "Pope's Own"

Timothy Taylor, "Silent Cruise"

R.M. Vaughan, "Swan Street"

13

2001

SELECTED BY ELYSE GASCO; MICHAEL HELM;

MICHAEL NICHOLSON (INDIGO BOOKS & MUSIC INC.)

Kevin Armstrong, "The Cane Field"*

Mike Barnes, "Karaoke Mon Amour"

Heather Birrell, "Machaya"

Heather Birrell, "The Present Perfect"

Craig Boyko, "The Gun"

Vivette J. Kady, "Anything That Wiggles"

Billie Livingston, "You're Taking All the Fun Out of It"

Annabel Lyon, "Fishes"

Lisa Moore, "The Way the Light Is"

Heather O'Neill, "Little Suitcase"

Susan Rendell, "In the Chambers of the Sea"

Tim Rogers, "Watch"

Margrith Schraner, "Dream Dig"

14

2002

SELECTED BY ANDRÉ ALEXIS;

DEREK McCORMACK; DIANE SCHOEMPERLEN

Mike Barnes, "Cogagwee"

Geoffrey Brown, "Listen"

Jocelyn Brown, "Miss Canada"*

Emma Donoghue, "What Remains"

Jonathan Goldstein, "You Are a Spaceman With Your Head Under the
   Bathroom Stall Door"

Robert McGill, "Confidence Men"

Robert McGill, "The Stars Are Falling"

Nick Melling, "Philemon"

Robert Mullen, "Alex the God"

Karen Munro, "The Pool"

Leah Postman, "Being Famous"

Neil Smith, "Green Fluorescent Protein"

15

2003

SELECTED BY MICHELLE BERRY;

TIMOTHY TAYLOR; MICHAEL WINTER

Rosaria Campbell, "Reaching"

Hilary Dean, "The Lemon Stories"

Dawn Rae Downton, "Hansel and Gretel"

Anne Fleming, "Gay Dwarves of America"

Elyse Friedman, "Truth"

Charlotte Gill, "Hush"

Jessica Grant, "My Husband's Jump"*

Jacqueline Honnet, "Conversion Classes"

S.K. Johannesen, "Resurrection"

Avner Mandelman, "Cuckoo"

Tim Mitchell, "Night Finds Us"

Heather O'Neill, "The Difference Between Me and Goldstein"

16

2004

SELECTED BY ELIZABETH HAY;

LISA MOORE; MICHAEL REDHILL

Anar Ali, "Baby Khaki's Wings"

Kenneth Bonert, "Packers and Movers"

Jennifer Clouter, "Benny and the Jets"

Daniel Griffin, "Mercedes Buyer's Guide"

Michael Kissinger, "Invest in the North"

Devin Krukoff, "The Last Spark"*

Elaine McCluskey, "The Watermelon Social"

William Metcalfe, "Nice Big Car, Rap Music Coming Out the Window"

Lesley Millard, "The Uses of the Neckerchief"

Adam Lewis Schroeder, "Burning the Cattle at Both Ends"

Michael V. Smith, "What We Wanted"

Neil Smith, "Isolettes"

Patricia Rose Young, "Up the Clyde on a Bike"

17

2005

SELECTED BY JAMES GRAINGER AND NANCY LEE

Randy Boyagoda, "Rice and Curry Yacht Club"

Krista Bridge, "A Matter of Firsts"

Josh Byer, "Rats, Homosex, Saunas, and Simon"

Craig Davidson, "Failure to Thrive"

McKinley M. Hellenes, "Brighter Thread"

Catherine Kidd, "Green-Eyed Beans"

Pasha Malla, "The Past Composed"

Edward O'Connor, "Heard Melodies Are Sweet"

Barbara Romanik, "Seven Ways into Chandigarh"

Sandra Sabatini, "The Dolphins at Sainte Marie"

Matt Shaw, "Matchbook for a Mother's Hair"*

Richard Simas, "Anthropologies"

Neil Smith, "Scrapbook"

Emily White, "Various Metals"